W9-BGB-785

LT MYST PAWLIK TOM
Pawlik, Tom, 1965-
Vanish
VISA

19 FEB 2010

VANISH

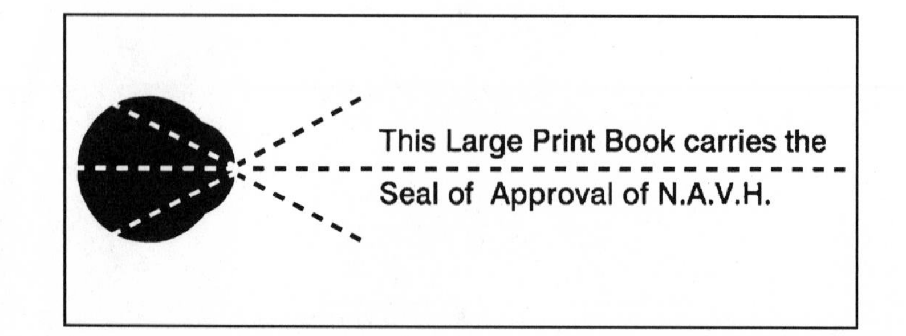
This Large Print Book carries the
Seal of Approval of N.A.V.H.

VANISH

TOM PAWLIK

THORNDIKE PRESS
A part of Gale, Cengage Learning

Detroit • New York • San Francisco • New Haven, Conn • Waterville, Maine • London

TULARE COUNTY LIBRARY

Copyright © 2008 by Tom Pawlik.
Thorndike Press, a part of Gale, Cengage Learning.

ALL RIGHTS RESERVED

This novel is a work of fiction. Names, characters, places, and incidents either are the product of the author's imagination or are used fictitiously. Any resemblance to actual events, locales, organizations, or persons, living or dead, is entirely coincidental and beyond the intent of either the author or the publisher.

Thorndike Press® Large Print Christian Mystery.
The text of this Large Print edition is unabridged.
Other aspects of the book may vary from the original edition.
Set in 16 pt. Plantin.
Printed on permanent paper.

LIBRARY OF CONGRESS CATALOGING-IN-PUBLICATION DATA

Pawlik, Tom, 1965–
Vanish / by Tom Pawlik.
p. cm. — (Thorndike Press large print Christian mystery)
ISBN-13: 978-1-4104-2221-7 (alk. paper)
ISBN-10: 1-4104-2221-6 (alk. paper)
1. Lawyers—Fiction. 2. Models (Persons)—Fiction. 3. Mechanics (Persons)—Fiction. 4. Homeless children—Fiction. 5. Mute persons—Fiction. 6. Storms—Fiction. 7. Large type books. I. Title.
PS3616.A9573V36 2009
813'.6—dc22 2009035814

Published in 2009 by arrangement with Tyndale House Publishers, Inc.
Published in association with the literary agency of Les Stobbe, 300 Doubleday Road, Tyron, NC 28782.

Printed in the United States of America
1 2 3 4 5 6 7 13 12 11 10 09

IT ALL BEGAN WITH A FEELING.
JUST AN EERIE FEELING. . . .

For Colette, who inspires me

ACKNOWLEDGMENTS

Many heartfelt thanks to . . .

. . . Colette, for being the example to our children of a godly wife. You are more than I had ever hoped for.

. . . Jerry Jenkins, for the opportunity of a lifetime and for your generous work with the Christian Writers Guild. May it continue to bear much fruit.

. . . Kathy Olson and Jeremy Taylor, for taking this story under your wings and letting me benefit from your talent and experience.

. . . Karen Watson, Stephanie Broene, and the many folks at Tyndale, for your encouragement and tireless work behind the scenes.

. . . and Les Stobbe, for your wisdom and counsel.

1

It all began with a feeling. Just an eerie feeling.

Conner Hayden peered out his office window at the hazy downtown Chicago vista. Heat plumes radiated from tar-covered rooftops baking in the midafternoon sun. A late-summer heat wave had every AC unit in the city running at full capacity.

He narrowed his eyes. Every unit except the one on the building across the street. On that roof, a lone maintenance worker in blue coveralls crouched beside the bulky air conditioner with his toolbox open beside him.

Conner watched the man toil in the oppressive August heat. Something hadn't felt right all day. Despite the relative seclusion of his thirty-ninth-floor office, Conner couldn't shake the feeling that he was being watched.

It had begun early that morning when he

stopped for gas. He could have sworn the guy at the next pump was staring at him. Conner saw his face for only an instant. But it looked strange somehow — dark, as if shrouded by a passing shadow. And his eyes . . .

For a moment, his eyes looked completely white.

Then the shadow passed and the guy turned away.

Conner dismissed it at first as merely an optical illusion, but he had the same experience with a truck driver on the Edens. Then there was the kid in the green minivan, the woman in the parking garage, and the guy on the elevator. Each time Conner only caught a glimpse, and each time he saw the same shadowed countenance with white, soulless eyes.

By the time he got to the office, he had been in full paranoia. His neck and shoulders were tense. He stopped at his secretary's desk. "Nancy, do you notice anything strange about me today? People have been staring at me all morning."

Nancy just curled an eyebrow. "You mean other than the horns sticking out of your head?"

"Very funny."

Nancy loved her lawyer jokes.

Conner had retreated to his office and closed the blinds but found himself peering through the slats every few minutes. He'd first noticed the maintenance man at nine o'clock. It was now almost three. Either the guy was hopelessly incompetent, or he wasn't really working on the AC unit at all.

It was ridiculous, of course. There was no way the guy could even *see* him from that position. Conner turned back to his desk and his work. He had a meeting with clients in a few minutes and desperately needed to focus. He tried to push the thoughts from his mind, but he was still on edge as he joined them in the conference room.

Annie Malone was a mousy redhead and her husband, Jim, a beefy blue-collar guy — not the sharpest tool in the shed. At least that was the way he came across. Conner had to remember to keep his words simple and his sentences short.

Annie was shaking her head as Conner sat down. "I just . . . I'm still really uncomfortable with this whole thing."

"I understand your misgivings, Annie," Conner said. "I do. But you lost your child and you're legally entitled to compensation for your pain and suffering. And mental anguish."

Annie bit her lower lip. "But Philipa

recommended we go with a C-section —"

Conner held up a hand. "Okay, first, it's Dr. Trent, not Philipa. You call her by her first name and suddenly the jury sees her as your friend —"

"But she *is* my friend."

"This isn't personal, Annie. This is about business. Dr. Trent charges you for her services, doesn't she? She's not treating you for free, is she?"

Annie hesitated. "Well . . . no . . ."

"And in exchange for your payment, you expect a level of competence. You should be able to trust that your doctor will give you sound advice. That she's looking out for your health and safety."

"Well, yeah . . ."

Conner leaned forward. "Look, Annie. This isn't like you're taking money from a friend. Doctors have medical malpractice insurance to cover them in situations like this. It happens all the time. It's a part of doing business."

Annie still looked doubtful.

Conner paused and turned to her husband. "Jim, you make, what, forty . . . fifty grand a year?"

Jim shrugged. "Around that."

"And you support four kids on that. You pay your bills. You try to live right," Conner continued. "Trent makes a six-figure salary. Part of her business pays for insurance that covers her in case something goes wrong like this. You're not taking money from her. Her insurance company compensates you. That's why she has it."

Jim just looked down.

Conner leaned closer. "A settlement could be in the millions, Jim. What would you do with that? You could retire on that. Pay off your house. Buy a bigger one."

The Malones exchanged glances.

Conner leaned back again. "There's nothing dishonest about this. You lost your child due to someone else's negligence. That's a pain no parent should have to endure. We can't bring Erica back. We can't make you whole. But I want to make sure you get some compensation for your grief and suffering. The law allows it."

In the end, the Malones said they wanted the weekend to think it over. *Pray* about it, they said.

Pray?

Conner felt his jaw tighten. He would never understand how people could live through such a terrible event and still come away trusting in some higher power.

They reminded him of his ex-wife.

As the Malones gathered their things,

Conner caught a glimpse of Jim. A shadow seemed to pass over his face, and for a split second, his eyes turned white. Then he looked away.

Conner frowned as he watched them leave. For a moment he thought he might follow them out and demand to know what was going on. Instead, he returned to his office and busied himself with paperwork. But now the sensation was stronger than ever. Like someone was standing right behind him.

He spun around and opened the blinds.

The maintenance guy was still there, crouched down, working on the AC unit.

Conner rubbed the tension out of his neck and watched for a few minutes. His gaze drifted down to the street, and when he looked up again, the repairman was standing. Toolbox in hand. Facing him.

Conner blinked. *Facing* him?

He jerked back in his chair. The guy was *watching* him!

He squinted and leaned closer. He had a hard time focusing but . . .

This guy . . . had no face!

The man stood there for only a moment and then stepped behind the AC unit. Conner rubbed his eyes. Was he seeing things? There were only shallow, fleshy indentations where the repairman's eyes and mouth should have been. The guy must be wearing a mask or —

"What are you going to do when you're alone?"

The voice drove a shudder down Conner's spine. He tore his gaze from the window to see Gus Brady in his doorway.

Conner narrowed his eyes. "What'd you say?"

Gus chuckled. "Did I wake you up? I said, 'What are you going to do with the Malones?' "

"Oh . . ." Conner shot a glance back at the empty rooftop. "They, uh . . . they said they wanted the weekend to talk it over."

Gus raised his eyebrows. "Talk it over? What's there to talk over? It's a slam dunk malpractice."

"Well . . . not quite. It seems Annie Malone's developed a bit of a friendship with her OB."

Gus rolled his eyes. "Oh, for pete's sake —"

"Don't worry. I'm working on them."

"Friendship's got nothing to do with it, Connie."

"I know."

"That's why they have malpractice insurance."

"I know."
"It's not personal."
"I said I'm working on them." Conner leaned back and stretched his neck.
"You okay?"
"Yeah . . . I just . . ." He was briefly tempted to tell Gus about the faceless maintenance man. "I'm fine."
"Hmm." Gus bit his lip. "Well, don't let this one get away. This one's huge."
Gus disappeared down the hall and Conner spun back to the window.
He surveyed the empty rooftop and shook his head. It must have been some kind of optical illusion, like how hot asphalt looks wet from a distance.
But still . . .
He dialed Nancy's phone. "Can you get me our building security office?"
"What?"
"I saw someone on the roof of the building across the street who looked a little suspicious and . . . I just want to see if everything's all right over there."
"You mean like a terrorist?"
"Just get me the number."
A minute later, Nancy called back and connected him to building security.
"Mr. Hayden?"
"Yes."

"Your secretary mentioned you saw someone on the roof of the Brighton building across the street."

"Yeah, it looked like a maintenance guy working on the air-conditioning unit, but he . . . well . . ." Conner wasn't quite sure how to describe it. "At one point he turned in my direction. He was just standing there, and it looked like he had some sort of . . . mask on."

"A mask?"

"Well . . . or like a nylon or something. Something was covering his face, I think."

"How good a look did you get at this guy?"

At that point Nancy came in and peered out the window too. Conner pointed to the rooftop. "Uhh . . . not too good. I mean, just for a second, but I thought it was kind of strange for him to be looking at *me.*"

There was a pause at the other end of the line. "Most likely he was just facing in your direction. I doubt he could see you from that vantage point."

"Well, I just thought it was a little strange."

"I see." Another pause. "We have someone on the phone with their building management. They, uh . . . they confirmed they were having some work done on one of their AC units. But it was their own maintenance guy. Apparently he checks out. They're going to send someone up to have a look anyway."

Conner sighed. "Okay. Sounds like a false alarm. Sorry to bother you."

"Not at all, sir. We appreciate you letting us know. Can't be too careful these days."

Conner hung up and Nancy chuckled. "You obviously have too much time on your hands if you can spend half the day staring out the window."

Conner shrugged. "I just happened to see him standing there."

Nancy nodded. "Mmmm . . . Well, anyway, your ex-wife called to find out if you had left yet. You're supposed to pick up your daughter for the weekend."

"Rachel." Conner swore and looked at his watch. "I was supposed to be there by five. Marta's gonna kill me."

He scooped the papers into his briefcase.

Nancy chuckled again. "I told her you weren't here. I said you were probably stuck in traffic."

"You're the best." Conner nodded toward the window. "Let me know if they find anything."

Then he was out the door.

Conner snaked his black Mercedes through the afternoon traffic, mulling over the excuses he could give Marta. He knew none of them would work. After fourteen years of marriage, she knew him far too well. He could picture the look on her face already. Marta always wore a sort of tight-lipped half smile when she was angry.

It was nearly five thirty when he pulled up her driveway in Lake Forest. He shut the car off and sighed. He'd given up the handsome brick Tudor to Marta in the divorce settlement two years ago. And been glad to do so. It had become infested with too many memories. Too many things he preferred to forget . . .

He knocked and let himself in the front door. "Sorry I'm late."

Marta's voice called out from down the hall. "In the kitchen."

Conner moved down the hallway into the breakfast nook. "I ran into some construction. You know how it goes."

"Yeah." Marta was rinsing some dishes at the sink. She turned around. Her lips were drawn tight in the familiar smirk.

Conner sighed. "What now?"

Marta shook her head. "It's just that there always seems to be construction or extra-heavy traffic or *something* that makes you late whenever you're coming to pick Rachel up. But when it's time to drop her off again, somehow you manage to be a few minutes early."

Conner shrugged. "That's because I'm always coming from *downtown* when I pick her up and from *home* when I drop her off."

"Mmm." Marta seemed to brush off his explanation and went to the back stairway. "Rachel," she called. "Your father's here."

"It's not a conspiracy, you know," Conner persisted.

"She hasn't eaten supper yet." Marta wiped the table.

"I've got it covered."

"And I'll be over Sunday at eight thirty to pick her up for church."

"Church?" Conner raised an eyebrow. "You make her go to church now too?"

"She wants to go. She even joined the youth choir."

"You sure *she* wanted that?"

"I haven't pressured her to join anything," Marta said. "You know Rachel. No one can make her do anything she doesn't want to do."

Conner frowned. "She sings, too?"

"She's got a beautiful voice. They're doing a special number this week. You should come."

Conner chuckled and shook his head. "Yeah . . . I don't think so."

"Not even to hear your own daughter sing?"

"That's pretty low," Conner said. "Using our daughter to get me to church."

"You know it's not always about you, Connie," Marta shot back. "Did you ever stop to think what it'd mean to Rachel? to have her father there to hear her sing?"

"You think I don't care about her?"

"No, it's just that for the past two years I've been watching you two grow more and more distant."

"Look —" Conner's expression darkened — "I'm doing my best here. Okay? It's not like I don't have any other responsibilities."

"This isn't about your work, Connie. It's about our daughter. Rachel's growing up — she's *fifteen* — and you're missing everything."

"I come to her birthdays," Conner offered. "I see her every other weekend."

"And even then it's like you're miles away. It's like she's just an imposition on you."

Conner rolled his eyes. "Oh, come on, Marty —"

"You had *two* children, Connie." Marta's tone iced over. "Only one of them died."

She pushed past him and headed for the hallway.

Conner caught her arm and spun her

around. "Don't take a cheap shot like that and just walk away." He loomed over her small frame. "You were the one who pushed me out of her life, so don't start complaining about it now!"

Marta didn't back down. "This started long before the divorce, Connie. After Matthew died, *you* were the one who pushed *us* away —"

"This doesn't have anything to do with Matthew!"

They turned to see Rachel in the back hall with her coat and backpack. She stared at them, chewing a piece of gum. Then she shook her head.

"I'll be out in the car."

As she walked away, the anger drained from Conner. He felt a little sheepish for having gotten so easily rattled. Why was it every conversation with Marta ended in an argument? "Look . . . I —"

"No, you were right," Marta said. "It *was* a cheap shot. I'm sorry."

Conner sighed. "I know I've been working a lot, but I was planning to spend the whole day tomorrow with her. We're going to the Cubs game."

Marta nodded. "She'll like that. And *talk* to her. You know, ask her about what's going on in her life. She's not a cynical teenager. She *wants* to be with you."

"It'll be good," Conner said. "We'll have a good time. We'll bond."

Conner and Rachel drove home in silence. Rachel stared out the window with her headphones on, humming to a song. Conner felt a bit relieved at not having to make small talk and a twinge of guilt for feeling relieved.

For all his efforts, he still couldn't shake the sensation that had plagued him all day. He found himself peering at every pedestrian and into every passing car. His behavior was so obvious it even prompted a remark from Rachel.

"You looking for someone, Dad?"

He chuckled a bit. "No, it's just been a very strange day."

They turned up the elm-lined boulevard to Conner's condominium.

They ate supper in further silence. The soft clinking of forks on plates was broken only by an occasional cough. Conner picked at his food, shifting his gaze between his plate and his daughter. He brooded over conversation topics with which to engage her other than the church choir. He didn't want to risk providing an opportunity for her to invite him to the service, but still he wondered whether her motives for joining were genuine or if her mother had pressured her. Finally, he decided to take the risk.

"So your mom tells me you joined a choir. . . ."

Rachel looked up and stared at him almost placidly, as if waiting for him to finish the sentence.

After a few grudging seconds, he obliged. ". . . at church."

Rachel smiled and nodded. "Mm-hmm."

He thought he saw a glint of amusement in her eyes. She went back to her meal, offering no further details. Conner drummed his fingers on the table, then tried again.

"So . . . you like it? Is that something you enjoy?"

Rachel smiled again. "Yep." And went back to her meal.

"Because . . . I just want to be sure it's something *you* wanted to do. Not . . . y'know, not because your mother–"

"I like it, Dad. Okay? I *wanted* to join."

"That's fine," Conner said. "It's just that your mom can be a little pushy about her religion. . . ."

Rachel rolled her eyes. "I can sign an affidavit if you want."

"Okay, okay."

"Take a polygraph?"

"Look, I just want to be sure you're

not . . ."

"Not what?" Her pleasant tone had evaporated. "Not being brainwashed? Is that what you think? I'm part of a cult or something?"

Conner's jaw tightened. "You're *my* daughter too, you know. And I think I have a say —"

"That doesn't give you the right to dictate what I can believe."

"I'm not trying to dictate anything. I just want to expose you to diverse points of view. And to appreciate the fact that there's more than one way of looking at the world."

"Then why don't you practice what you preach?"

Conner shook his head. *"What?"*

"Why don't you even *try* to respect Mom's beliefs?"

"I've never denied your mother the right to her own beliefs. I just don't want her pushing them off on you to the point where you're biased against my views."

Rachel leaned back and stared at him for several seconds. "Do you know why I started to go to church with Mom? Because I watched how you both reacted when Matty died. All you did was get angry. It was like you didn't even want to look at us anymore. But Mom found something that gave her comfort."

Conner scowled. "Comfort in an outdated book written by religious bigots?"

"Comfort in God," Rachel said softly.

"God?" Conner leaned over the table. "Let me tell you something about God. If He has the power to create the universe but can't spare a few seconds to keep a little boy from drowning in his own pool — if He even exists at all — He's either too selfish or stupid to care about what happens to any of us!"

Rachel's eyes widened. She opened her mouth as if to answer him but couldn't seem to find the words. Finally she shook her head and got up. "I think I've had enough pleasant conversation for one night."

Conner blinked and looked down at his clenched fists, white knuckled on the table. He straightened up. What had come over him? "Rachel, I —"

"You know, I don't even know who you are anymore."

She left the room and Conner sat staring at his plate. He shook his head, dizzy from his rant.

A half hour later, he had retreated to the solace of his study and retrieved a bottle of Scotch from his liquor cabinet. He downed his first glass, poured a second, and sank into his leather armchair.

Outside, the low rumble of thunder signaled the approach of a late-summer storm. Conner rolled his neck. He had been sore all day, and his squabble with Rachel hadn't helped any.

As he downed his second glass, his eye caught a framed photograph on his desk across the room. It was Rachel's picture from her tenth birthday. Conner moved to the desk and frowned. Ten? Rachel was fifteen now. He picked up the picture and ran his finger along the frame. Had it been that long since he had gotten an updated photograph of her?

His gaze drifted to one of the lower drawers. He slid it open and retrieved another photograph. It was the last picture they had taken together as a family. Five years ago at Disney World. He couldn't stand to look at it, but he couldn't bear to throw it out.

His finger cleared a path through the veil of dust on the glass. Matthew gazed back at him like a phantom. Tousled blond hair. Mischievous grin. Blue eyes squinting in the sunlight . . .

Conner's gaze moved to Marta: the slope of her nose, the curl of her lips. His chest ached as he tried to pinpoint exactly when during the last five years he had stopped loving her. It was as though a hedge had sprouted the day Matthew died and grown taller day by day. Their grief kept them from even speaking in the days after the funeral. But days soon turned into weeks and weeks into months. Eventually they were miles apart under the same roof.

Conner had withdrawn into his work, refusing to talk or even to see a counselor as Marta had suggested. He didn't want to console or be consoled. His anger consumed him. Anger at circumstance and blind chance. And at a God he didn't believe was there. Soon he found himself avoiding Marta and Rachel altogether. He watched their suffering but could find nothing to say to them. His anger allowed him no room to comfort them. When Marta turned to religion, his anger found a new target. And when she tried to push her faith on him . . . that was the end.

Thunder rumbled louder now, low and sustained. Flashes of lightning lit up the night sky. Conner went to the patio doors.

Something wasn't right. For one thing, no rain had been predicted in the forecast he'd heard earlier. For another, this storm was rolling in from the east. Off Lake Michigan. The clouds churned and billowed like the black, acrid smoke of a chemical fire.

Lightning flashed inside the billows. Long, sustained flashes of multiple hues. Red, amber, and blue.

Conner's frown deepened. He called back into the house. "Rachel? You see this?"

The cloud bank extended north and south as far as he could see, rolling westward quickly. Like a blanket stretching over the sky. The peals of thunder grew louder as it approached.

Conner stood, gaping at the sight. "Rachel," he called again. "Come take a look at this."

It rolled over the house. No more than a couple hundred feet, Conner guessed. The clouds swirled directly overhead and the deep rumbling shook the house.

Conner's mouth went dry. This was no storm. . . .

2

"It wasn't anything personal, Helen. They were just looking for someone a little . . . younger."

Helen Krause leaned back and leveled a gaze at her agent. "They're a brokerage firm, Rex. They're advertising an IRA. A *retirement* account."

Rex gave Helen what she could tell was a forced smile. "Well, y'know . . . they wanted it more geared to people who're just *starting* to think about retirement."

"They said they wanted a middle-aged career woman. What exactly do they consider *middle-aged?*"

"Uh . . . well . . ." Rex's smile evaporated. "Thirty."

"Thir—" Helen started to laugh but then just stared. *"Thirty?"*

"Well . . ." Rex squirmed in his seat. "Thirty-*ish.*"

"I see." Helen folded her arms. "So . . . at

forty-seven, what does that make me?"

Rex started to say something, but Helen cut him off. "Don't answer that."

Maybe forty-seven wasn't exactly accurate. But she didn't need Rex to remind her.

They sat in silence. Helen finished her drink and looked around the lounge. A perky twentysomething blonde chatted with a businessman at the bar. A dozen other couples engaged in small talk dotted the pub, oblivious to each other. Helen couldn't see anyone who looked older than forty. Other than the man across from her. But then again, Rex was sixty going on twenty-one.

Finally Rex spoke up. "Y'know, Helen, you've really become successful *behind* the camera. You're one of the few models who've managed to transition into . . . other roles."

Helen grunted. "Other roles?"

Rex sighed. "Look, it's a tough business. You know that. When you started thirty years ago, you were taking jobs from other models past their prime. You weren't too concerned about *their* feelings at the time, were you? So the cycle continues. I thought you were content moving on. You've done well as a consultant. You've got a great eye.

What's so terrible about moving into the next stage of life?"

"I know." Helen's voice softened. "It's just . . . I was hoping for another gig. I miss it. I miss being in front of the camera. It was hard enough to think of myself as *middle-aged.* Now I find out I'm too old even for *that.*"

"I know it's hard, sweetie." Rex nodded. "You were one of the top models in your day —"

"You're not really helping, Rex."

He looked down. "Sorry, kiddo. I'm just trying to cheer you up."

The sun had set by the time they left the bar. The downtown streetlights cast an amber glow onto the pavement, and a cool breeze wafted in off Lake Michigan. Rex walked Helen to her car. "We'll keep our eye out for something," he said. "There'll be other opportunities."

"Yeah," Helen chuckled. "Maybe a Depends ad or Geritol."

Rex laughed and gave her a hug.

Helen got into her Tahoe and waited until Rex was around the corner. Then she let her tears come.

Twenty-five minutes and a good cry later, she pulled into the parking garage of her apartment building off Lake Shore Drive.

She rode the elevator alone to the thirty-seventh floor, let herself into her apartment, closed the door . . .

And gasped.

A tall figure stepped out of the shadows of the dining room. It was a man in his twenties, holding a pink carnation.

"Happy birthday, Mom."

Helen stepped back, her mouth open. "Kyle . . . what're you doing here?"

"You didn't think I'd forget your birthday, did you?" He grinned and kissed her cheek.

Helen recovered and laughed. "You just scared a few years out of me."

"Come here." Kyle led her to the dining room, where a candlelit table had been set and a few decorations taped up. "Ta-daaa."

"Sweetheart," Helen said, "you're the best thing in my life."

"Yeah, I know." Kyle poured some wine. "I ordered in Chinese, and I even bought a cake." He peered at her closely and his smile faded. "You've been crying."

Helen waved the comment off. "I'm all right. . . ."

Kyle frowned. "No one remembered your birthday, did they? Not even Rex?"

Helen shrugged. "It's okay. When you're my age, you don't *want* anyone to remember."

Kyle pulled out her chair. "Why don't you fire that knucklehead? Least he could do is give you a card."

Helen sat down. "Because we go way . . . Because we're friends."

Kyle brought out two steaming plates. "Well, forget about him. We'll have a nice dinner by ourselves."

Helen traced her son's face with her eyes. She knew every inch. He looked so much like his father: strong jawline, deep brown eyes, and thick, Italian eyebrows. His dark hair was nearly shoulder length but neatly groomed. After college he'd begun working at an ad agency in the northern suburbs. She had a tough time when he moved to his own apartment, but they still saw each other regularly. He really was the best thing in her life.

They chatted over supper, and soon Helen had forgotten about Rex and losing the modeling gig. She nearly laughed herself out of her chair at a few of Kyle's jokes and dead-on celebrity impressions. He was always trying out new material on her. His not-so-secret ambition was to be a stand-up comic. She had often encouraged him to go to the open-mic night at one of the local comedy clubs, but Kyle could never seem to muster the courage. She had even asked

Rex once if he'd consider representing her son or at least help him find an agent. But Rex only gave her a strange look and steadfastly maintained that he didn't *do* show business, nor did he have any contacts, which she found hard to believe.

She stared at the cake in front of her. Two slices had been carved out. One sat uneaten on her plate, and all that remained of the other were a few crumbs on the plate across from her.

Kyle was clearing the dishes, rinsing and stacking them in the dishwasher. He came out of the kitchen and stood over her, frowning at the uneaten slice.

Helen shrugged. "I wasn't very hungry."

"You barely touched your supper, too."

"I ate some of it. . . ."

"You're not on one of those weird diets again, are you?"

Helen sighed. "No. It's just . . ."

"What is it? Work?"

She shook her head. "No. It's this day. I've been dreading it."

Kyle kissed her on the forehead. "Y'know, it's just fifty."

Helen grunted. "Say that when *you* turn fifty."

"But you're healthy. Beautiful. You have a good job." Kyle gestured around him.

"You've got a great apartment here — I mean, look at that view." He went over to the balcony door and pulled the drape aside. "You can see Navy Pier from here, watch the sunrise over the lake."

He turned back to her and shrugged. "You could be fat and lonely and living on welfare in a trailer park. So, y'know . . . look on the bright side."

Helen smiled. "Even if I was a fat welfare queen, as long as you were my son, I'd be happy. You mean more to me than all this."

Kyle was silent for a moment; then his gaze fell. Helen glimpsed him bite his lip. He always did that when he had something on his mind. Something he had to get off his chest. Bad news was coming.

"You know, Mom, I —"

"Did I tell you your father called?" Helen said quickly. She scooped up the remaining plates and brought them into the kitchen. "Yeah, he called this morning to wish me a happy birthday. We actually had a nice chat. He seems to be doing well."

Kyle followed her. "Mom . . ."

"I know you put him up to it." She started rinsing the plates, keeping her back toward him. "Not that . . . not that I'm not grateful."

"Mom, I have something to tell you."

Helen shut off the water and stared at the sink. She took a breath, forced a smile, and turned around. "What is it, Son?"

Kyle avoided her eyes. "I . . . uh, I got a job offer."

Helen's smile faded. "Where?"

"At Baker and Associates," he said. "It . . . it's in New York."

Helen steadied herself against the sink and put a hand to her chest. "New York?"

"It's a great offer," he said. "Creative director. I . . . I couldn't pass it up."

Helen took a breath. "Creative director — that's great. . . ." She was suddenly at a loss. "When do you start?"

"I'm moving on Thursday. They found me an apartment, and they wanted me to start as soon as possible."

"*Thursday?* You're leaving Thursday?"

Kyle's shoulders slumped. "I . . . I didn't know how to tell you."

"So you thought you'd wait to spring it on me now?" Helen turned around. "Is this your idea of a birthday present?"

"I'm sorry, Mom. I thought maybe this would soften the blow. I know it's gonna be rough on you, but it . . . it's a great opportunity for me. Can't you see that?" He drew up behind her and put his hands on her shoulders. "I can't stay here forever. You gotta let me go sometime."

Helen felt her heart racing. She tried to calm herself. "It's just that you really are the best thing in my life. I don't . . . I don't know what I'm going to do with you so far away."

"It's not so far — just a couple-hour flight. I'll fly out every few months. I promise."

Helen went to the balcony and looked out over Lake Shore Drive. A cool breeze had picked up. Thunder rumbled in the distance and lightning flashed over the lake.

"You know, when your father left, I thought I was going to die. I hadn't realized how much I had come to depend on him. The only thing that kept me sane during those years was you. Knowing I still had you.

"I don't think you'll ever know how much I love you. How much love a parent can have for their child. It's not like anything else you ever experience. No other relationship is like it. Nothing can prepare you for it. And from the day you were born, I knew . . . I knew you'd have to leave someday and go out on your own. I just kept thinking that day would never come. Sometimes you want to stop time and keep your children with you. Keep that love you feel."

Kyle stood in the doorway of the balcony.

"Mom, are you all right?"

She shook her head. "You really are the best . . ."

Helen glimpsed the storm front moving toward shore. The low rumble of thunder grew louder as it approached. Thick clouds rolled westward like a giant wave washing across the sky. Prolonged flashes of lightning blazed inside the billows — red, blue, and amber. Her frown deepened.

She had never seen a storm like this before. . . .

3

"Dude, you're not gonna make it in time."

Mitch Kent glanced at his watch and then down at the pieces of the motorcycle engine splayed on the garage floor. "D'ya think?"

Stan crammed another fistful of cheese curls into his mouth. "She gets off in like a half hour."

"I know when she gets off work." Mitch shot a glance over his shoulder. "Instead of stuffing your face, why don't you give me a hand?"

"I didn't have no supper. Why don't you just take my car?"

Mitch sighed. "Linda never thought I'd get it running and I want to surprise her, okay? It's probably the most important night of my life, and I'm *not* gonna pick her up in your car."

"All right, don't go spastic on me." Stan dumped the last of the cheese curls into his mouth and wiped his hands on his pants.

"So, where're you gonna ask her?"

Mitch took off his baseball cap and swiped his long, sandy hair back across his scalp. "I found a nice, quiet spot down by the lake. I bought a bottle of Merlot, and we're going to sit on the rocks."

"You couldn't spring for some champagne?"

"Linda likes that cheap blackberry Merlot, so get off my case."

"Dude, you're so romantic."

"Shut up."

After a few minutes, Stan spoke up again. "Rizzo says he's moving to Arizona next year."

"That's his plan."

"You still gonna buy this place?"

"That's *my* plan."

"So . . . like, are you gonna fire me when you take over?"

"You kidding? I need someone to just sit around all day and eat. I'd make way too much money otherwise."

Stan chuckled. "You gonna get one of them slushy-drink machines?"

"If that's what it takes to keep you on."

Mitch tightened the last of the spark plugs and connected the battery. Then he held his breath and thumbed the ignition switch. The engine turned, sputtered, and finally roared to life.

Stan nodded and shouted over the din. "She's gonna love it."

Mitch gunned the throttle a few times and let it idle while he ran upstairs to his apartment over the garage to wash up. He changed his shirt, put on a clean pair of jeans, and snatched a small, velvet box from the dresser. He opened it and inspected its contents. It was only cubic zirconia, but it was the best he could do. He'd bought it a week ago from a friend of a friend who sold them out of his car. Maybe in a couple years, after he bought the garage, he'd be able to afford a real diamond.

He was headed out the door when the phone rang.

Mitch hesitated and checked his watch. It might be Linda.

He picked up. "Hello?"

For a moment, there was silence on the other end.

"Mitch? Mitch . . . it's . . . it's your father."

Mitch froze as a wave of emotions washed over him. His eyes narrowed. "What's wrong?"

"I've been trying to get in touch with you all week. But you haven't returned any of my messages."

Mitch had gotten the messages. And

deleted them. "Yeah, well . . . I've been kinda busy lately."

"I understand. I just . . . I was hoping we could get together to talk."

"Talk?" Mitch could sense the hesitation on the other end. If this really was his father, it wasn't the man he remembered. "What's there to talk about?"

"It's a little complicated. I just want to try to resolve whatever issues we've got between us. I can't . . . I don't want to let it go any longer."

"And you think you can do that with a phone call?"

"No, no. But I thought maybe we could get together for a bit. Can we do that?"

"Yeah, well . . ." Mitch sighed and rubbed his eyes. "Y'know, I really don't have a lot to talk about."

"Son, I just want you to know I don't have any . . . I'm not . . . I'm not angry with you. I know I said things. Terrible things. We both did. And I wanted to apologize."

"Apologize?" Mitch stifled a laugh. This had to be some kind of prank. Maybe the guy was drunk or had finally gone off the deep end. He glanced at his watch. "Look, I'm glad you feel like you gotta get stuff off your chest and all, but I really don't have time to —"

"Son, I'm dying."

The words hit Mitch like a slap in the face. He stood with his mouth open, unable to think of a response. He stammered, "You . . . you're . . . what?"

"I'm sorry. I didn't want to tell you like that. Over the phone. I wanted to tell you in person."

"What's wrong?"

"I found out a couple weeks ago. I've been trying to think of how to tell you. It's cancer. It was in my liver. But now it's spread."

Mitch closed his eyes. "How . . . how long do you . . . ?"

His father chuckled on the other end. "You know, they never tell you that exactly. But my doctor said probably a matter of months."

"Months?"

"So, I was thinking . . . I was hoping we could get together. Maybe tomorrow? Would you be willing to come over?"

Go back? Back home? "Uh . . ."

His father went on. "I know how you feel about me, Mitch. I know I wasn't the best father . . . or the best example of my faith. And ever since you left, I knew I needed to get in touch with you and get our relationship back. But I just kept putting it off. I couldn't get past . . . I just couldn't forgive you. But God has a way of . . . well, of getting our attention."

Mitch felt his jaw tighten. This whole conversation was surreal. He shook his head. He couldn't listen to any more. He had to get off the phone. He had to get going. Linda was waiting. "You know . . . I don't know what you want from me. If you're calling to ease your conscience, then fine. But I don't want anything from you. I don't need anything from you."

His father's voice softened. "Look, Son, I know this is a lot to dump on you all at once. But I just don't want us to be enemies anymore. I . . ."

There was a pause.

"I love you, Mitch."

Mitch blinked. Had he just heard what he thought he'd heard? "I . . . uh . . . Look, I'm just on my way out to pick up my girlfriend from work. She gets off in a few minutes, and I don't want her waiting outside. Why don't I call you tomorrow? Okay?"

"Okay. Tomorrow. Good-bye, Son."

Mitch hung up and stared at the phone. He had just spoken to his father for the first time in more than five years — only to discover that the man he had hated for so long was now dying. His head was spinning as he returned to the garage. Stan was back on his stool with his feet up on the work-table, eating a candy bar.

Mitch walked up, shaking his head. "You want to hear something really bizarre? My dad just called."

Stan nearly fell off the stool. "No way."

Mitch nodded. "I'm serious. My old man."

"You haven't talked to him in, like, five or six years, right? Did he want to yell at you some more?"

Mitch frowned. "No . . . no, he didn't yell."

"What did he want? Did he preach at you?"

"No. No preaching."

"Well, what did he want?"

Mitch ran his hand through his hair. "He said he wanted to try to patch things up between us."

"You mean he just called you out of the blue to make amends. Just like that?"

"Something like that."

"Dude, you're like in the Twilight Zone."

"Tell me about it."

"So what did you say? Did you tell him where to go?"

Mitch stared at the floor. "I didn't know what to say. He kind of caught me off guard." He shook his head. "He said he was dying."

Stan stopped chewing. "Whoa . . . dude. *Dying?*"

"Yeah. Cancer, I guess." Mitch went to the refrigerator in the back of the garage and retrieved the bottle of Merlot.

Stan watched him, his mouth open. "You're not still gonna propose tonight, are you?"

Mitch shrugged. "Why shouldn't I?" He wrapped the bottle in a towel and packed it gingerly into the cycle's leather side bag along with a pair of plastic coffee mugs.

"You . . . you just found out your old man is *dying.*"

Mitch slid his jacket on. "He's been dead to me for six years."

"Dude, that's cold."

"Whatever. I'm late. Linda's waiting."

Stan grew more earnest. "But it's like bad karma or something, y'know? It's like an omen. I don't think you should propose tonight."

Mitch's expression darkened. "So I gotta put all my plans on hold because my old man got sick? When did he ever do that for me?" He swung a leg over the bike and gunned the throttle. "I got my own life to live."

Things were just starting to work out for him. He was going to marry Linda and buy the garage from Rizzo. He was going to keep moving forward. He cast a glance back at the building as he rolled out onto the highway. *North Chicago Muffler and Brake.* Next year there would be a big, glowing sign that read *Kent Auto.*

Or something like that.

Mitch headed north and checked his watch. Linda worked at an out-of-the-way bar and grill just across the Wisconsin border. It usually took him fifteen minutes from the garage, and Linda had finished her shift five minutes ago.

After a few miles, he glimpsed lightning flashing in the sky off to his right. Lightning? He swore and pulled to a stop along the highway. A bank of clouds was rolling in off the lake.

Mitch's shoulders slumped. *It can't be a storm. The news predicted a clear night.* This was going to ruin everything. Their ride on his vintage Harley. His late-night proposal at the lake. Maybe Stan was right. Maybe his father's news *was* an omen.

Mitch peered up at the storm front and frowned. The curtain of black clouds moved low and fast on a westward course. Too fast. Thunder rumbled deep and steady over the sound of his engine. Lightning flashed inside the churning billows. Long, bright flashes. Red, blue, and yellow.

The storm front rolled overhead with a deafening roar. His chest vibrated with the noise. This wasn't like any storm he'd ever seen before. Without warning his motor died. The headlight and gauges blinked and went out. Mitch sat in the darkness on the empty highway as the clouds swirled overhead. Suddenly a light blazed in his face. Everything flashed white.

And then everything went black.

4

Conner woke from a deep slumber. His head throbbed and the ceiling spun above him. After several moments, he recognized his surroundings. He was sprawled out on the wood floor of his study, but the room swayed like the deck of a ship.

What had happened? The last thing he remembered was . . .

He couldn't recall the last thing he remembered.

His tongue felt thick like his mouth had been stuffed with cotton. After a minute, he managed to stagger to his feet and survey his surroundings. His suit coat was tossed over a chair, and a half-empty bottle of Scotch sat on his desk. He stumbled to the patio doors and tugged the drapes aside. Sunlight drove shards of pain through his skull. A wave of nausea forced him back into the chair at his desk.

Running a hand through his hair, Conner

strained to remember anything from the previous day.

Rachel.

He had picked up Rachel for the weekend.

No, he had been late picking her up. And Marta had been none too happy about it. He and Rachel had eaten alone in the dining room, and he had ended up in the study because they had argued about something. He lost his temper and had gone to his study for a drink.

The storm.

Conner frowned. He had watched a bank of clouds roll in off the lake. He recalled the lightning flashing. It was the strangest thing. . . .

His nausea subsided and he peered outside.

The backyard was bathed in the amber morning sunlight. The patio abutted a small flower garden and fountain. Beyond that, a dense carpet of sod stretched out a dozen yards, ending abruptly at the forest that encircled the whole condo complex.

Conner shook off the last tendrils of sleep and stumbled to the kitchen. He put on a pot of coffee and went out to get the paper.

He stood on the stoop, scowling. The paper was always there by seven o'clock. Always. Conner searched in the bushes and out on the driveway. Maybe Rachel had brought it in already, though he'd never known her to be an early riser. Then again, he was finding he really didn't know her at all anymore.

He went back inside.

"Rachel, did you get the paper in already?"

Silence.

"Rachel?"

He made his way upstairs to the spare bedroom.

"Rachel?" Conner knocked and peeked inside. Rachel's bags lay at the foot of the bed. The blankets were crisp and tidy. The bed hadn't been slept in.

"Rachel?" His voice sounded strange in his ears now. Like a man growing more frantic each second. He hurried downstairs. "Rachel!"

He checked all the rooms, the garage, and back outside.

He returned to the kitchen and dialed Marta's number. After four rings, her voice mail kicked in, and Conner swore. Marta's voice sounded detached and mechanical.

". . . so leave a message at the tone, and I'll get back to you as soon as I can."

"Marty," Conner began. "Marty, I can't . . ."

He stopped. Can't what? He couldn't very

well leave a message saying their daughter had disappeared.

He hung up and dialed her cell phone. No answer there either. It kicked him back into her voice-mail service.

Conner hung up and swore again, louder.

He stared at the phone a few seconds longer, then dialed 911. He knew the police wouldn't be able to do much at this point. Particularly when they learned Rachel was the daughter of divorced parents. Teens like that were always acting up, running away just to get attention.

The phone continued to ring. Conner stared at it in disbelief. Had he misdialed?

He dialed again. *9-1-1.*

No answer.

Conner sat at the kitchen table, staring at the phone. The ring tone droned on.

He returned to the living room and switched on the TV. The screen was blank and static hissed through the speakers. He thumbed through a dozen channels. Nothing.

He returned to his study and flipped open his laptop. While it booted up, he dialed half a dozen other numbers — friends, people from the office, anyone he could think of. Each number he called sent him into voice mail.

When his laptop was ready, he tried connecting to the Internet. A pop-up error message informed him the server was not available. He tried several more times, growing more frustrated with each failed attempt.

Conner sat at his desk for a moment, trying to clear his head. What was going on? He could understand how his cable and Internet service might both be down at the same time — maybe affected by the storm. But his phone was working; it was just that no one was answering.

His mind started to reel, and he struggled to think logically. His first priority was to locate Rachel. There was no sign of a break-in or struggle, so wherever she had gone, she had gone willingly. His car was still in the garage, which meant she had either walked or . . .

Or someone had come to pick her up.

Had Marta come to get her? Or one of her friends?

He had to get out of the house to find some answers. He walked to his neighbor's door. It was 8:35 when he rang the doorbell. He could hear the chime inside and waited. No answer. He rang a few more times and knocked as well. He peeked inside the front window but couldn't see any sign of his neighbors.

Conner returned to his condo and dialed Marta's number again. Again he got her voice mail. This time he decided to leave a message.

"Marta, it's Connie." He paused, trying to decide how much to tell her. "Listen, I need you to call me back as soon as possible. Okay? Call me back on my cell."

He hung up and gathered his wallet and keys. As he backed out of his driveway, he turned on the radio. He listened to AM 1020 every morning in to work. Now static hissed through his speakers. He pressed the Seek button and the LCD screen scrolled through all the frequencies without stopping. He tried the same on FM with the same results.

Conner headed down Baltic Avenue to Columbus. His first stop would be the police station. It might be a bit premature, but it was the place he'd most likely get some answers.

He had driven less than a mile before he realized his was the only car on the road. He rolled past strip malls and grocery stores with empty parking lots, gas stations void of customers. There were no other cars in sight. No pedestrians. No signs of life anywhere.

A sick feeling grew in the pit of his stomach. This was more than just his daughter missing. Everyone else seemed to be missing as well.

Conner rolled to a stop in the middle of the road and got out. He was in the heart of the Lake Forest business district on a Saturday morning and not a soul was in sight. Silence surrounded him. No sounds of traffic. No planes overhead. Nothing.

The sun blazed down from a hard, blue sky, and a warm breeze tugged at his clothes. It was a beautiful day. Other than the fact that he seemed to be the last man on earth . . . it was a beautiful day.

5

Helen stood on her balcony. Lake Michigan spread out under the morning sun like a vast, diamond-studded carpet to the horizon. Thirty-seven floors below, Lake Shore Drive snaked its way south to Navy Pier. A cool breeze wafted off the lake and tousled her hair.

It was a daily ritual for her as soon as the weather turned warm enough in the spring: enjoy a cup of steaming coffee and the newspaper as the city stirred to life.

Helen normally drank in the vista with pleasure, but this morning she had no pleasure, no coffee, and no morning paper. She drummed her fingers on the railing and stared out over the city. She couldn't see a soul on the streets below. No traffic, no people. No sign of life anywhere.

She had awakened from a deep slumber ten minutes ago, groggy and disoriented. Apparently she had fallen asleep in the deck chair on the balcony. She found no morning newspaper in the hall and had gotten no answer when she called management downstairs.

Helen tried to reconstruct the events of the previous evening, but it was all still a little fuzzy. Kyle had come over — surprised her with a birthday dinner. They had eaten and . . . and Kyle had mentioned his job. He was moving to New York. She now recalled the anxiety she had felt coming to grips with her son moving so far away. She had gone to the balcony for some fresh air when . . . when she saw the storm.

And that was the last thing she could remember.

She went back to the kitchen and called Kyle's cell phone. After two rings, an automated message came on: *"If you'd like to make a call, please hang up and dial again."*

Helen frowned. Had he switched off his cell phone? He never shut it off. It should've at least sent her into his voice mail. She tried again, hoping she had only misdialed.

"If you'd like to make a call, please hang up and dial —"

Helen slammed the phone down and swore. Where was he?

After several minutes, she ventured back into the hallway. She hesitated at her neighbor's door and then knocked.

"Walter?"

She knew Walter Kiel casually — he was a divorced investment banker or something, also in his fifties. They only spoke in passing or on the elevator.

He didn't answer.

Helen pressed her ear to the door but could hear nothing on the other side.

She knocked again. Still no answer.

She went around the corner to Jeff and Susan Russel's suite. They had moved in a few months earlier, and Helen had developed a somewhat amiable relationship with Susan, though she had yet to meet Jeff.

No answer there either.

She moved on to the next door. Felicia Wilcox was always home. Helen had met the reclusive author after retrieving her shih tzu from the stairwell a few years earlier. They visited once or twice a month.

She knocked. "Felicia? Are you home?"

No answer.

She pounded. "Felicia?"

Her heart raced now and she paused to regain her composure. Closing her eyes, she leaned back against the door and focused on her breathing, just like her yoga instructor had taught her.

Where was everyone? Had they evacuated

the whole building last night? Had no one thought to even check on her?

She was used to being alone, but this was surreal.

There had to be someone else in the building. Surely the whole of Chicago hadn't been completely abandoned.

She returned to her apartment and shut the door. Her hands trembled. There had to be a logical explanation. She just needed to stay calm. Her first order of business was to contact Kyle. His apartment wasn't too far away. She'd stop there first.

Helen changed quickly into a pair of jeans and a clean blouse. She grabbed her keys and was headed for the door when a thought struck her. She might not be home for a while. She rushed back to the bedroom and stuffed a few items into an overnight bag.

Then she was out the door.

6

Mitch opened his eyes and found himself staring up at a cloudless blue sky. A patch of weeds and tall grass surrounded him, and the ground rose sharply on either side. He struggled to sit up. A strip of gravel and an asphalt highway lay to his left, and several yards to his right rose a wall of foliage and trees. Sunlight glinted off the chrome of a motorcycle, parked on the gravel shoulder several yards away.

Mitch frowned. That was *his* motorcycle.

His head spun as if he were fighting off a hangover, but he couldn't recall drinking last night. In fact, he couldn't recall much of anything.

The sun was just topping the trees. It was still fairly early in the morning. Around nine or so. He must've been out here all night. He climbed out of the ditch, staggered back to his bike, and inspected it for damage. Everything seemed fine.

He found a bottle of blackberry Merlot in the leather side bag, along with two plastic coffee mugs and a small, velvet box.

Memories flitted back to him. He had been on his way to pick up Linda. He was going to propose last night. He had planned to take her down to the lake and . . .

No, there had been a storm. He recalled the strange cloud bank. Lightning flashed inside — but not lightning. Lights. . . . It was like . . . like something was inside.

Mitch scanned the highway. Not a single car had gone past since he had awakened. He was in a rural wooded area near the Wisconsin border. A new subdivision was going up on the west side of the highway. A bulldozer and a backhoe stood silent amid a few large mounds of dirt.

A Mobil sign rose over the trees a quarter mile back down the road. He remembered passing it last night.

Mitch swung a leg over his bike. He had to call Linda and let her know he was all right. In fact, he was surprised she hadn't called the police. For that matter, why hadn't any state trooper or sheriff's deputy bothered to stop during the night? Seeing an abandoned motorcycle along the side of the road should have caused someone to investigate.

Mitch thumbed the ignition switch and swore. The key had been on all night, so the battery was dead. After several attempts with the kick start, he managed to fire up the engine. He turned around and headed back to the Mobil station. Maybe he could use the phone there.

Rolling to a stop under the pump canopy, Mitch bit his lip as he surveyed the gas station and quick mart. They stood amid several wooded acres with a dense tree line just beyond the parking lot. He shut off his bike and peered into the trees.

The mesh of trunks and branches caught his eyes, drawing his gaze deeper. Something about it didn't look right, like one of those pictures that had other objects hidden within a scene.

Everything was still. No sounds of traffic, no birds. Nothing. Just a slight breeze wafting through the upper branches. Then his breathing quickened — he thought he heard something. Like the branches clacking in the wind. Or snapping underfoot . . .

Mitch tore his gaze from the trees and headed into the store.

"Hello?" His voice sounded strangely distant as he entered. "Anybody here?"

No one answered. He spotted a phone behind the counter, next to the register, but couldn't quite reach it from his side. He looked around.

"Is anyone here?" he called again, louder. "I just need to use your phone."

Mitch drummed his fingers on the counter. Finally he slipped around back and dialed Linda's number. After several rings, her answering machine kicked in.

"Hey, Linda, it's Mitch," he said. "I . . . uh . . ." He was suddenly not sure what to say. "I'm sorry I didn't get there to pick you up. I, uh . . . I had some problems with my bike on the way and . . . I'm headed back to my place, so you can call me there, okay? I . . . I love you."

Mitch hung up and eyed the cash register. He tapped the phone absently, wondering how much money was in the drawer.

After a moment, he shook his head. These places all had surveillance cameras. He wasn't about to ruin his whole life over the prospect of a few easy bucks.

He was heading back out to his bike when he heard another sound in the woods. A branch snapped. A shadow flitted amid the tree trunks. He peered closer. It hadn't looked like a squirrel or a raccoon. In fact, he thought it had looked big enough to be human.

A rustling off to his right drew his attention in time to see a second shadow duck behind a tree. This one was definitely big enough to be human. *Probably just some kids goofing around,* he thought, but a chill shuddered through him nonetheless. The empty highway and gas station were beginning to creep him out.

Mitch heard a third sound to his left. Whispering. He turned to see a figure standing in the shadow of one of the trees. It was tall — over six feet — and thin. He peered closer but couldn't make out any distinct features. It was a gray silhouette in the shadows. It stood still for a moment and then slipped back behind the tree.

"What . . . what do you want?" Mitch tried to sound gruff, but his voice wavered.

No one answered. Nothing moved.

Mitch backed away from the trees. His mouth went dry. "Wh-who are you?"

A soft breeze blew through the trees, and amid the rustling of leaves, Mitch thought he heard more whispering. First one voice. Then another in reply.

Mitch scrambled to his bike and jumped on the kick start. The engine sputtered.

He glanced at the trees. Three gray figures stood at the edge of the woods. They were no more than fifty feet away, but he couldn't make out any distinct features. Only that they were tall and thin.

Mitch swore and jumped on the kick start again. This time the engine fired up and he spun around, out of the station, back onto the highway.

7

Conner pulled into Marta's driveway and stared at the house. Sunlight filtered down through the branches of the big ash tree in the front yard and cast patches of light and shadow onto the doorway.

Conner made his way around back to the patio door. Marta kept a key under a potted plant. He found it and let himself in.

"Marty?" he called but his voice sounded flat and small. He walked through the kitchen into the hallway. Ahead of him was the foyer and to the left was the living room. She hadn't redecorated much since the divorce.

He peered up the stairway. "Marty?"

No answer. The house was silent.

Conner was just about to head up the stairs when his legs stiffened. His body convulsed as pain tore through him. Intense and sharp. It felt as if a giant knife had pierced his chest and cut down straight through his torso. His neck and arms stiffened. His jaw clenched. He felt himself topple forward onto the tiled floor. An intense pressure built inside his chest and neck. His ribs felt as if they were going to snap. White light seared through the corners of his eyes, blotting out the hall and the room beyond. The pressure mounted. The pain was so intense that it paralyzed him. He felt his tongue clenched between his teeth. He couldn't even scream.

Then, as suddenly as it started, the pain left. The pressure was gone and Conner went limp. He lay on the floor, unable to move, gasping for breath. The white light faded and his vision slowly returned. It was as if someone had flashed a powerful spotlight in his eyes in the middle of a dark room and then turned it off again. Now he saw only spots. Large white blotches that turned amber and red. He heard himself moaning. But his voice was muffled and distant, as though his eardrums had burst.

He lay gasping for breath for several seconds. His body limp, his cheek pressed against the cold ceramic floor tile.

Then something moved past him. A small, bare foot touched softly on the tile right in front of his face, then lifted and was gone.

Conner was too numb to react. He tried

to lift his head. To see who had just walked past him. He struggled to move but his limbs wouldn't respond. Every nerve ending tingled from his convulsion. Using his shoulders and all of his strength, he managed to roll onto his side. His arms flopped about like deadweights.

He glimpsed a figure moving through the kitchen, small and waiflike. He couldn't see any features, though. It moved quickly, silhouetted in the sunlight that streamed through the patio door. Then it was out of sight.

Conner tried to talk. "Hey . . . ," he moaned.

A second later, the figure flitted back across the kitchen.

As his paralysis slowly abated, Conner struggled to his feet, clutching the walls to steady himself. His head spun like he'd just spent the last several hours on a Tilt-A-Whirl ride. He stumbled into the kitchen, bracing himself against the doorway.

His vision was still blotchy, but he heard the flap, flap, flap of bare feet on the tile floor. Conner lurched to the cooking island in the center of the kitchen. From there, he saw the figure standing in the breakfast nook, shrouded in the sunlight.

It turned and ran toward him.

Conner jerked backward, fumbling for something to protect himself if need be. A small body emerged from the light and sprinted past Conner, back down the hallway, out of sight. Sunlight glinted off a bouncing mop of blond hair.

"No!" Conner stood frozen, clutching the granite countertop to keep himself from falling.

He cried out again. Louder this time. Shock had turned to fear. And fear into rage.

"No!"

His heart pounded and he gulped for air. He tried to move but his legs buckled under his weight. His anger was slowly giving way to something else.

Conner clung to the island. Clutching it, leaning his weight on top of it. His gasps for air turned to sobs.

He tried to speak again. This time his voice was only a whimper.

"Matthew?"

8

Helen got out of her car and peered up at the apartment. Kyle lived in a small one-bedroom on the fifth floor. There had really been no need for him to move out of Helen's condo, but he had wanted his space. He was twenty-four and needed his own space.

Helen looked back down the street. A few cars were parked along the curb, but like everywhere else, no people were in sight. The sun cast the whole street in an amber glow. The sidewalk and shops along the block were punctuated by the shade of evenly spaced trees. It would have been a cheerful scene, were it not for the conspicuous lack of people.

She turned her attention back to Kyle's building, steeled herself, and went inside. Letting the door close behind her, she stood in the foyer, listening. No music, no muffled voices, no sounds of life anywhere in the building.

There was no elevator, so Helen paced herself up the four flights of stairs.

She got to Kyle's floor and found his apartment. Number 503. She knocked and listened. No sounds inside.

She knocked again. "Kyle?"

No answer.

"Kyle," Helen called louder, but she could hear her voice quivering. "Please."

She pulled on the doorknob and pounded harder. "Kyle!"

Tears stung her eyes, and she pressed her forehead against the door. Why would he have left without even calling her? Where had everyone gone? What was going on?

"Mom?"

Kyle's voice broke through the silence with jarring abruptness.

He stood at the end of the hall, staring at her, almost as if he was surprised to see her.

Helen ran to him. "Kyle!"

She threw her arms around his shoulders and hugged him. But he just stood there, arms at his side.

Helen wept now, unable to control her emotions. Her mind reeled with a thousand questions, but she couldn't even think what to ask him first.

After several seconds, she stepped back

and wiped her eyes. "Where were you? Do you know what's going on?"

Kyle looked confused and shook his head.

Helen frowned. "What's wrong?"

"I . . . I don't know." Kyle looked down at his hands. "What's happening to me?"

Helen reached for his hands but he withdrew.

"What's wrong?"

Kyle just shook his head.

Helen took a step toward him. "Kyle, honey, what's the matter?"

Kyle winced in pain and took another step backward. "Mom . . . what's happening to me?"

He held his hands out. His palms were blistered and red.

"Kyle!" Helen gasped. "What happened to you?"

"I don't know."

"Let me see them —"

"No!" Kyle pulled away and backed up further.

"Honey, I'm not going to hurt you. Just let me see them."

Kyle winced again. His hands stiffened. Helen saw the blisters crack and begin to bleed. Kyle gritted his teeth and groaned. "It hurts!"

Helen's eyes widened. The blisters were

spreading across her son's hands even as she stared at them. Blood dripped onto the floor.

Kyle threw his head back. "What are they doing to me?"

He turned his hands over. The blisters were spreading onto his wrists and forearms. He screamed, "It burns!" He tucked his hands under his arms and doubled over. "Why are they doing this?"

Helen was in tears. "Kyle, who? Who's doing this? What happened to you? Where were you?"

But Kyle was no longer listening. He moved away, clawing at his shirt. Helen could see the blisters spreading onto his neck. He screamed again and bolted past her, down the hall.

"Kyle!" Helen called after him, but he was already down the stairs.

She followed him, her mind now growing numb from shock. What was happening? She could hear his cries echo up the stairwell.

In a panic now, she hurried down the stairs. Kyle's voice grew fainter.

"Kyle!" she screamed. This had to be a bad dream. Or some kind of hallucination.

Helen reached the bottom and ran out into the street, where she was met with the same silence she had encountered earlier. Kyle was nowhere to be seen. She ran up the street, calling out for him. After three blocks she stopped, out of breath. She stood there, gasping for air and listening.

No answer. No screams. Nothing.

9

Mitch rolled into the garage and shut off his bike. The double bay doors were still open, exactly as he had left them last night. His tools were still out on the workbench, and the radio was still on, though only static hissed through the speaker now.

And there was no sign of Stan. Not that Mitch was surprised. He hadn't seen a single car or pedestrian the entire way back to the garage. It was as if the northern suburbs had been evacuated. Mitch adjusted the radio on the workbench, scanning all the frequencies, AM and FM. Static hissed back at him. He shut it off.

This all had to have something to do with that storm last night. If it *was* last night. Who knew how long he might have been lying in that ditch. It might've been days.

His heart pounded and his mouth was dry. He shuddered as he recalled the creatures he had seen — or thought he had seen — at the gas station. Were they even human? That had been no storm and no lightning in the clouds. There had been something inside. Was this some kind of invasion? Had everyone been evacuated? Or had something worse happened to them? More to the point, why had *he* been left behind?

"This can't be happening." The sound of his voice seemed odd in the eerie stillness of the garage.

Mitch shook his head. The whole thing was surreal. He closed his eyes and tried to think. What to do next?

He went into the office and dialed Linda's number again. Again he got her answering machine. This time he hung up.

He stared at the phone, biting his lip. After a moment, he picked up the receiver and dialed another number. It rang four times before an answering machine clicked in.

"You've reached Walter Kent. I'm sorry I'm not able to take your call right now, but if you leave a message, I'll get back to you."

"Dad . . ." Mitch's voice broke. How long had it been since he had addressed his father? He was at a loss. "Dad, I don't know if you're going to get this message, but I . . . I'm just a little sc —"

Scared? He wasn't about to admit that to his father.

". . . a little . . . I mean, things are a little weird here. I don't know where everybody is. I don't know what happened, and . . ." He paused again and swallowed. His throat was dry. "I . . . I'm going to head down to the city to see if I can find anyone. I don't know what else to do. If you get this . . . I just wanted to let you know that I . . . uh, where I went."

Mitch hung up and returned to the garage, sitting down to gather his thoughts.

First of all, he had to see if Linda was home, though deep down he knew she most likely wasn't. Still, he felt obligated to make sure. Maybe there would be some clue as to where she had gone. Whatever had happened to her, she hadn't called or left a message. He couldn't even remember the last time he had seen her. Or the last thing he had said to her.

Next, he would stop by his father's house. After that he would continue south into the city. There had to be people there. There's no way they could have evacuated all of Chicago.

He went up to his apartment to pack a few things. Then he retrieved Rizzo's .45 and a box of bullets from the drawer under the register. He tucked the gun into his belt, started up his bike, and pulled out of the garage, heading south. Linda lived just a few miles from the garage.

Mitch shook his head. Last night, he was going to propose to her. He was making plans to buy the garage. Today, he was just hoping to find someone — *anyone* — still alive.

He cast a glance in his rearview mirror. Well, someone human at least.

He pulled up in front of Linda's house and looked around. She still lived with her parents. She had just turned twenty and was working her way through technical college. He had wanted her to move in with him, but she refused. She was old-fashioned that way — or at least her folks were. But she had said it'd be smarter for her to live at home while she was in school than to move out and just add to her expenses. Mitch liked that about her. She had her head screwed on straight.

The front door was unlocked. Mitch went inside.

"Linda?"

The only sound was the grandfather clock ticking in the corner. Mitch checked upstairs and then in the basement. Nothing. Two sets of car keys hung on a small key rack on the kitchen wall. They hadn't taken their car. Clothes were still in the closets.

No sign they had left in a hurry or tried to pack anything. The whole house was tidy and undisturbed.

He went back onto the porch and surveyed the street. Everything looked normal, except for the fact that there were no people anywhere.

Mitch got back on his bike. His father lived in Lake Bluff, several miles south. Mitch cruised through town before getting on the highway. His stomach was knotted, but his head felt clouded and numb.

The four lanes of Highway 41 were completely empty. Normally it was crowded with traffic, one of the main arteries from the northern suburbs down to Chicago. Mitch cruised along, scanning the businesses and parking lots on the way. Straining to see any sign of life.

He turned off to Lake Bluff, where he had grown up. He hadn't been home in six years. Not since . . . not since the argument.

He'd left home right out of high school, fleeing his father's tyranny. His father had gotten into politics when Mitch was only five, having made a successful bid for Congress. And so he was rarely home during Mitch's childhood. And when he was, his father spent most of the time in his study. The only family time Mitch recalled growing up was going to church — and then it seemed like a facade to Mitch. An attempt to appear pious and conservative for his constituents. His father was open and affable in church or while campaigning. But at home, he was stern and brooding.

Mitch had always resented the hypocrisy. The dual personality. He had been forced to conform to a set of rules and religious beliefs not for pursuit of virtue but solely to appease his father. He had always promised himself that as soon as he was old enough, he would leave. And at eighteen, after he'd gotten the job at Rizzo's and secured the apartment over the garage, he let his old man have it. Both barrels. All the frustration and rage that had been building for years.

Then he left and never looked back.

Mitch pulled up his father's long, tree-lined driveway and shut off the bike. The majestic house was big and brooding — much like his old man — and the spacious yard was still perfectly manicured. The trees were larger than he remembered, but otherwise, it was all the same. He felt sick, in a way. As though everything he had wanted to escape from had suddenly drawn him back.

The big front door was locked, but Mitch

went to a side entrance, surrounded by ivy. That door was never very secure, and with a few slams of his shoulder, it snapped open.

He stood just inside the entrance and listened. The house was silent.

"Dad?" His voice echoed though the rooms.

Nothing. He went into the dining room and looked around.

"Hey, Dad, it's Mitch."

Somewhere upstairs the floor creaked.

Mitch pulled the gun from his belt and flipped the safety off. He stood, listening, holding his breath. After several seconds, he exhaled. Maybe it had been his imagination.

Memories flooded his mind. Memories of a childhood that had been happy once. Very early on . . .

The floor creaked again.

Mitch slipped down the hall into the front foyer and peered up the winding staircase.

Upstairs, a door closed.

His heart pounding and hands trembling, Mitch paused to wipe the perspiration from his forehead. He shook his head. Something inside screamed for him to leave, but something else — something stronger — drew him on. He moved up the stairs.

The upstairs hallway was wide and carpeted. Four doors opened off the hall, two on each side. One of them was closed. The last one on the left. The door to his father's bedroom.

He inched his way down the hall. Mitch's old bedroom looked tidy and untouched. His father had converted the second bedroom into an office.

Mitch paused and listened at the door to his father's bedroom. Then, with the gun held steady, he turned the knob and opened the door.

10

Conner sat on the front stoop of Marta's house. His gaze was unfixed.

He had spent the last fifteen minutes searching the house from top to bottom but found nothing. No sign of his son. No sign of any explanation for his ghostly hallucination. He was at a loss for what to do next.

And as perplexing as everything else was the seizure he had experienced. The pain had been excruciating. It had most likely triggered the hallucination of Matthew. But what had caused the seizure? Was this some act of terrorism? Had there been some biological or chemical weapon released? Or was his convulsion merely a symptom of something worse yet to come?

Several minutes later, Conner stood up. He had to find some answers, though he had no idea where to look. He returned to his car and backed out of the driveway.

He decided he would return home. Maybe

a solution would present itself. Maybe he would find someone else along the way. But before going home, he had to make a stop.

Fifteen minutes later, Conner pulled into the Forest Hills Cemetery. A narrow gravel road wound through the maze of granite monuments and headstones. After several turns, he came to a stop near a small mausoleum. A miniature statue of Jesus stood at the front. It was weathered and cracked. Above it, seven words were etched into the stone.

I am the Resurrection and the Life.

Conner sneered at the statue. It wasn't what he had come here to see.

Beyond it, he spotted a small headstone, barely visible in the grass. Three rows back, second stone to the left. Under the shade of an old ash tree.

But Conner just sat in the car, his hand clutching the door handle. The last time he had actually stood at the grave was five years earlier, at the funeral.

Five years. One month. Thirteen days.

He had not seen it since. He couldn't muster the courage to see Matthew's name again, engraved in stone with two dates only four years apart.

At length, he forced himself out of the car. After his hallucination at the house, he needed to see it. If for no other reason than to be sure the grave was still there.

It was. Just as he remembered it. Small red flowers sprouted from fresh dirt on either side of the headstone. Probably Marta's doing. Conner bent down and ran his hand over the smooth granite. His fingers traced the letters.

"Matthew." Conner's voice was barely a whisper. His eyes stung as tears welled up and dripped down his cheeks. He had worked so hard to forget. To detach himself from those memories. To sever all the strings, all the chains that bound him to it.

From the corner of his eye, Conner glimpsed something move. A dark shape slipped behind a tree. Conner gasped and lurched backward. He thought he could see the crest of someone's arm and shoulder around the tree trunk.

"Who are you?"

Conner stood, frozen, chest pounding, not sure of what to do. Maybe it was someone who had answers. Or, more likely, it was someone out looking for them, just as he was.

Or . . . could it be Matthew?

After a moment, Conner's curiosity won

out and he took a few cautious steps. A diminutive shape darted out from the tree and dashed behind a row of gravestones.

Conner lunged after it, sprinting along a parallel course.

"Wait!"

He caught only fleeting glimpses of the figure as it raced behind the headstones. It was fairly small, more the size of a boy than an adult.

Conner pursued it to the end of the row, where it dove behind a mausoleum. He stopped at the front, gasping for air.

"Wait! I don't want to hurt you. I just —"

He never finished the sentence.

Without warning, his back arched and his legs stiffened. A sharp bolt of pain sliced through his torso just as it had before, paralyzing him. He felt himself fall backward onto the grass. The pressure built inside his chest, neck, and jaw, growing so great that he felt he was going to burst. His muscles tightened, frozen up like steel. White light pressed in from the corners of his vision along with what felt like an ice-cold blast of air.

Then it was gone, passing over him like a wave. The light faded, and the cold, and his vision returned.

Groaning, he rubbed his eyes. He could

just see the outline of someone's face, silhouetted against the sky. Someone leaning over him. Slowly it came into focus. Eyes, nose, and a mouth.

Conner opened his mouth but couldn't speak. All he could do was lie there, moaning and gasping for breath.

11

Helen sat in her car, staring ahead. Her eyes were red but her face was expressionless. She had searched the streets for nearly an hour, looking and listening for Kyle. Hoping for any sign of him. She had circled the block where he lived and continued in an outward spiral, widening her search.

The image of her son was seared into her memory. The blisters spreading across his body and his agony. It was as if he was burning alive. The encounter was no hallucination; that much she knew. She had touched him, thrown her arms around him. But what was happening to him? Who was responsible? Why were they torturing him?

Her mind culled through every possible explanation. Was it some government agency? The military? How had they evacuated the entire city? Was it some sort of bioweapon? A virus unleashed on the general populace? If so, was she infected as well?

Helen now found herself driving north on a deserted Michigan Avenue, her senses numb in disbelief. She crossed the river and finally stopped in the middle of the Ohio Street intersection. She got out of her car and leaned against it.

Buildings loomed around her, silent and empty, surrounding her with a canyon of concrete, steel, and glass. But not a soul in sight.

A sick feeling rose in the pit of her stomach. A growing fear replaced the numbness that had been there earlier. She had to find someone. She had to find some answers. She had called 911 several times on her cell phone, but to no avail. No one answered. She found a public phone and paged through the phone book, dialing every government agency and emergency number she could find. But each time she met with a dead-end recording or no answer at all.

At length, she fell onto a curbside bench and buried her face in her hands. Her sobs came in convulsions as she thought of Kyle, suffering somewhere out there all alone. Was he even still alive?

Finally she regained a grip on her senses and went back to her car. She leaned in the door and pressed the horn.

"Help me!"

She blared the horn again and screamed.

"Can anyone hear me?"

She paused to listen a moment and then repeated it.

After several more times, she heard something, faint and distant.

Voices.

Helen looked around. It *was* voices. But not faint. Not distant. They were merely soft. Quiet. Almost like . . .

Whispers.

She held her breath. The whispering was soft at first, like remote echoes, reverberating off the buildings. She couldn't tell which direction it was coming from. She spun around and strained to listen, tilting her head.

One voice whispered off to her left. Another replied to her right.

Helen peered into the storefront windows and doorways on either side of the street. But no matter which direction she turned, the voice seemed to come from behind her. It was as if someone was watching her. Toying with her. She couldn't make out any words. Just whispers.

Fear flowed up like a fountain inside her, flooding her veins with ice. Something wasn't right. Whatever these voices were, somehow she knew they weren't friendly.

They weren't trying to help.

Then she turned and caught a glimpse of movement across the street. A shadow slipped into a doorway and out of view. Her heart jumped. Was that Kyle? She peered at the doorway. Why would Kyle try to hide from her?

Another voice whispered behind her.

Helen's eyes widened. She wasn't alone. And something told her she wasn't safe.

She jumped back in the Tahoe and started it up. A moment later, tires squealed on the pavement as she tore off, east onto Ohio Street.

Helen drove for several blocks, glancing in her mirror but catching no sign of anyone following her. She wasn't even sure what she had seen or heard. Maybe she was imagining things. But still, she thought she had better err on the side of caution. She had no idea who — if anyone — was out there. Who were they and what did they want? And why were they watching her?

She shook her head. In a matter of seconds, she had gone from desperately trying to be found to just wanting to hide. She drove another few blocks before feeling safe enough to slow down. Spotting a convenience store, she screeched to a stop.

She suddenly felt vulnerable. She needed

a weapon. She needed a gun. Something to protect herself.

Helen ran inside the store. These places usually kept a gun by the register. She slipped behind the counter and rummaged through the shelves. Far back in the shelf beneath the register, she spotted the rubber grip of a handgun. She reached in; her fingers closed around it. . . .

Then something hard pressed against the back of her head.

"Don't move."

12

Mitch cracked open the door to his father's bedroom. His heart pounded. His mouth had gone dry, yet his hands were damp with perspiration. He switched his grip on the gun and dried off his palm on his pant leg.

He pushed the door open further. A musty warmth brushed against his face and with it came a pungent scent. Bile and rot. Mitch winced. The curtains were drawn, and though he could not see anything in the muted light, he did hear something: a gentle, intermittent rattling. Soft but steady.

His eyes adjusted to the subdued lighting enough to make out the shape of the bed against the far wall. Then he heard a rustle of linen.

Something stirred beneath the quilt.

A chill ran down Mitch's spine and he froze. The rattling he heard was the sound of breathing. Labored and gargled.

Mitch stood in the doorway, unable to

move. After a moment, he gathered the courage to whisper, "Dad?"

The wheezing continued unabated. Mitch swallowed and took a step into the room.

"Dad? Is that you?" he whispered louder. "It's me. It . . . it's Mitch."

The quilt moved slightly, but the breathing did not alter.

The stench grew stronger as Mitch moved into the room, and he found himself fighting back a gag reflex. He covered his nose and mouth.

Something inside him urged him to leave. To get out of this house. But there seemed to be another force compelling him forward.

Mitch moved around to the side of the bed and tugged the quilt down.

His eyes grew wide. "No!"

He stumbled backward against the wall.

It was a woman's face, gaunt and sunken — little more than a skull covered with a veil of pallid skin, mottled by lesions. Her eyes were open wide in an unfixed gaze. Dark circles ringed her sockets. All that was left of her strawberry blonde hair hung in frail wisps on her scalp. Her breathing came in gargled rasps from the fluid in her lungs.

"Mom?" Mitch's horror slowly turned to rage. He pointed the gun at her face. "No," he hissed through clenched teeth. "You're not real!"

The woman's gaze slowly turned and fixed on Mitch. Her cracked lips parted, revealing yellowed teeth. She reached a withered hand out toward him. Her breathing grew more labored as she opened her mouth as if to speak. The fluid in her lungs rattled like a rake across gravel.

Mitch shook his head and lowered the gun. His eyes filled with tears. "No."

This couldn't be real. His mother had died ten years ago. He had watched her suffer as the cancer devoured her. This couldn't be happening again.

A sliver of sunlight shone between the curtains on the window across the room. Outside, a shadow passed by, blocking the light momentarily, and then moved away.

Mitch brought the gun up and fired at the window. Bullets tore through the curtains, shattering the glass. Smoke filled the room. He lunged for the window and tore the curtain aside. Sunlight poured in, blinding him for a moment. He heard a thump overhead followed by a heavy scraping, like claws skittering across the shingles. Then another series of thuds and then . . .

Nothing.

Squinting in the light, Mitch peered out the window. Nothing moved in the yard below. He turned back to the room. Through the haze of smoke, he could see that the bed was empty. The quilt was pulled down, but all that remained was a pillow. No indentation, no other sign that his mother's body had been there. He looked out the window again and then back to the bed.

Mitch blinked and stormed into the hall. Enough of this. They wanted to mess with his head? He'd give them something to mess with!

He ran down the stairs and outside, circling the house, pointing the gun in front of him. He checked the roof, the shrubs, and the tall hedge that enclosed the spacious backyard. Nothing moved. No sign of life.

"Who are you?" he shouted. "What do you want with me?"

His voice dissolved into silence. Nothing moved in the yard or out on the street. He heard nothing but his own labored breathing.

Mitch shook his head and his voice softened. "Why are you doing this?"

He returned to his motorcycle, swung a leg over, and sat for a moment.

He *had* seen his mother in her bed. It couldn't have been a hallucination. He had *heard* her breathing. The stench of death was as thick as it had been all those years ago. She looked exactly as she had then. He was fourteen when she died, and he remembered vividly the suffering she had gone through. And how horrible she looked.

And he remembered his father — the congressman — sitting at her bedside, praying and reading the Bible to her. The man's piety revolted him.

Mitch had never accepted his father's faith. It was never anything more than a set of rules and regulations. He had given God one chance to prove Himself. To show He was more than just empty religion. Mitch had prayed for his mother to be healed. For seven months he prayed. And when it was obvious she wasn't going to get better, he prayed for at least a quick and merciful death. But even that prayer was not answered. She died slowly. She lingered for more than a month in that condition.

Mitch grimaced. It was as if God wanted to show off His handiwork. Like He took delight in her suffering.

The morphine had done little to ease her pain toward the end. And his father would read that stupid Bible to her as if it would bring her some comfort. She was lying there, moaning, and he just kept reading. It was as if no one could see her suffering. And no one would do anything about it.

That was when Mitch learned prayer was useless. God did what He wanted. He couldn't care less. Mitch had hated God with every fiber of his being.

And he hated his father for keeping his faith.

Mitch ran his hand through his hair. What was going on?

It must have something to do with the cloud he'd seen last night. Or more specifically, whatever was *inside* the cloud. He shook his head and grunted. As weird as it seemed, there had to be some kind of alien presence at work.

Whatever was happening, Mitch knew he wasn't alone. Someone . . . or some*thing* . . . was following him. *Watching* him. It was as if they were trying to make him see things, to scare him. Maybe just to see how he would react.

He felt a light breeze brush back his hair. And on the breeze, he heard something. A chill crawled down his spine.

Whispering.

Just as he had heard in the woods at the gas station.

One voice whispered something Mitch could not make out. Another voice whispered back.

He thought he glimpsed a shadow moving behind the shrubs in the neighbor's yard. A voice inside his head screamed, *Get out of here!*

Heart pounding, Mitch thumbed the ignition and snapped the bike into gear. The rear tire squealed and the back of the bike spun around, laying down a circle of rubber.

The next instant Mitch tore off down the street.

13

Conner lay on his back, groaning and unable to move.

Slowly the face leaning over him came into focus.

It was a boy, no more than nine or ten years old and rail thin. Large brown eyes peered at Conner from under a thick mop of dark, matted hair. He wore an old flannel shirt a few sizes too big for him and torn jeans.

This wasn't Matthew.

Conner struggled to sit up. His head was spinning. "Wh-who are you?"

The boy backed away from him, crouching down beside the mausoleum. His gaze darted around the cemetery and back to Conner.

Conner rubbed his eyes. "Did you hear me? Who *are* you?"

The boy lifted an arm and pointed in the direction of Conner's car.

Conner shook his head. "What's the matter? Can you understand me?"

The boy narrowed his eyes for a moment, then pointed to the car a second time.

"You need a ride?" Conner nodded. "I can give you a ride. Are your parents nearby?"

The boy was looking around the cemetery again. His face was grim and focused.

Conner got to his knees and stood up. The ground seemed to sway beneath him. He took a few shaky steps toward the boy. "Do you have any family? Have you seen anyone else around here?"

The boy slowly moved away from the mausoleum and circled Conner, keeping his distance. He pointed again toward the Mercedes and motioned Conner to follow.

"I just want to know who you are," Conner said. "Can you speak English?"

The boy peered at Conner's mouth. As if trying to understand what he was saying.

Conner nodded. "English? Do you speak English?"

The boy shot a glance beyond Conner and his eyes widened.

Conner spun around. The cemetery was empty. Nothing moved.

He turned back to the boy. "What's wrong? What's going on?"

The boy lunged forward and caught hold

of Conner's arm. Conner tried to pull away but the boy's grip clenched around his wrist.

"I said, I need —" Conner stopped. The boy was still looking past him and Conner suddenly felt a chill. He turned around and gasped.

Something was standing beside a large headstone twenty yards away.

Conner stumbled back into the boy. "Who — who is that?"

He couldn't make out any details. It was no more than a fleeting gray silhouette that ducked behind the stone. Then from the corner of his eye, Conner spotted a second shadow just as it moved behind a tree.

"What is it? What's going on? Who are they?"

The boy tugged Conner's arm. Harder now. Conner's chill turned to fear.

The kid knew something. He knew enough to be afraid of whatever those things were.

They hurried to the Mercedes. The boy crawled over the driver's side into the passenger seat. Conner got in and started the engine.

"Just tell me what's going on. Who are they?" Conner's voice quivered. He tried to maintain his composure.

The boy peered through the window and

shook his head. His expression was more stern than afraid.

"Maybe they have some answers."

The boy glared at Conner and pounded on the dashboard.

Conner glanced back out the window. His eyes widened.

One of the figures was standing over Matthew's grave. This one made no attempt to seek cover. It just stood there. Watching them.

Conner squinted and rubbed his eyes, but it was as if he were looking at it through an out-of-focus lens. Everything else was clear; he just couldn't seem to focus on the figure itself.

Then it moved!

It walked toward them with wide, deliberate strides. Conner threw the car into gear and stomped on the accelerator. Tires spun, kicking up grass and gravel as they tore down the path. He glanced in the rearview mirror but couldn't see anything.

The road wound an erratic course through the cemetery. Conner's hands sweated with raw panic now. What was going on? What were those things? He gunned the accelerator, skidding around turns, sideswiping a large mausoleum and toppling a Virgin Mary.

They had reached the main entrance when something lunged out in front of them. Conner caught a glimpse of a tall, shadowy torso, arms held out, and a head . . . a head with no face!

Conner cried out as the Mercedes plowed into it. The creature bounced off the fender with a sickening thump. He swore and spun the wheel hard. Tires screaming, the car roared into the street, fishtailing as Conner fought to keep control. He glanced in the rearview mirror. A gray mass rolled across the pavement, off to the side of the road.

Just before the creature disappeared from view, Conner thought he saw it getting back to its feet. He jammed the accelerator to the floor and headed toward the highway.

14

Helen felt the cold, hard metal of a gun against her skull. She took a breath and raised her free hand. Her other hand was jammed in the shelf, her fingertips still closed around the gun she had found there.

"Get both your hands where I can see them!" the voice snapped.

Helen released her grip on the gun and removed her other hand. The voice had the harsh timbre of a street thug, probably just a teenager, but that gave her no comfort. Her heart pounded as she straightened up and put both hands in the air.

"I . . . I don't have any money —"

"Shut up!"

A second set of footsteps approached, and Helen reflexively turned her head.

"I said, *don't move!*"

A second voice let loose a string of profanity.

"What you gonna do? You gonna shoot her?"

"What if she's one of *them?*"

"She ain't one of them."

"How do you know? You don't even know what they look like for sure."

There was a pause.

"Yo, lady. What's your name?"

Helen turned to face them.

Two black kids stood over her. Both were tall and lanky. The first one — the one with the gun — wore a black White Sox sweatshirt with the hood pulled up. The other one wore a gray Nike T-shirt and jeans. Neither of them was older than eighteen, she guessed, twenty at the most.

"Helen," she said, leaving out her last name.

"Where you live, *Helen?*" White Sox snapped.

Helen shook her head. "I'm not giving you my address."

White Sox pointed his gun in her face. "Lady, I ain't foolin' with you. Tell me where you live!"

"In the — in the Hudson, on — on Lake Shore! Thirty-seventh floor."

White Sox sneered and leaned closer. "Who won the World Series last year?"

"What?" Helen shook her head. "I don't

know! I don't follow baseball!"

"Yo, man — just chill out!" The other kid pushed the gun away. White Sox shoved him back.

Helen closed her eyes as the two argued through a barrage of expletives. She tried to concentrate on her breathing, control her emotions, and clear her head.

The kid in the gray T-shirt argued that they should leave now and get out of the city. And though he seemed to be the older of the two, and probably the leader, White Sox was not going to be easily persuaded. He must have felt Helen had information about what had happened to everyone. They were as clueless as she was, and just as scared, if not more so.

"Please," Helen interrupted, doing her best to sound calm. "I don't know what's going on either."

Nike turned to her. "You seen anyone? Anyone following you?"

Helen shook her head. "I — I haven't seen anyone." She decided against telling them about her encounter with Kyle. For all she knew, it had been her imagination. In either case, it would only pique their interest and extend this ordeal.

Nike crouched down. "Lady, someone's out there. I don't know who it is or what they want. They been following us all day." He paused and looked down for a moment. "I don't think they're human. And I don't think they're friendly."

"What're you saying?" Helen peered at him.

White Sox swore. "You need us to spell it out for you? *Aliens,* lady. They're aliens!"

Helen nodded. "The storm. Did you see the clouds moving in off the lake last night?"

"Yeah, we saw it." White Sox lifted his sweatshirt, revealing a dark purple rash covering his stomach and chest. "And they did something to me! I want to know what they did to me!"

It wasn't a burn like Helen had seen on Kyle. This looked more like a rash or a bruise. "What is it?"

"That's what I'm trying to find out!" White Sox's voice was gruff, but Helen could see fear in his eyes. "I woke up this morning with this on my chest. And now it's spreading."

Helen backed away. "Does it hurt?"

He lowered his shirt. "A little. Like a burn. But it's cold. It feels cold."

Helen shook her head. "I . . . I'm not a doctor. I don't know what —"

White Sox put his hand up, slipped over to the door, and crouched down. "Listen," he said. "You hear that?"

Nike followed him. Helen could see a gun under his shirt, tucked into the back of his jeans.

Now she heard it too. Outside. Soft at first, like a breeze moaning through the empty buildings. *No,* thought Helen, *not wind. More like . . .*

Breathing.

A long, slow inhale started softly but grew steadily louder until it reached a deafening crescendo — like a jet engine — and then stopped suddenly.

White Sox turned around, his eyes wide. "They're here!"

The next instant, the window and door shattered. Shards of glass shot across the room. Helen ducked behind the counter and covered her eyes as glass rained down.

The store erupted in shouting and gunfire.

When she looked up again, she saw a tall figure standing in the doorway. Tall, thin, and gray. It loomed behind White Sox and wrapped a pair of long arms around his chest, crushing him in a bear hug. The thing had no face that Helen could see, like a blurred shadow. But it had substance.

White Sox screamed and kicked. Helen watched as his face and hands changed color. His skin turned purple. As if the rash or bruise — or whatever it was — had suddenly spread across his entire body.

The creature lifted White Sox off his feet and stepped back through the shattered doorway. The boy continued to struggle and scream as it carried him around the corner of the building. It was the high-pitched, blood-chilling scream of a terrified kid.

Nike had drawn his gun and was firing at a second figure, crouched in the aisle in front of him. The creature made no effort to elude the barrage of bullets. It slowly straightened up and stood still. Helen could see bullets pummeling its body, but they disappeared into the gray flesh, leaving no holes and no damage.

The creature lunged forward, caught the boy by the neck, and lifted him up, peering at his face. It turned him slightly as if inspecting him. Nike tried to scream but could manage only a gargled whimper.

Helen gathered her senses and scrambled for the gun under the register. She reached into the shelf and felt her fingers close around the grip. She turned to take aim.

But the creature was gone. And the boy lay on the floor, gasping for breath.

15

Conner sped through town, flying though empty intersections. His eyes flicked reflexively from the road to the rearview mirror and back.

Had he seen what he thought he had seen? He'd struck one of the gray men — men if in fact it was a man — going at least thirty miles an hour and sent him flying off his fender. Conner watched him roll across the pavement, only to see him get up again as if nothing was wrong.

He glanced at the boy in the seat next to him. The boy who couldn't — or wouldn't — talk. "You know what's going on, don't you?"

The boy just stared at him. He could obviously hear Conner but didn't seem to understand what he was saying.

Conner tried again. *Habla Español?*

The kid didn't look Hispanic. His black hair and dark eyes made him look more

Middle Eastern, maybe . . . Iranian or Palestinian.

Conner tried to focus his attention on the road, but his thoughts returned to the creatures in the cemetery. Were they after them? Was it both of them they wanted or just the kid? And why couldn't he get a clear look at them? They seemed to be wearing some kind of camouflage. It had all happened so fast, but still . . . it was as if they were out of focus. Just enough to prevent him from making out any identifying traits. Maybe it was some sort of high-tech camouflage device. And why not? Anyone who could make an entire population disappear would certainly be able to do something like that. Conner's mind reeled.

He recalled the repairman on the roof. That had been *before* the storm. Before everyone had disappeared. Maybe it wasn't an illusion after all. Maybe this was some sort of orchestrated attack.

But an attack by whom?

As irrational as it all seemed, was there something extraterrestrial at work? What else could explain the bizarre cloud bank? Or cause his hallucination of Matthew?

He turned onto the highway and headed back home. Maybe he'd be able to find some way to communicate with this kid. He obviously knew something about these creatures. Maybe he had been captured by them and had just escaped.

Conner shook his head. He was a skeptic's skeptic and now here he was, entertaining theories of, what? Government conspiracies? Alien abductions?

Up ahead, sunlight glinted off of something metallic, coming toward them. It was another vehicle. He saw a single headlight.

A motorcycle!

Conner flashed his lights and slowed down. A knot tightened in his stomach. What if it was just more of the creatures? How many more of them were out here? What if they were tracking him or following him?

The motorcycle passed by. The rider was a muscular guy in a black T-shirt, jeans, and a leather jacket. A long blond ponytail fluttered behind him. He slowed down and peered at them from behind dark glasses; then he turned around and came back.

They both came to a stop on either side of the median.

"Stay put." Conner motioned to the boy while he got out of the car.

The other man had gotten off his bike and reached behind his back. A moment later he had produced a handgun and pointed it directly at Conner. "Don't move!"

Conner swore. Just his luck — the second person he came across today was some freak who was going to shoot him!

"Whoa, whoa!" Conner put his hands up. "Take it easy!"

The man scowled at Conner. "Who are you?"

Conner stared at the gun. "Uh . . . my name's Conner. I . . . uh . . ." He wondered how much to tell this guy. "I live right up in Lake Forest. . . . Look, I'm in the same predicament you are."

The man leaned forward, keeping the gun pointed at Conner's face. "How do *you* know what kind of predicament I'm in?"

Conner forced a grim smile. "Well, let me guess. You woke up this morning to find everybody had disappeared."

"And what do you know about it?"

"Nothing. That's just what happened to me. I'm out looking for answers, same as you."

Conner could feel the stranger's gaze boring through him from behind the dark glasses. "Look . . ." Conner softened his voice. His lawyer skills were kicking in. He needed to persuade this guy to put his gun away. "Look, I'm freaked out here too, okay? But let's not do anything rash. I mean, we'll both do better if we can work together, y'know? I just want some answers. Same as you."

The man lowered the gun slightly. "What'd you say your name was?"

Conner nodded. He was making progress. "Hayden. Conner Hayden. I . . . I'm a lawyer. What about you?"

The guy bit the inside of his cheek for a moment. "Mitch," he said finally.

"Mitch." Conner nodded again. "Good . . . good. Uh . . . look, Mitch, would you mind just pointing that thing down or something? I'll stay right here; I'm just a little nervous with you aiming that gun at me."

Mitch hesitated a moment, then lowered the gun.

Conner breathed a sigh. "Good. That's good."

Mitch removed his glasses. His face was solemn. "We're not alone."

"What do you mean?"

Mitch looked up and down the empty highway. "I mean, someone's been watching me. Maybe following me. I don't know. I don't think they're . . . human."

Conner nodded slowly. "I think I ran across a couple of them a few minutes ago."

"I never got a good look at them."

"Neither did I," Conner said. "I think they're using some kind of . . . camouflage or something. Did they come after you?"

"What do you mean?"

"Did they try to chase you?"

"No." Mitch shook his head. "No, they just seemed to be watching me. But I got the distinct feeling they weren't friendly."

Conner gestured toward the dent in his fender. "Well, one of them stepped out in front of my car."

"Where?"

"We saw some of them in the . . ." Conner paused, wondering whether he should tell this stranger that he had just come from a cemetery because he'd been hallucinating.

"We?" Mitch's expression turned dark. "I thought you said you were alone?"

Conner bit his lip. "Uh . . . yeah, I was." He hesitated, then opened the driver-side door and motioned to the boy. "Until I found him."

Mitch raised the gun again. "Who's that?"

"Take it easy," Conner said. "I don't know who he is. I just came across him a little while ago. But he seemed to know that those things were after us."

Mitch's brow remained furrowed. "What do you mean you 'just came across him'?"

"Well," Conner said, "I guess it'd be more

accurate to say he found me."

"How do you know he's not one of them?"

Conner glanced at the boy. The kid was leaning across the seat, staring at both of them. His brown eyes wide and haunting. Conner turned back to Mitch and shrugged. "I guess I don't."

"Maybe they're after *him.*"

Conner shook his head. "Maybe. But I don't think he speaks any English. At least he doesn't seem to understand. And I couldn't get him to speak at all."

"Where'd you find him?"

Conner drummed his fingers on the roof of the car. This guy was pretty sharp for a biker. "In the, uhhh . . . in the cemetery."

"The cemetery?"

"Yeah." Conner wasn't quite sure how to explain why he had gone there. He didn't want to appear unstable. "I had . . . a sort of hallucination or something and . . ."

Mitch seemed to perk up. "Have you seen things too? People you . . . used to know?"

Conner raised his eyebrows. "Uh . . . yeah."

Mitch lowered his gun and stared off down the road. "I saw my mother. I stopped by their house and . . ." He turned back to Conner. "She's been dead for ten years."

Conner frowned. This guy's dead mother.

Conner's dead son. There must be some connection. At length he said, "I saw my son. He, uh . . . he drowned five years ago."

"He's dead too?"

Conner nodded. "So I stopped by the cemetery to see . . . you know, if his grave was still there." Then he looked up. "Did you have any . . . pain or convulsions?"

Mitch shook his head. "No, nothing like that. But it was so real. I mean, I could *hear* her breathing. She was right there, just as real as you are now."

Conner rubbed his neck. "I had this . . . this pain. Twice now. It was so intense, I thought I was going to pass out. It was like a pressure inside my chest. I can't explain it. I never felt anything like it before."

"And then what happened?"

Conner shrugged. "It just stopped. I was dizzy, lying on the floor. And then I saw Matthew. He . . . he walked right past me."

Mitch's shoulders slumped. He sat back on his motorcycle, shaking his head. "I don't get it. What's going on?"

"I wish I knew." Conner fell silent for a moment. He suddenly realized how hungry he was. He hadn't had anything to eat all day, and it was getting close to noon. "Listen, are you hungry? Have you eaten anything yet today?"

Mitch looked up and shook his head.

"Why don't we head back to my place and get something to eat. Then maybe we can figure out what to do next."

16

Helen leaned against the counter, dazed. The kid in the gray shirt sat up, moaning, and looked around the store.

"They took your friend," Helen said.

She watched his expression turn from disbelief to shock. He scrambled to his feet and ran outside.

She heard him yelling. Calling for his friend. He ran up the street a little way and then back the other direction, shouting at the top of his lungs. His voice echoed among the buildings.

Helen watched him, but she felt no emotion. After everything she had just witnessed, she felt oddly detached, as if she were watching a movie. These *creatures* had crashed through plate glass, but there was no blood anywhere. They had been shot at — and hit — but the bullets had no effect.

What were they? What did they want? And why had they only taken the boy? It must've had something to do with the rash on his chest. She recalled seeing it spread across his face when the creature touched him. Those things must have caused it somehow. Some sort of virus maybe?

She felt dizzy, unsure of what to do next. Her main priority was still to find Kyle. Had these things taken him as well? Were they torturing him? Would that explain his burns that seemed to appear out of nowhere?

After a few minutes, the kid came back to the store, out of breath. "Did you see which way they went?"

Helen shook her head. "It happened so fast. . . ."

He stared at her. Helen could see his eyes slowly fill with tears. He turned away and crouched in the doorway. "What's happening?" he said. "Why are they doing this?"

Helen drew close behind him. "I'm sorry."

The boy sank against the doorframe, his face buried in his sleeve. Helen watched him for a moment. She couldn't just leave him here. They would both be better off staying together. Whatever was going on, they were safer if they stuck together.

"We . . . we should go," she said after a moment. "They might come back again. Maybe with others."

"It don't matter. They're gonna find us

wherever we go. We've been running from them all morning."

Helen looked around. "Maybe we should get out of the city, like you said. We could head north. See if we can find others . . . other survivors."

The kid shook his head. "I gotta find Terrell."

Helen hesitated a moment. This was a thug with a gun, but somewhere inside she knew he was also just a kid who had lost his friend. "How old are you boys?"

He glanced at her over his shoulder, then back at the street. "Sixteen."

Sixteen? Helen peered at the boy and shook her head. "What's your name?"

He seemed to ignore her for a moment, looking up and down the street. "Devon," he said at length. "Devon Marshall."

Helen's voice softened as she knelt behind him. "Devon, maybe we can help each other. I lost someone too. I lost my son. I've been looking for him all morning. And I just want to find out what happened to him."

Devon looked at the gun in his grasp. "I shot that thing at least eight times. I know I hit it. It didn't even bleed. Not one drop of blood."

"That's why we shouldn't wait around for

them to come back."

Devon shook his head. "Lady, those things probably got your son already, like they got everyone else. We're the only ones left. And I bet they'll come for us, too."

Helen stood up. "Well, I don't believe it. We can't be the only ones left. There have to be others somewhere. Maybe just as confused and scared, but I bet they're out there somewhere." She stepped around him and headed for her car. "And I'm going to find them."

"Lady," Devon called after her. "Yo, lady."

"And you know something?" Helen turned around. "My name is Helen. You got that? Your ghetto act is getting a little old."

"Helen." Devon stood up. "I'll come with you."

17

Mitch found himself headed back north now, following the guy in the Mercedes. He still wasn't sure if he could trust him. After what he had seen at his father's house, he wasn't going to trust anything he saw. Especially since this guy had obviously tried to hide that kid from him.

Maybe he had kidnapped the boy. Or maybe he was just trying to protect him. Mitch had to admit his own hulking, tattooed appearance didn't always make a good first impression.

They turned off the highway and headed through a residential area, past a golf course, and finally into a gated condo community. Mitch had only seen places like this from the outside. Way outside.

The palatial condominiums were impressive — homes to rich empty nesters or childless professionals, Mitch guessed. Or at least they had been once. Now they stood stark and silent in the sunlight. For all the wealth represented here, Mitch felt like he was driving through an Arizona ghost town.

They pulled up to a particularly large condo. Part of a three-unit building. They stopped at the farthest one. The backyard butted up to the golf course.

The lawyer and the kid got out of the Mercedes. Mitch ran his hand across the fender. He could tell the kid was watching him intently. Big brown eyes stared out from under a low mop of black hair.

Mitch pointed to the dent. "You say this just happened?"

The lawyer nodded. "Yeah. Just a few minutes before we came across you."

"The paint's chipped off," Mitch grunted. "It's rusting already. Looks a few months old at least."

Conner shrugged. "Well, I don't know what to tell you. It just happened a few minutes ago."

Mitch scraped a chip of paint off and narrowed his eyes.

"Look," Conner said. "I just bought this car three months ago. I've got the paperwork to prove it."

Mitch stood with his hands on his hips, biting the inside of his cheek. He didn't trust this guy. Not at all. But then again, there didn't seem much reason to be afraid of him either. His hair was mussed and his clothes were disheveled. It looked like maybe he'd slept in them. Maybe he was a lawyer. Maybe he wasn't. Either way, he didn't look like he weighed more than one seventy, one eighty, tops. Mitch had several inches and nearly fifty pounds on him.

Besides, Mitch had the gun. He wasn't going to give up the gun.

He followed them inside.

Conner went to the kitchen. "You want a sandwich?"

Mitch followed close behind. If the guy had a gun stashed around somewhere, he wasn't going to make it easy for him to get it. "A sandwich is fine."

Conner brought bread, meat, cheese, and mayo from the refrigerator.

The kid sat at the table, watching them. Conner made a roast beef sandwich and set it in front of the boy.

The kid just stared at it.

Conner motioned with his hands. "Go ahead; eat."

The kid pushed the plate away.

Conner frowned. "What is it? What's wrong?"

"Maybe he's a vegetarian," Mitch muttered.

Conner picked up the sandwich. "No, it's okay. See?" He took a bite. Then promptly gagged and spit it back out.

"What's the matter?" Mitch sniffed the package of beef and winced. The scent was strong with rot. "Dude, your meat's bad."

Conner shook his head. "I just bought it a couple days ago. It can't be bad already." He looked at the date on the label. Then he sniffed the bag of turkey cold cuts and grimaced.

Conner rummaged through all the food in his refrigerator, sniffing and grunting.

Mitch inspected a slice of the bread. Green spots peppered the crust. "Y'know, I'm no biologist or anything, but this looks like mold to me."

Conner scratched his head. "The power's on. But everything smells. Meat's rotten. Milk's sour."

"So much for lunch, huh."

Conner began searching his cabinets. "I gotta have something here that's not spoiled or stale."

Mitch shook his head. "Look. Dude. I'm not even hungry anymore. And I don't think we should be wasting our time just sittin' around here. I was headed into the city. I figure there's gotta be more people there."

"Fine." Conner nodded. "But I think we

should stick together. I think we're safer — you know, better off, if we stick together."

"Whatever." Mitch shrugged. "I just want to find some answers."

"So do I —" Conner stopped and stared through the glass doors of the breakfast nook.

Mitch peered outside. A dense grove of trees and foliage lined the back of the property. Patches of sunlight and shadow mingled with a tangle of branches and tree trunks. Something about the scene drew Mitch's gaze further in.

"Do you see that?" Conner whispered.

"Uhhh . . . I'm not sure. . . ." Mitch squinted but couldn't make out what had drawn the lawyer's attention.

Then something moved in the shadows.

Mitch gasped involuntarily. He could see one of the creatures in the shade. It stood so still that it blended in among the tree trunks and branches.

Conner moved closer to the window. "It looks like it's watching us."

Mitch fingered the grip of his gun. "They're all over the place."

"Maybe, but I only see one of them."

Mitch found his chest pounding. His hands bristled with cold sweat. "I don't think they're ever alone. When I saw them this morning, there was at least three of them."

Conner shook his head. "I think it's time to stop cowering and see what they want."

"What?" Mitch said. "You're not going out there?"

Conner nodded. "And I'll need you to come with and cover me."

"Are you *nuts?*"

"You said you wanted to get some answers. My guess is they —" Conner nodded out the window — "may have some."

"Yeah, but I — I meant to find some other *people.*" Mitch found himself stammering. "Not *them!* You said you ran into one of them with your car. How do you know they're not . . . y'know, hostile or something?"

"That's just it. I think if they had wanted to harm us, they could've done that at any time. It just looks like they're watching."

Mitch's jaw tightened. He hated being debated into a corner like this. It reminded him of the arguments he used to have with his father over politics and religion. He could feel the same sense of frustration growing in him now. Growing to anger. It was like trying to talk to a wall. A robot, preprogrammed with an opinion.

He glared at the lawyer, but the man just

looked back at him with a placid expression. The look of someone who was certain he was right, regardless of the truth.

After a moment Mitch looked away. "Fine," he said through his teeth. He was out of excuses. He took a breath and pulled his gun out of his belt.

As Conner slid the door open, the boy jumped from the stool and gripped his arm. He shook his head, wide-eyed.

Mitch snorted. "Y'know, maybe he knows something. Maybe we should listen to him."

Conner clutched the boy's shoulders. "It's all right. We'll be all right. We just want to try to talk with them. You stay here."

But the boy refused to let go. Conner set him firmly into a chair. "Stay here!"

They stepped out onto the patio and inspected the yard. Mitch peered into the foliage along the back of the lot. He could see only the one figure standing in the trees, still as a statue.

Mitch held the gun at his side, safety off, finger on the trigger. Fifty feet of thick grass led up to the tree line. It felt like a hundred and fifty.

They moved toward the trees. About halfway, Conner began talking to the creature.

"We . . . we just want answers," he said.

"We just want to find out what you want. What are you looking for?"

They inched closer. The thing didn't move.

Conner whispered to Mitch, "He's not trying to hide, but he's not coming out."

Mitch nodded. "He's staying in the shade."

"The ones I saw at the cemetery all kept to the shade too. I wonder if they're trying to avoid direct sunlight. Maybe it affects them."

"Same with the ones I saw."

They stopped a few yards from the trees. The creature remained motionless.

Mitch squinted. It was tall, probably over seven feet. And thin. Its torso was no thicker than Mitch's thigh, and its gangly limbs bulged at the joints. Mitch couldn't make out distinct hands. Just fleshy appendages that looked like mere extensions of its arms.

The creature didn't appear to have any clothing, nor did it seem to need any. There was no face, no genitals, no distinguishing marks of any kind. Its gray skin was thick and leathery. Only shallow indentations appeared where its eyes and mouth should have been.

Mitch brought his gun up. His hands shook.

Conner's voice trembled as well. "We . . . we don't mean any harm. We just want to try to know what you want —"

Mitch saw a gray blur, and the next thing he knew, the creature had lunged forward in one fluid movement and clutched Conner's wrist. Several multijointed fingers — like large spider legs — wrapped around his flesh. Mitch cried out and tumbled backward to the grass. His limbs went numb, as if he'd been dunked in ice water.

Conner's face was frozen in a mask of terror, eyes round, teeth clenched.

The creature drew Conner's arm into the shade and leaned its head forward. Two dark slits suddenly appeared where its eyes should have been, as if invisible razors were slicing into its gray skin. Then the slits peeled open to reveal white eyes. Cold, soulless, and empty.

Fear uncurled in Mitch's abdomen like a giant snake uncoiling. It paralyzed him. He watched the creature pull Conner into the shadow, but he couldn't move. He tried to close his eyes or will his limbs to move. . . .

From the direction of the house, he saw a flash of movement. The dark-haired boy dove for Conner, folded his arms across his waist, and threw his weight backward.

At that moment, Mitch found his strength

again. He brought the gun up, took aim at the creature's head, and pulled the trigger.

18

Helen made her way to the Edens and headed north. Why north, she couldn't say. Somehow it just felt right. As if the answer to this nightmare was in that direction. She reached into her overnight bag and felt the gun she had taken from under the cash register. She didn't know much about handguns, but she knew how to use one. Even though guns appeared useless against the creatures, it still gave her some comfort to know she had one.

Beside her, Devon slouched back in his seat, staring out the window.

"You said you saw the storm last night too?"

Devon nodded.

"What do you remember about it?"

He shrugged. "I don't know. It was just a weird-looking storm."

"Where were you when you saw it? Do you remember the time?"

"We were in Terrell's ride. I don't remember what time. Nine thirty maybe."

"Did you see anything inside it?"

Devon shook his head. "Naw. Just lights. Didn't look like lightning, though. But we never got a good look. Then the next thing I remember was waking up this morning. The sun was up, and I felt like I had a hangover."

Helen tapped the steering wheel. "Was it just you and Terrell in the car?"

"Yeah. We drove around awhile. Everything was like a ghost town. We thought it was fun at first, but then we knew something was wrong. We drove around all of downtown. Then we saw one of those things in an alley. We just thought it might be someone who knew what was going on. So we went after it."

"Did you get a good look at it?"

Devon frowned. "No. We went down this alley but we couldn't find it. We could hear them whispering, though. Talking to each other."

"Then what happened?"

"Then we saw them in doorways and windows. They were all over."

"Did they attack you?"

Devon shook his head. "We didn't stick around. We got back in the car and took off. But everywhere we went, we kept seeing them, hiding out. Watching us. And whispering. Then we heard you honking your horn and screaming down on Michigan. We followed you to that store."

He rubbed his neck and winced.

Helen could see dark blotches, like bruises, on his skin. "Looks like you're bruised."

Devon flipped the visor down and peered at his neck in the mirror. He touched one of the bruises and winced again. "Feels like it's burned or something. That's just what Terrell had!"

"That's where that thing grabbed you." Helen looked closer. The marks were long and uneven, encircling his neck. As if made by the creature's fingers. "They weren't there a few minutes ago, were they?"

Devon was still staring in the mirror. "I don't know." He winced again.

Helen swerved the Tahoe down the next exit.

Devon tumbled in his seat. "What're you doing?"

"It's probably some reaction to contact with these things. Some kind of chemical or even a virus."

"Virus?" Devon's eyes widened. "Wh–what do you mean, *virus?*"

Helen shook her head and kept her eyes on the road. "I don't know, but I think we should clean it off. Get some antiseptic or something."

"You don't think it's some kind of flesh-eating thing, do you?"

"I don't know what it is, but I think we should clean it with something, just to be sure."

She pulled into a drugstore. "Come on."

They searched the shelves and gathered containers of alcohol, hydrogen peroxide, and antibacterial ointments. Helen also grabbed several rolls of gauze and other supplies she thought they might need.

She rubbed the discolorations with peroxide first. It foamed up a little and Devon complained that it stung. Then she squeezed some antibacterial ointment on his skin and wrapped the gauze around his neck.

"Let's leave it there for a while and see if it does anything," she said. Then she spotted a snack aisle. "Have you eaten anything today?"

"Nope."

They went through the aisle, gathering candy bars, chips, and salted nuts. Helen also found boxes of bottled water in the stock room. She made a few trips and loaded up the back of her Tahoe.

Devon opened a bag of corn chips and stuffed a handful in his mouth. He made a face. "They taste kind of stale."

"They're probably just old," Helen said as they pulled back onto the highway. She peered into the distance and frowned. Far off, a purple ribbon of clouds clung to the horizon. "Looks like a storm front moving in."

Devon grunted. "Hopefully not with another one of their ships inside."

19

Conner stood in the breakfast nook of his old house. Sunlight poured in through the bay windows and bathed the ceramic-tiled floor in a warm glow.

How had he gotten back here? He had been in his condo. He thought he had gone back to his condo. But now . . .

Something moved behind him. Footsteps scampered across the floor. Bare feet slapped on tile.

Conner spun around and glimpsed a small shape darting across the kitchen, down the front hall. His heart pounded.

Not again.

"Matthew?"

He rushed to the hallway. It was empty. Footsteps thumped up the stairs. A voice giggled. He recognized that laughter. Mischievous and carefree. His chest ached. It felt like an eternity since he had last heard it. And he now realized how badly he missed it.

Conner shook his head. His eyes clouded with tears. "Please, don't do this to me."

He followed the sounds to the stairs. Footsteps pattered from room to room. A soft giggle echoed in the hallway.

Conner climbed the stairs. "Matty!"

The last door on the left slammed shut. It was Matthew's old room. Marta had turned it into a sewing room or something. Through the crack at the floor, Conner saw a shadow move.

He took a step toward the door but felt something pulling him backward, as if he were moving against a strong current. He needed to open that door. . . .

Somewhere in the distance, thunder echoed. A deep pounding.

Boom! Boom!

"No!" He strained against the force. His eyes stung with tears. "Please, just let me see him once more."

Boom! Boom!

He lunged forward one last time, but the force pulling him back was too strong. The doorway receded from him. The hallway seemed to stretch farther and farther. He felt his feet slip and he tumbled backward, down the stairs. . . .

Conner opened his eyes and found himself lying facedown on the grass, gasping for breath. The distant pounding he had heard was now clear and nearby.

The crack of a gunshot exploded in his ears and died away.

Conner struggled to his hands and knees and looked around. The dark-haired boy lay in the grass beside him, eyes closed, chest heaving. To the other side, Mitch was also sprawled out on the grass, holding the gun in both hands. Smoke twirled up from the end of the barrel.

"What happened?" Conner's head spun.

Mitch looked at him, wide-eyed. "It . . . it grabbed you."

Then Conner remembered. They had tried to make contact with one of the creatures. Tried to communicate. He turned and peered into the trees. No sign of it anywhere.

"Where is it? Where'd it go?"

Mitch's complexion was white. He shook his head. "I — I don't know. It just disappeared!"

"What do you mean, *disappeared?*"

Mitch turned to Conner. His expression grew dark. "I mean it vanished! It let go of you, turned around, and *disappeared* into the trees. I shot the thing in the head four times and it didn't have any effect."

Conner frowned. "Why did it let go?"

Mitch nodded to the boy. "He pulled you back into the sunlight. I think we were right about that. I don't think they like the light."

Conner helped the boy to his feet. "Thank you."

The boy narrowed his eyes and nodded.

They went back inside. Conner sat down at the table and rubbed his head.

"I had another hallucination. It was so real. I was back at my house and my son was there again."

Conner winced. His wrist stung. His skin looked like it was starting to bruise where the creature had touched him.

Mitch frowned. "That's where it grabbed you."

Conner examined the marks. Long, parallel bands wrapped around his entire wrist. "Maybe that's how they communicate."

"What?"

Conner looked up. "I think we can assume these things have been responsible for our hallucinations. Maybe they're trying to communicate with us. By using images from our memories."

Mitch shook his head. "It didn't look like it was trying to talk to you. When it grabbed you, I saw its eyes. I don't know. It didn't look very friendly."

"Look, we're most likely talking about a completely alien life-form here. We can't jump to conclusions about their intentions. . . ."

Mitch snorted. "Conclusions? Dude, *everybody's disappeared!* What kind of conclusion should we jump to?"

"I'm just saying we don't know anything about them. How do we know what their intentions are?"

"I don't know about you —" Mitch leaned back and folded his arms — "but I'd rather err on the side of caution."

Conner rubbed his temples and tried to clear his head. Everything that had happened over the last few hours was too much to process. He kept hoping it was all just a bad dream. Rachel and Marta were both gone, the only two people he cared about in the world, and now he wondered if he would ever see them again.

And then there were his seizures and hallucinations. Maybe they were related or connected somehow. Still, Mitch had not experienced any convulsions or physical pain during his hallucination. Maybe it was something specific to Conner. Or his memories of Matthew.

But why? Why would they be showing him

visions of his son?

Conner looked up suddenly. “Matthew! I was thinking about him right before the storm came. I was looking at his picture! Maybe they were able to detect that somehow.”

“What are you talking about?”

“These hallucinations,” Conner persisted. “Maybe I’m having visions of my son because I had just been thinking about him when the storm came last night. What about you? Were you thinking about your mother at all last night? You said she died when you were a kid? Was that a traumatic — ?”

“No,” Mitch growled. “I wasn’t thinking about her. I hadn’t thought about her for years until . . .”

“What?” Conner pressed him. “Until what?”

Mitch turned away. “My dad called me last night,” he said after a moment. “I hadn’t talked to him in years. We had a fight when I was eighteen, and I left home.”

“What did you fight about?”

“Everything.” Mitch rolled his eyes. “What does it matter?”

“Did it have anything to do with your mother?”

Mitch’s jaw tightened. He didn’t respond.

But Conner went on. He was sure he was

on to something. "Maybe the phone call evoked some memory of your mother on a subconscious level. . . ."

"So what?"

"So maybe that's how they're trying to communicate. Maybe they're able to scan our memories and —"

"You're saying they can read our minds now?"

Conner paused at the absurdity of the thought. But was it really so absurd? "Why not? Maybe they're able to detect brain waves. It's not out of the realm of possibility. Maybe they're just replaying them back to us to get our attention."

Mitch got up and peered out the patio doors. "I still don't trust them."

"Maybe," Conner said. "I agree we should proceed with caution."

Mitch turned around. "So then, what do we do now?"

Conner thought for a moment. Their first priority should be to try to locate others. He made a mental note not to call them *survivors*. That would imply everyone else was dead. And he wasn't ready to accept that yet. There was no evidence of mass destruction or death. That was what was so odd about the whole experience. Other than these creatures, the rest of the world seemed completely untouched.

"I think we should stick to your plan," he said at last. "We need to try to find anyone else that may still be around."

Conner went to his room to change and throw a few items into an overnight bag. He had no idea how long he'd be gone or when he'd be back. He glanced around the room, running through a mental list of anything he might need.

Then he went into the bathroom and examined his wrist. The purple bruises had grown more distinct and tender. His discolored skin, however, was oddly cool to the touch. He frowned. He had made contact with an extraterrestrial life-form. How could he possibly know what kind of effect it would have on his own physiology? He washed his wrist several times and wrapped it with an Ace bandage. Then he gathered a few first-aid items as well.

He went back downstairs, where Mitch and the boy were waiting.

Conner looked at the kid for a moment. His flannel shirt looked a few sizes too big. His jeans were tattered, and his sneakers looked equally worn-out. "I think Junior here could use some better clothes. And we still need to find some food."

"Right." Mitch nodded. "We'll make a few stops first."

20

As they stepped outside, Conner peered at the sky and shook his head.

"Looks like another storm is coming." He nodded to the horizon.

Mitch frowned. "That's not a good sign. If sunlight's been keeping them to the shadows, they may get more aggressive if clouds roll in."

Conner bit his lip. "To say nothing of what may happen after sundown."

They looked at each other for a moment. Conner could see a grim resolve grow on Mitch's face. "Let's get moving."

The boy climbed into Conner's car and Mitch opted to stay on his motorcycle. They agreed it would be best to use both vehicles. Maybe they could split up and cover more highway space.

They headed back into town. Mitch pulled on ahead, following the main street into the business district. Conner could see he was scanning the stores on either side of the road.

After a few miles, he swerved into a large strip mall and parked outside Earl's Sporting Goods. Conner pulled up next to him.

"I thought of a few things we might need," Mitch said. "There's a Jewel over there if you wanna get some dried goods and water."

"Right."

Conner and the boy headed into the grocery store and perused the aisles. Conner grabbed a shopping cart and began stocking up on snack crackers, granola bars, and beef jerky. Anything he thought might last without being refrigerated. Neither he nor Mitch had acknowledged it, but eventually the electricity was bound to go out with no one manning the power plants.

Conner made a mental note to stop by a hardware store to find a gas-powered generator. He'd also need plenty of gas cans and floodlights. If their theory was correct, they would need as much light as possible after sundown.

Then Conner realized he had lost track of the boy.

"Hey, kid?"

A moment later the boy showed up in the aisle grinning and lugging an armload of bottled water.

Conner nodded. "Good thinking."

All in all, they filled two shopping carts with supplies and wheeled them out to the car, where Mitch was waiting.

Mitch showed them what he had picked up at Earl's: three rifles, a pair of shotguns, three handguns, and a few dozen boxes of ammo.

Conner raised an eyebrow. "I thought you said your bullets didn't faze that thing?"

Mitch shrugged. "My aim may have been a little off. Never hurts to be prepared." Then he showed them a pair of two-way radios he had also found. "I figure we'll need to keep in touch if we have to split up."

Conner scratched his head. "You know, I was thinking we may need to get a generator, too, and some floodlights. The power's bound to go out eventually."

Mitch eyed Conner's car and shook his head. "You're gonna need a bigger vehicle."

They looked at each other and then at the auto dealership across the street.

Fifteen minutes later, Conner rolled out of the lot in a spotless black Hummer.

The boy ran his hand along the leather seat and looked at Conner. Conner just shrugged. "I left them my credit card."

A few blocks farther down, he pulled into

an Ace Hardware store. They loaded the back of the Hummer with two gas generators, ten halogen floodlights, a dozen gas cans, and a few other items they had thought of along the way. Then they stopped at a Shell station across the street and filled up the Hummer, the gas cans, and Mitch's tank as well.

Mitch started up his cycle and gestured over his shoulder. "I'll head over to the tollway; if you want to, park someplace on Highway 41. If anyone's heading into Chicago from the north, they're bound to take one of those routes."

Conner nodded. "Sounds good." He held up the two-way. "I'll be on channel two."

"Gotcha." Mitch pulled out and headed west.

Conner turned east. After a few more blocks, he connected with Highway 41 and turned south. He figured he'd stop at the point where he had first encountered Mitch. He wasn't normally superstitious, but it seemed as good a place as any.

He rolled to a stop in the middle of the southbound lane and shut the engine off. The cloud bank was getting closer and showed no sign of clearing up.

He surveyed their surroundings. They were a good distance from any type of shade, so if there were any of those creatures about, they wouldn't get too close. That is, if their sunlight theory was accurate.

Conner switched his radio to channel two. "Mitch, you there?"

A moment later the radio crackled and Mitch's voice sputtered through. "I'm here."

"I'm going to scan the channels for a minute to see if I can pick up any other signals. See if anyone else is out there."

"Good idea."

Conner switched through successive channels repeating a hail. "Is anyone receiving this signal?"

Only static returned. Conner went through a second time with the same results. Finally, he switched back to channel two, reported the results to Mitch, and set the radio down beside him.

The boy pulled out a box of granola bars from a plastic shopping bag at his feet. He handed one to Conner along with a bottle of water.

Conner smiled. "Thanks, kid."

The granola tasted a little stale, but the water was okay.

Conner closed his eyes for a moment and tried to clear his head. He felt oddly detached from the bizarre nature of what was happening. Here he was, maybe one of the last three people on Earth, sitting in a stolen Hummer in the middle of the highway, waiting for something to happen. But what exactly? The whole scenario seemed more like something from a 1950s end-of-the-world B movie.

He glanced at the boy. "Sorry, kid, I was going to find you some better clothes. Guess I forgot."

The boy leaned his head back against the seat.

"Guess you had a long day too, huh?"

The boy just rubbed his nose.

"What are you, about nine or ten?" He was a lanky kid, Conner thought, a little undernourished. "You like sports? You look like you play soccer."

The boy didn't reply.

Conner's gaze drifted off. "My son loved soccer. He was always kicking that thing around." He sighed. "He would've been about your age by now. Sometimes I wonder what he would've looked like."

Conner remembered one of the items he had thrown into his bag. The family picture from his desk — the one he had been looking at last night.

"You want to see a picture of him?" He grabbed his duffel bag from behind the seat and rummaged through it. "Here it is."

He handed the picture to the boy, pointing to Matthew's face.

"That was my son. Matthew."

The boy peered at the picture for a moment and smiled. He pointed to Matthew's face and looked back at Conner.

Conner nodded. "Yeah. Matthew. That was my son."

The boy looked back at the picture and said, "Matthew."

Conner's eyes widened. "What did you — ?"

He lurched back in his seat as another convulsion hit him. This one was stronger than the others and took his breath away with its intensity. His muscles tightened as the pressure built in his chest. His neck arched uncontrollably as the white light pressed in again from the corners of his vision. A frigid blast of air ripped through him. It roared in his ears. Thunderous, like a waterfall.

But through the din, the pain, and the blinding light, Conner thought there was something else. Some other sound. Indistinct, beneath the rumble of the wind.

Then it passed and Conner slumped forward, gasping for air as the white light faded. He felt a small hand on his arm. He leaned back and groaned.

The boy was leaning over, peering at him. His brown eyes seemed filled with concern.

Mitch's voice crackled over the radio.

". . . you there? Come in. . . . Repeat, I see a car approaching from the south. . . ."

21

". . . you there?" Mitch's voice persisted. "Dude. Conner. Come in. . . ."

Conner fumbled for the radio. "I . . . I'm here."

"I had a red SUV approach from the south. They just passed by."

"They didn't stop?"

"They didn't see me. I'm parked on the overpass. I was trying to keep out of sight. I'm going to follow them."

"Where are you?"

After a pause, Mitch's voice came back over the rattle of his motorcycle engine. "Take 137 over. You should be able to cut them off."

Conner rubbed his temples as the last of his dizziness left him. He started up the Hummer, turned it around, and headed north. Just a few miles up he could cut over to the tollway. He flew through intersections doing more than eighty miles an hour.

His thoughts quickly returned to his seizure. They had been getting progressively worse. It had been nearly two hours since his last one in the cemetery and only a half hour between his first two. They came on with jarring abruptness and with such intensity that Conner didn't think he could survive many more.

Then he remembered what had happened just before his convulsion. He frowned at the boy. "So you can talk, huh?"

The boy looked up at him, his brown eyes registering no sign of comprehension.

"Matthew. You said 'Matthew.' "

The kid held up the picture but didn't say anything.

Conner nodded. "That was my son."

The boy just stared at the picture.

Conner swerved west onto 137 and gunned the accelerator. In another mile or so, he'd come across the interstate. He increased his speed.

Helen stared at the eight empty lanes of highway. They had left the city twenty minutes ago and had not seen a single vehicle since then. She found her jaw aching and suddenly realized how tense she had become.

Something had compelled her northward.

She thought it was her own instinct, but now she was beginning to doubt. They were almost to the Wisconsin border but had yet to see any signs of life. Should she just keep driving? Through Wisconsin and then where? Canada?

She shook her head. Every mile was taking her farther from home and from where she had last seen Kyle, yet somehow she didn't feel like she was getting any farther from him. Or any closer.

Devon fidgeted in the passenger seat, rubbing his neck and peering into the mirror every few minutes.

Helen glanced over. "Does it hurt?" She tried not to sound worried.

"A little," he muttered, lifting the gauze slightly. "I think it's spreading."

Helen kept her eyes on the road. "It's just a rash."

"How do you know? That thing was an alien. Who knows what kind of disease I got."

"Because it *looks* like a rash. Like an allergic reaction. Poison ivy or something."

"Poison ivy," he muttered. "Ain't no poison ivy."

"We'll stop and get you some —"

Helen saw something flash in her rearview mirror. Like sunlight glinting off metal. She looked back. A motorcycle was racing down the on-ramp they had just passed and was closing in on her.

Devon turned around and swore. "Hey, someone's following us!"

"I know."

"Dude's coming up fast."

Helen gripped the steering wheel, her heart racing. "Is it one of *them?*"

Devon pulled out his gun. "No. Looks like some guy. He's coming up on your left."

Helen slowed down slightly as the motorcycle pulled up alongside them. The guy looked big. Tattoos covered most of his thick arms. Long, blond hair whipped behind him. Dark sunglasses hid his eyes. He looked as though he was trying to peer into her car, and Helen was thankful for her tinted windows.

Devon peered back at him and pointed suddenly. "The dude's got a gun!"

"What?"

"Tucked in his belt!"

Helen's slammed her brakes, sending Devon into the dashboard. Her throat went dry. The cycle pulled ahead and braked as well.

Helen shook her head. "We have guns too. It doesn't mean he's gonna shoot us. He's probably out looking for people, just like we are."

"Lady, you're way too trusting."

Helen pulled onto the shoulder. "Let's just see what he wants."

They rolled to a stop. The motorcycle turned around and came back. He stopped about fifty yards in front of them. Helen saw him reach around to his back.

Devon beat the dashboard. "He's pulling his gun! He's pulling his gun!"

Helen could see the gun in his grasp. A moment later, he put his other hand up near his mouth. He was holding something. Helen peered closer. A two-way radio! He was talking to someone else!

She reached back into her bag and slid her gun out.

Conner pulled up to the overpass and peered north and south at the empty lanes. There was no sign of any vehicles.

He got on the radio.

"Mitch, I'm at 137. Did you pass by yet?"

A moment later, Mitch's voice responded. "No, they saw me behind them and stopped. We're just south of you. Half a mile or so."

"Who are they?"

"Don't know. Looks like two people, but they aren't getting out."

Conner turned down the exit ramp and headed south on the northbound lane. "They're probably as paranoid as we are. Don't do anything. I'll be there in a few seconds."

In a moment, Conner spotted Mitch's bike parked in the center lane. Beyond it was a red Tahoe pulled off on the shoulder. Conner slowed to a stop and got out.

"Stay put," he said to the boy and shut the door.

Mitch sat on his bike, his gun drawn but held down at his side.

Conner shook his head as he approached. "Y'know, no offense, but you don't exactly make the best of first impressions."

"What?" Mitch got off the bike. "I didn't do anything."

"Just stay here. And put your gun away."

Mitch muttered something and slid his gun back into his belt.

Conner approached the Tahoe slowly, both hands in view, and peered through the windshield. From what he could tell, there were only two occupants, as Mitch had said. A white woman and a young black man. A teenager.

Suddenly, both front doors swung open and the occupants slipped out, each one crouching behind a door for cover. Conner glimpsed a flash of steel in the sunlight.

"They got guns!" Mitch shouted and ducked behind the Hummer.

A woman's voice shouted from behind the driver-side door. "Put your gun down! I swear I'll shoot you right now. Put it down!"

"Yeah, you first, lady!" Mitch shouted back.

"Whoa, whoa." Conner positioned himself between Mitch and the Tahoe. "Let's all keep calm here! We're not looking for trouble. We're all in the same boat."

"Then tell him to drop his gun!"

Conner turned. "Mitch, lower your gun. We don't want to start a shoot-out here."

Mitch glared at him from behind the front fender. "I ain't giving up my gun!"

"I'm not telling you to give it up. Just lower it, okay?"

"I said *drop it!*" The woman's voice was gruff but hardly authoritative. She wasn't a cop, Conner guessed, maybe just trying to act like one. Whoever she was, she was obviously as frightened as they were.

Conner cleared his throat. "Look, there's no way he's dropping his gun for you. And we don't expect you to give up your weapons. Let's just agree not to shoot each other for the moment, okay?"

After a pause the woman spoke. "Who are you?"

Conner nodded. Good, at least she was reasonable. "My name's Conner."

The woman pointed in Mitch's direction. "Who's that?"

Conner glanced back. "Uh . . . that's Mitch. He and I just met a little while ago too. We crossed paths over on 41."

"Why was he following us and why'd he pull his gun on us?"

Conner had to shrug. "Look, lady, we don't want to hurt you. We're just playing it safe. I assume that's why you both have guns too."

She didn't answer. Conner decided to go further.

"I assume you saw that storm last night? And, uh . . . and you woke up this morning and found that everyone had vanished?"

"Do you know what's going on?"

Conner shook his head. "I — I don't know. We're just out looking for some answers, y'know. We're just trying to find others."

"Did you see anyone else?"

"Uhh . . ." Conner paused, wondering how much to tell her. "Well, we . . . we had some interesting experiences. We've seen, uh . . . well it's a little hard to explain."

"Aliens!" The kid on the passenger side finally spoke up. "Aliens, man. They killed my friend!"

Conner turned to the kid. "They *killed* him? What did they do? Did you see them?"

"They attacked us," the woman said. "They crashed into a store — through plate glass — and grabbed his friend and . . . and disappeared."

"What do you mean *disappeared?*"

The woman shook her head. "It pulled him out of the store, out into the street. But then we couldn't find any sign of them."

Conner frowned. Mitch's distrust of the creatures was proving to be accurate. "I'm sorry about your friend," he said. "But don't you think we should try to work together?"

No one said anything.

"Look . . . ," Conner tried again. "We have to trust each other, okay? Why don't we all put our guns away and try to figure out what to do next."

The woman eyed him for a moment. Conner guessed she was still distrustful of Mitch. He turned around. "Hey, Mitch, just put the gun away and come out."

Mitch muttered something, but Conner couldn't hear what it was. After a moment, Mitch stuck his gun into his belt and stood, showing his hands.

Conner turned back to the woman. "Okay? Are we agreed?"

She stepped out from behind the door with her gun at her side. She was a brunette. Maybe his own age — midforties — Conner guessed. Maybe a little older.

The black kid came out as well. He was tall and lanky, wearing a Nike T-shirt and baggy jeans. He had a layer of gauze wrapped around his neck. He glared at Conner and Mitch but kept his gun at his side.

"Good." Conner nodded. "Good. I . . . uh, I don't think I got your names."

"Helen," she said.

The kid didn't say anything. After a moment, Helen added, "He told me his name was Devon."

Conner stuck a thumb over his shoulder, back at the Hummer. "We also found a boy. Just a kid. He's inside, but I don't know who he is. I don't think he understands any English."

Helen peered into the Hummer and frowned.

"Those things," she said. "I think they're going to be coming for us."

Conner nodded. "You're probably right."

"What are they?"

Conner hesitated. "The only thing I can

say at this point is that they're some kind of extraterrestrial species. I tried to communicate with one of them, but . . ."

"What happened?"

"It grabbed me." Conner lifted his wrist. "We're not sure what it wanted, but it left a mark on my wrist. Like a bruise." He nodded to Devon. "That what happened to you, too?"

Devon rubbed his neck. "I popped eight rounds into one of 'em. Point blank. It didn't even flinch!"

Conner nodded and cast a glance back at Mitch. "Yeah, it would seem bullets don't have much of an effect."

Mitch just shrugged.

"Did it grab you too?" Conner asked, pointing to Devon's neck.

Devon nodded and lifted the gauze slightly. Conner could see discolored markings around his neck.

He looked at Helen.

"You wouldn't happen to be a nurse or a doctor or anything?"

Helen shook her head. "They broke through a plate glass window. There wasn't a drop of blood anywhere. They didn't even feel the bullets."

Conner nodded. "We noticed they seem to keep to the shadows. Avoid direct sunlight. We think that may be a weakness. But it's just a theory."

Helen seemed to think for a moment. "The store was on the east side of the street. It may have still been in the shade at that time. I guess I didn't really notice."

Devon brightened. "Every time we saw them before, though, they were hiding in buildings and alleys. They never came out in the sun."

Mitch peered at the sky. "This is all well and good, but even if it's true, those clouds aren't gonna help us any."

The front was moving east quickly. They had maybe a half hour or so before the sky completely clouded up. Not to mention what might happen after sundown.

"I think we should find some shelter. Someplace secure maybe." Conner nodded to the Hummer. "We borrowed some halogen floodlights for tonight. I don't know if they'll help any, but it's the best we got right now."

Helen shook her head. "I don't feel safe inside anywhere. Not the way they broke into that store. I don't want to get trapped."

Conner shrugged. "I don't think we'll be any safer outside. I suppose we could just keep driving. . . ."

They all fell silent for a moment. Conner

felt a growing sense of helplessness seep into his thoughts. Should they hole up somewhere or flee? If they left, where would they go? What direction should they head? There was no guarantee they'd be any safer on the road than in a building somewhere. Maybe a bank vault or . . .

Then Mitch spoke up. "You think they can swim?"

22

Mitch nodded toward the east. "A buddy of mine has a boat. A cabin cruiser, down at the marina. What if we head out on the lake?"

Conner glanced at Helen and rubbed his jaw. There was no guarantee they'd be better off on the water. He shrugged. "I don't know. . . . We can't be sure we'd be any safer. Not without knowing more about these things."

Mitch frowned. "Well, given the fact that I don't want to study them up close, I say we risk it. It can't be any more dangerous than staying on land. We already know what they can do *here.*"

Helen nodded. "Might not be a bad idea. Maybe they have some kind of aversion to water."

"We just don't know enough about them," Conner said.

"Dude, sometimes you just gotta take a

chance and make a decision." Mitch swung a leg over his motorcycle. "I'm going to give it a shot. The rest of you can do whatever you want."

Devon piped up. "I say we take the boat."

Helen stared at Conner for a moment. "We don't really have the luxury of learning anything more about them. Whatever we're going to do, we need to hurry."

Conner sighed. She was right. He hated making decisions without knowing all the possible consequences and minimizing his risks. Unfortunately, he didn't have that option at the moment.

"All right," he said to Mitch. "We'll follow you."

They headed east toward the lake. Mitch led them back through North Chicago and into Waukegan. Conner hated this area. A lot of low-income, graffiti-laced, crime-riddled neighborhoods. Normally, he wouldn't be caught dead in either town.

They arrived at the marina and Mitch rolled past several newer boats, finally stopping at a large cabin cruiser tied to the dock. The fiberglass hull was scraped-up and stained by algae. *Hey Lady* was painted across the stern in bold letters.

Conner raised an eyebrow. It wasn't exactly a luxury boat. "You sure he's got the key on board?"

Mitch climbed aboard and disappeared below. He emerged a moment later, waving a key ring on a wooden block. "Freddy practically lives on board during the summer. He makes some extra cash taking rich lawyer types out fishing."

"Nice. You know how to drive this thing?"

Mitch shrugged. "I've been out a few times."

Helen got her things out of the Tahoe and eyed the boat. "A few times?"

Devon just jumped aboard. "All right; let's go."

Mitch shrugged again. "What's with you people? It's a boat. All you do is start it up and steer. You coming or not?"

Conner sighed. "Give me a hand with these supplies."

They transferred one of the gas generators on board along with several floodlights and all the gasoline, food, guns, and ammo. The dark-haired boy stood on the dock, shaking his head.

"Come on." Conner motioned. "It's all right. It's safe."

The boy still shook his head. His brown eyes were wide. Conner finally grabbed him by the arm and hauled him over like a piece of luggage.

Ten minutes later Mitch had the motor rumbling and untied the lines. He climbed up into the captain's chair and pushed the throttle forward. They pulled away from the dock, out into the main channel.

Conner called up to him. "How much gas do we have?"

"Half a tank," Mitch said. "There's a fuel station up here. I'll stop to fill up."

Conner watched the dock recede and all their vehicles along with it. He bit his cheek. He hated burning his bridges, rushing into decisions that offered no way back. And he had the nagging feeling he would never be back this way again.

He wondered if they had made the right decision leaving land. Had they fully considered all the options? All the consequences? Mitch and Helen were right, though. It wasn't as if they had an abundance of time. The sky had clouded up, gray and dismal. And the afternoon would soon turn into evening.

Mitch stopped at the fueling pump and started filling the tank. Conner set about running the floodlights along the sides of the boat. Three on each side, connected to the generator by extension cords.

Twenty minutes later they were headed out of the marina into open water.

Conner stood at the stern, peering back at the shoreline. Mitch and Devon sat up at the bridge. Mitch had agreed to just take them a mile or so. Conner wanted them to keep the shore in sight. None of them had much experience navigating on open water.

They came to a stop after ten minutes and waited. They all kept watch on the water and the shoreline. The water grew calm. Nearly smooth as glass.

The afternoon stretched on into evening, and eventually Mitch broke out a couple of boxes of granola bars and some beef jerky. They probably had enough food and water for several days. Conner shuddered at the thought. How long would they be out here?

The boy had curled up on the bed in the cabin below deck and had fallen asleep. Conner looked in on him and sighed. He wondered if he'd be able to sleep tonight himself. He went back on deck and sat down at the stern, staring at the shore.

The sky was starting to grow dark when Helen approached and gave him a bottle of water. "So when you woke up this morning, did you expect to spend the night out on Lake Michigan?"

Conner chuckled. "After what I've seen today, I'm learning to expect anything."

Despite the hellish day they'd all had,

there was something about adversity that seemed to draw people together. A few hours ago, they had all been on the verge of shooting each other. Now they were working together.

Conner sighed. "I'm just hoping we survive the night."

Helen rubbed her arms and shuddered. "And what if we do? Tomorrow we'll still be in the same predicament."

Conner shook his head. "There have to be others. I have to believe that."

"I hope you're right."

"Look at us. Five strangers, and we all managed to find each other in just half a day. I think the more we look, the more we'll find."

"What do you think happened?"

"I have no idea," Conner said. "None of this makes any sense. There's no purpose to it. How were they able to make millions of people just disappear overnight? Why did they leave us here and why are they watching us? What do they want? Where do they come from?" He shook his head. "All I have are questions. I've got no answers."

Helen fell silent for a moment. "Do you have any family?"

Conner nodded. "Yeah, a daughter and my ex-wife. But they're gone like everyone else. You?"

"I have a son. Kyle. He's twenty-four. We had dinner last night." Helen's voice broke. She put her hand to her lips.

"I'm sorry," Conner said. "Look, I'm sure we'll find some answers soon —"

"No." Helen cleared her throat. "It's not that. It's . . . I . . . I saw him this morning."

"What?"

"I went to his apartment, looking for him. I was worried sick. Scared to death. But then I saw him standing in the hallway." Her lips drew tight. "I *saw* him. He talked to me, and I hugged him. I *felt* him in my arms."

"What happened?"

Helen peered out at the water and shook her head. "He had something . . . They were doing something to him. He had . . . burns. . . . They just appeared out of nowhere on his skin."

"Burns?"

Helen nodded. "He was in such pain. He wouldn't let me help him. He ran away, out into the street. I was searching for him all morning."

Conner held out his wrist and peeled back the gauze. "The burns — did they look like this?"

"No. No, they blistered and bled. They

spread all over his body right in front of my eyes." A tear rolled down Helen's cheek. "He was in such pain and . . . and I couldn't do anything to help him."

She wiped her eyes.

Conner hesitated, then put his hand on her shoulder. "I think they're just manipulating us somehow. I saw things too. So did Mitch."

"But I *felt* him. I *touched* him. . . ."

Conner nodded. "I know. It seemed real for me, too."

Helen looked up at him. "What did you see?"

Conner's jaw tightened. "I saw *my* son. But he died five years ago. It was as real as you are sitting here right now. It happened twice. The second time was when one of those things grabbed my wrist. . . ."

"What happened?"

"One minute I was outside and . . . suddenly I was standing in my old house. I could hear Matthew running around and laughing." Conner fell silent for a moment. "Did you experience any pain?"

"What do you mean?"

Conner described his convulsions, but Helen only shook her head. She hadn't experienced anything like that. Conner's worry deepened. What was happening to him? Their experiences were all so similar, except for the convulsions. He was the only one having them. Were these creatures doing something just to him?

Was this all some sort of . . .

". . . experiment," he said.

"What?"

"What if this is all just some kind of experiment? The hallucinations, my seizures — they've got to be doing this for a reason."

"But why?"

Conner shrugged. "Maybe just to see how we react or to see what makes us angry. Or what frightens us. I don't know."

The gray light of dusk was fading, and a milky fog had settled on the dark water. Conner straightened up. "I better fire up the generator before it gets too d—"

Thump!

The boat lurched and shuddered as something bumped hard against the hull.

23

Conner and Helen steadied themselves against the rail and peered into the water. Nothing moved on the surface.

"What was that?" Helen gasped.

"I don't know." Conner said. "I have to get the generator started!"

Mitch slid down the ladder from the bridge. "What happened?"

Conner made his way forward. "Something's in the water. I can't see anything out there. Get the engine started; I'll fire up the generator."

Mitch swore and climbed back up to the bridge. Conner had set the generator at the bow, where the noise would be minimized. He had strung a series of extension cords to a power strip that was plugged into the generator's AC output.

He had tested the engine earlier, and after a few tugs of the pull-start, it fired right up. He switched on the power strip, and immediately the fog around them lit up in the bright amber glow of the halogen floodlights. He double-checked the cord connections and the lights, then returned to the back.

"See anything?" he called up to Mitch.

Mitch shook his head. "Can't see anything in this fog."

Helen had backed away from the rail. "Let's just go."

"Where?" Conner said. "You want to go back to land?"

Devon poked his head over the rail. "Man, anything's better than just sitting around here."

Mitch was trying without success to get the boat's engine started. Conner could hear intermittent curses between the sounds of the engine chugging.

"Don't flood it," Conner said.

Mitch muttered something about a lawyer trying to tell a mechanic how to start an engine.

Conner looked over the side. The floodlights lit up the mist but couldn't penetrate the surface of the water. He tried to aim one of the lights down, into the water, but with no luck. The water was too dark and murky.

After a moment, Helen joined him at the

rail. "Do you see anything?"

"No," Conner said. Then he called again to Mitch. "Does this thing have any underwater lights?"

Mitch nodded toward Devon. "There's a couple under the bench in the cabin."

Devon slid down and disappeared inside the cabin. They could hear him rummaging around. He emerged a moment later with a pair of battery-powered light cases, each connected to a length of rope. He held them up. "These them?"

Mitch nodded. "Freddy uses them for night diving."

Conner turned on the lights and lowered them over the side. A wide ring of light lit up the water on each side of the boat.

"That's good!" Conner called. He paced from side to side, peering into the water.

Mitch slid down the ladder again, now issuing a steady stream of curses. He ransacked the cabin and dug out a toolbox.

"What's wrong?" Conner said.

But Mitch appeared in no mood to talk. He loosened the cover to the engine compartment and looked inside.

Back on the bridge, Devon threw up his hands. "Man, that's just great. Now we're stranded out here!"

"Everybody just shut up!" Mitch growled

as he tinkered with the engine.

Conner paced the deck, gazing out into the mist. A sudden chill came over him. It was the same sensation he'd had the day before in his office. Somewhere in the mist, something was watching them. He felt trapped.

Cornered.

Suddenly, Helen screamed and backed away from the rail. "There's something in the water!"

Everyone froze.

Conner shook himself back to his senses and rushed to the side where Helen had been watching. "What was it? What did you see?"

Helen's face was pale, her eyes wide. She tried to answer but her lips only quivered.

Conner grabbed her shoulders and jolted her. "What did you see?"

"I don't — I don't know," she stammered. "It was big!"

Devon swore. "Was it one of those things?"

"I don't know what it was. . . ."

"Keep an eye on the left side," Conner called up to Devon while he peered into the water on the right. "Mitch, we really need to get this engine running."

"I'm working on it!"

Then Devon said, "There it is! Just went

under the boat!"

A large shadow darted out from underneath them, jerking awkwardly side to side. It was distorted in the water, a murky shape, silhouetted by the underwater light.

"Whoa!" Conner shouted. "I see it!"

It was big, but it moved too quickly for him to get a good look. It had no limbs or fins, nor even a tail.

"What is it?" Mitch called out from the engine compartment. "Is it one of them?"

Conner shook his head. His heart was pounding now. "I don't — it moved too fast. I couldn't get a good —"

"There's another one!" Devon called out.

Helen disappeared into the cabin and returned a moment later, rifling through her bag. She pulled out her gun and leaned over the rail, next to Conner.

Under the boat, a shadow emerged, then halted. A moment later it slid laterally along the hull toward the back. Helen fired three shots into the water. The bullets streamed down, missing the target.

Conner pulled her arm back. "You don't have a clear shot."

Then the rope from one of the underwater lights tugged and they heard a muffled pop. The water on one side of the boat went black. Conner blinked. He couldn't see anything now beneath the surface.

"It broke the light," he said. "They're breaking the lights!"

A moment later there was another bump under the hull and a second pop.

Devon swore again. "They got the other one!"

Now the water was completely black. Impenetrable. The mist seemed to curl in tighter. The fog thickened, like a glowing curtain in the halogen lamps.

From out of the fog came a heavy thump. The boat rocked slightly, dipping toward the front. Conner scrambled toward the bow. "The generator! They're going for the generator."

He stopped suddenly and his eyes widened.

A tall figure squatted at the bow, dripping wet. It stood motionless for a moment, outlined against the fog, as the boat rocked gently. It seemed to tilt its head as if listening for something. Then it bent down, lifted the generator off the deck, and leaped backward over the rail.

Ker-thwoosh!

The extension cords trailed along after it, snapping off the front set of lights and disappearing over the rail. There was a bright pop of electricity, and then all the lights went out.

24

Mitch sat in the darkness. Somewhere in the distance he heard a woman scream. Voices echoed far away.

Gradually his eyes adjusted and he could make out his surroundings again. But he was no longer on the boat.

Boat? What boat?

His mind staggered, disoriented. He sat on the cedar chest at the foot of his mother's bed. He could hear her slow, labored breathing and the gurgling of the fluid in her lungs.

"Mom?" His voice was soft. Slightly higher pitched. But it was his voice.

He felt dizzy, sitting on the chest. Like the whole house swooned beneath him. For a moment he had imagined he was a grown man. Had he been dreaming? His mind had felt small, lost inside a large body. . . .

She stirred beneath the sheets. She was awake, he knew. She rarely slept anymore. A sound came to his ears. Like a mouse's feet scraping lightly across the kitchen linoleum.

"Mitchy?" She was trying to answer him.

Mitch slid off the chest and went hesitantly to the bedside, swallowing hard to keep from gagging at the musty stench. He kept his eyes lowered. He didn't want to look at her.

Her hand brushed against his arm. A frail, bony touch.

"Son," she whispered. "Go on outside. . . ."

Mitch shook his head. "No, Mom. I don't feel like it."

"You can't stay here."

"There's nothing to do outside." How could he even think of going out when he knew she was in here. Suffering.

"Mitchy," she said, "I'll be okay. . . . I just need a . . . need a nap."

Tears stung his eyes. He shook them away.

"I was praying. I asked God to make you well again."

There was a pause. "God always answers . . . prayers, Mitch, . . . but sometimes He . . . He makes us wait . . . a little while."

Mitch squeezed his eyes tight and tears dripped down his cheek. He shook his head. "I don't think He heard me, Mom." His voice turned hard. "I don't think He was even listening."

"Oh . . . Mitch . . . don't . . ."

"He doesn't care if you're suffering, Mom. Neither does Dad or the doctors. Nobody cares. Nobody but me."

The door opened and his father strode in, eyes glaring down at Mitch.

"I told you to go *outside,*" he rasped through clenched teeth. "Quit waking her up. She needs her rest!"

Mitch glared back. Defiant. "I don't want to go outside!"

His father's eyes widened, then narrowed to slits. His lips trembled, like a volcano ready to erupt. "Don't talk back to me!" he boomed.

Mitch just folded his arms.

"Mitch!"

Mitch held his ground. He'd make the man force him out. Drag him out by his arm.

"Mitch!"

Mitch frowned. That didn't sound like his father. The room grew dark.

"Mitch!"

His father's face was fading. Out of the darkness, two hands clutched Mitch's shoulders firmly. They shook him.

"Mitch! Get the engine fixed."

Mitch blinked and shook his head. "What?"

A face appeared where his father's had been a moment before. A stranger's face and yet somehow familiar.

"Wake up! Get the boat started!"

Mitch looked around. He was sitting on the boat again. It was dark. . . .

Memories snapped back into his head. He recognized the face. The lawyer.

Mitch looked down at the socket wrench in his hand and the engine. The boat. The lake. The aliens! The memory of his hallucination faded like a nightmare.

He looked up at Conner. "Get me a flashlight. In the cabinet over the sink. *Quick!*"

Conner dashed off. Mitch could hear him fumbling around inside the dark cabin. There was another person on deck, standing at the rail. The woman was peering into the darkness. Disjointed memories fell back into place like random pieces of a puzzle. Yeah, they had found the woman and a black kid.

A light flashed on inside the cabin. Conner returned a moment later.

Mitch tapped the engine. "Shine it down here."

He popped the socket wrench onto the spark plug and finished tightening. He had two more to finish. The gaps were charred and filthy, unable to generate any spark. He had tried to scrape some of the debris away with a screwdriver. There was no guarantee they were going to fire any better now.

He glanced up at the lawyer. "What happened to the generator?"

Conner frowned. "They pulled it over the side."

Mitch's eyes widened. "Pulled it over?" He was going to ask for a better explanation, but he knew his priority was getting the engine running again. He nodded at the rail. "They're out there?"

Conner shook his head. "I don't see anything."

Mitch tightened the last of the plugs and replaced the wire caps. Then he got up and climbed back onto the bridge. Devon was staring out into the fog. Mitch turned the key. The motor chugged, fired, and died.

He pulled the choke out and was about to try again when he heard something. It was soft at first, coming from the mist. From all around him. He froze. A chill shuddered down his spine. He had heard this before.

Voices. *Whispering.*

He looked down at Conner. "You hear that?"

No one spoke. Conner and Helen stood back to back, staring into the fog.

The whispers seemed to swirl around them. Hundreds of them. Some sounded as if they were right next to him. Others seemed like echoes in the distance. Were they speaking to him or to each other? Mitch strained to hear what they were saying. To catch just a word. But he couldn't make out anything discernible.

Devon swore and pointed off to the side. "Tell me I am *not* seein' *that!*"

Something had risen out of the water. Mitch could barely make it out in the darkness. A head, shoulders, and torso. Like someone standing waist-deep in the lake.

A second, identical shape rose up beside it. Then a third.

"There's more over there." Helen's voice sounded oddly detached. Like she was describing something to them from a picture.

"They're all around us," Conner said.

Mitch tried the key again. The motor chugged.

"They . . . uh . . . they're getting closer." Devon had lost his thug facade. Now he sounded like a scared teenager.

Mitch peered into the mist. The kid was right. They looked closer now than they had a moment ago.

"Uh . . . Mitch?" Conner's voice was shaky.

Mitch cursed and slammed his fist on the panel.

The engine popped, then fired up. He clicked the throttle into neutral and gently pressed it forward. The engine sputtered a little but was running nonetheless. He pulled it back again until he felt the prop engage.

They were completely encircled now.

Conner began shouting, "Go! Go! Go!"

Mitch grimaced and pushed the throttle forward again. The boat lurched ahead through the mist.

Mitch felt a thump of bodies slamming into the hull, but he didn't see any of them trying to climb over the rail. Up ahead, swirls of mist rushed toward them. Behind them, the prop churned a solid wake. The boat lurched and bumped, and after several minutes, Mitch relaxed a bit and eased back on the throttle. The engine sounded like all the pistons were firing.

Conner's voice came up a moment later. "I don't see any of them anywhere. . . ."

That was good, Mitch thought. But he had no idea what direction they were headed. He glanced down at the compass.

"What the — ?"

It was spinning like a top.

25

Helen huddled inside the cabin. They had been traveling for over an hour now. Mitch had said something about the compass not working, so he didn't want to risk going too fast.

Conner had gone up on the bridge. The boat had a mounted spotlight there, and Helen could see the beam sweeping back and forth in the foggy darkness.

She couldn't see more than a few yards beyond the edge of the boat. She closed her eyes but could still see the creatures rising out of the water. Encircling them. She recalled how the idea to get away from land had at first seemed like such a good one. But now the gloom and the hellish attack had caused a serious reevaluation.

It was as if everything they tried to do only made things worse for them. Only put them into a more dangerous predicament. Now they were lost somewhere on Lake Michigan, not knowing what direction they were headed in or what to do next. If they stopped, how long would it take for those things to find them again? All they could do was keep moving until . . .

Helen shook her head. Until what? Until they ran out of gas? Great.

The dim bulb inside the cabin flickered. Helen sat at one end of the U-shaped bench around a cluttered table. The cabin itself served as a meager kitchenette with a small sink and microwave across from her. But it was also cluttered with fishing gear. A narrow set of stairs led down to the cramped forward berth.

Helen rubbed her temples. Her head throbbed. She was exhausted but couldn't sleep. She had tried to close her eyes. She tried her breathing techniques, but nothing relaxed her. She had long since given up hope that the whole ordeal was a nightmare. That she'd wake up in the morning and everything would be restored. That Kyle would be back.

Kyle.

For twenty-four years her life had revolved around him. She had always been protective, perhaps overly so. It had been more than a little difficult juggling her modeling career and raising a child alone. But she had been too proud to ask for help.

The light in the cabin flickered again. And went out.

Helen sighed. "Come on." She reached up and tapped the plastic cover.

It flicked back on. Kyle was sitting across from her.

His face was covered with dark blisters, cracked and bleeding. His eyes were nearly swollen shut. His beautiful black hair was matted with blood.

Helen tried to scream, but her throat was numb. Her chest pounded and she tried to get up, to get out of the cabin, but she was unable to move. Her limbs were suddenly paralyzed.

Kyle sat there. Motionless.

After a moment he opened his mouth. "Mom?"

Helen shook in fear and rage. She struggled vainly to move. She closed her eyes tight. "No! You're not here. This isn't happening!"

"Why are they doing this to me?" His voice was a hoarse whisper.

Helen opened her eyes again. They flooded with tears. "Please stop. Please go away!"

"Why did you let them do this?"

Helen blinked back her tears. She tried to will her limbs to move. "What do you want?" she sobbed. "What do you want from me?"

Kyle shook his head. "I thought you loved me. . . ."

"What are they doing to you, baby?" Helen rasped through her tears. "Who are they? What do they want?"

"Why did you do it?"

"*I didn't do anything!* Kyle. Baby. Please tell me!"

"Why, Mom?"

Helen now wept uncontrollably. She had tried to steel herself against these mind games, but it was no use. They were messing with her head. They had found the one person she loved most in the whole world and were using him against her. She could only sob.

Kyle stood up and walked out into the darkness. A moment later, Helen's control returned. She screamed and lunged after him. Kyle stood at the rail, looked back at her for a moment, then folded over and fell into the water. Helen cried out and dove over the rail.

Suddenly an arm reached out of nowhere and caught her around the waist.

Helen opened her eyes. It was daylight. Her hands were grasping the boat rail, and Conner was clutching her waist.

She struggled against his grasp, screaming. "Kyle!"

"Stop it!" Conner strained to pull her back.

"Let me go! I have to save him!"

Mitch and Devon appeared. They forced her back onto the deck. She struggled with them, teeth clenched, hissing curses at them.

Then someone slapped her. Her cheek stung.

"Helen!" It was Conner. "There's no one out there. You were dreaming! Snap out of it!"

They had her pinned. She lay there, panting, sobbing. She tried to stop. She had to control herself. She couldn't lose it in front of these strangers. These men. She wasn't going to be the weak one.

After a moment she calmed down and they let her go.

"It was Kyle." She sat up, choking back her tears.

She felt an arm slip around her shoulders and a soft voice on her neck. "It's all right. It's over now."

"It was so real," she said after a moment. "He was right there. He was in the cabin with me."

Conner helped her to her feet. "It's them," he said. "They're doing this to us. They're just trying to scare us."

Devon grunted. "And doin' a pretty good job too."

Helen looked at the overcast sky and frowned. "What time is it?"

"A little after six," Mitch said, surveying the water. "Looks like the fog is letting up a little too."

Mitch and Devon returned to the bridge, and Conner helped Helen back into the cabin.

She sat down again at the table. "I'm going crazy."

Conner got her a bottle of water. "It's happening to all of us. We're all in this together."

Helen shook her head, wishing she could erase the image of her son from her memory. "He talked to me. He sat there and talked to me just like you are now."

"Your son?"

Helen nodded. "He was covered with burns. He looked horrible. It looked so *real.* How are they doing that?"

Conner sat down. His eyes were fixed at the table. "I don't know exactly, but they must be able to detect our brain patterns somehow. Maybe they're scanning our memories and reproducing images so real. Touch, smell . . ."

"But why? What do they want?"

Conner shook his head. "I don't know. I've been trying to figure any logical reason for this."

Helen ran her hand through her hair. "It's like they're using the people who were closest to us to . . . I don't know. To torment us."

"What did he say to you?"

Helen looked down. "He kept blaming me for what was happening. He said I was letting them hurt him somehow."

They fell silent for several minutes, listening to the rumble of the motor. Helen shuddered as she tried to push the image of her son from her mind. Or at least to convince herself it wasn't real. Kyle couldn't just appear out of thin air. Conner was right — they had to be manipulating her mind somehow. She knew she needed to convince herself.

She downed most of her water. She had been so thirsty lately.

Finally Conner spoke up. "So, you, uh . . . you lived in Chicago long?"

Helen glanced at him a moment and nodded. He was obviously trying to make small talk. Maybe just to get her mind off her hallucination. "About thirteen years."

Conner nodded. "What do you do?"

"I'm a modeling consultant. I help girls

get started with their portfolios."

"Did you used to be a model?"

Helen sniffed. *Used to.* "Yeah. I did some modeling. Even a little acting."

"You have family there?"

"No. I grew up in Boston. My parents are both dead. I have a sister in Montana, but I haven't spoken to her in twenty years."

"What about Kyle's father?"

Helen stared out the window into the mist. "Nick was a photographer. We, uh . . . we met on a photo shoot in Hawaii. I fell for him hard. I thought he was going to ask me to marry him."

"You loved him?"

Helen's jaw tightened for a moment. She nodded. "He was the only man I ever really loved."

"So what happened?"

"Kyle. I got pregnant." Helen shook her head. "Nick said he wasn't ready to settle down. Wasn't ready for that kind of commitment." She sighed. "So it's just been me and Kyle his whole life. My parents disowned me when I went into the modeling business. It didn't conform to their morals."

"What did they think about Kyle?"

Helen frowned. "They never knew about him. My father died before I even got pregnant, and my mother . . . Well, I never told her. She passed away ten years ago. She never even knew she had another grandson."

Conner was silent for a few moments. Then he spoke up again. "You think about that much? Ever regret not telling your mother?"

Helen raised an eyebrow. "Are you trying to psychoanalyze me now?"

Conner chuckled. "No. I'm just trying to figure out why they're using your son —"

Mitch started yelling from the bridge. They rushed out of the cabin.

"The depth finder," he was saying. "We're starting to shallow. I think we're getting close to shore!"

Helen closed her eyes. A wave of relief washed over her. At this point, if she had a choice between being on land or water, with these creatures after them, she would have to choose land.

She turned to Conner and gasped.

His face had gone completely white. His eyes were round and his teeth clenched hard. His body contorted suddenly. Arms and legs stiffened. His back arched violently as he collapsed to the deck.

26

Brilliant, white light flooded Conner's vision. And a thunderous roar, like a violent wind, howled in his ears. But beneath the roaring was another sound. Muffled. Changing in pitch and volume. It sounded at once so completely alien and yet somehow vaguely familiar. . . .

But he was freezing. Numb, bone-chilling cold.

And then it faded.

The white light dissolved into a gray curtain of clouds. Faces stared down at him. A familiar band of strangers he had met only yesterday.

"Conner? Can you hear me?"

"Dude. You okay?"

"Yo, man, I think he's dead."

Conner rolled his head and groaned. "I'm okay."

Mitch helped him back into the cabin and sat him down at the table. Through his haze and confusion, Conner heard Mitch say something about the depth finder showing the lake was shallowing. Then he and Devon headed back to the bridge to keep an eye on the horizon.

Conner's head spun, though he couldn't tell how much of that was from his seizure and how much was from being on the boat.

Helen brought him another bottle of water. "Is that what you were telling me about? The seizures?"

Conner nodded. "I don't know what's causing it. They're getting farther apart but more intense."

"You're not epileptic, are you?"

"No, this is something else. It just started early yesterday. I see this bright light and there's a loud noise. Like a waterfall or something. It's deafening. But there's something else too. Another sound. It sounds like something I maybe heard before, but I can't quite tell what it is."

Helen shook her head. "I don't know what to tell you."

Conner grunted. "Just tell me I'm not going crazy."

"Do the seizures trigger your visions? your hallucinations?"

Conner thought a moment. "The first one did, but not since then. The first two were within a half hour of each other. Then the third was yesterday afternoon. Just before we met."

"And this one was over twelve hours later," Helen said. "If there's a pattern there, maybe you can calculate when the next one will happen."

"Maybe . . ."

"What about your visions? What are they like?"

Conner leaned back and closed his eyes for a moment. His head throbbed. "I was back at my old house in Lake Forest. And I saw my son running through the house."

"Did he say anything? try to communicate with you?"

Conner shook his head. "No. It was like he was playing hide-and-seek or something. I never even got a good look at him."

"But you're sure it was him."

"Yeah. Yeah, I'm sure."

They both fell silent. Conner rubbed his eyes. He had been up all night staring into the fog and now felt worn out. Yet somehow he wasn't sleepy. He took another drink. He had been so thirsty lately.

At length Helen spoke again. "So . . . your son? You said he died a few years ago."

Conner felt his jaw tighten. It really wasn't any of her business. Still, he had just made her share details from her personal life with him. After a moment, he rubbed his temple. "Yeah. Five years or so."

Five years, one month, fourteen days.

"And . . . ?"

Conner took a breath. "He drowned. He was just four, and he couldn't swim very well yet. He fell into our pool. In the backyard. I . . . I dove in and pulled him out . . . but he wasn't breathing. I called 911, did CPR. But I couldn't get him breathing again."

Helen's eyes lowered. "I can't imagine how horrible that must have been for you."

Conner was staring out the window. He suddenly felt numb. "He was just a child. They should've been able to revive him. They do it all the time."

"I'm sorry, Conner."

Conner shook his head again. "You know, I never knew what it meant to really love someone until my first child was born. Rachel." He almost managed a smile. "You have this little baby. No personality yet, completely helpless and dependent on you. You give it everything and it can't pay you back. It can't even say thank you. But it doesn't matter. Before you know what hit you, you're in love. I don't think there's any purer form of love than what a parent feels for their child. It's completely unconditional. You know?"

Helen nodded. "And there's no worse pain than to lose a child."

Conner looked at her. "I was angry."

"What do you mean?"

"I promised myself I wouldn't go through that again. I wouldn't let myself get that close to anyone ever again."

"What about your daughter and wife?"

Conner fell silent for a moment. "Marta dealt with it her way. I dealt with it mine. She found her religion. Started going to church. I focused on my work. I guess I thought if I kept busy, I could make myself forget."

Helen looked away. "That never really works, does it?"

"We just grew apart after that. We never really connected again. We got divorced a few years later."

They heard Mitch calling from the bridge. "I see the shoreline! I can see land."

They hurried out and peered into the mist. Conner could see several silhouetted shapes but didn't recognize anything.

"It looks like another marina or something," Mitch said. "I can see other boats."

They drew steadily closer, and soon Conner recognized the shapes as well. It was a small harbor. He could see several buildings along the shore. But it definitely didn't look like Chicago. More like the business district of a small town.

Conner felt a wave of relief wash over him, followed by a twinge of fear. It would be good to get off the water, but there was no guarantee those creatures wouldn't be waiting for them here. In any case, he'd be glad to get off this boat.

He suddenly remembered the dark-haired boy. He had forgotten all about him in the tumult. The kid had gone below to rest last evening. Had he slept through all the excitement of the past several hours? Conner sighed. At least one of them had gotten some rest.

He went below and stopped on the stairs. The bunk was empty. The blanket was balled up and tossed aside. The pillow was on the floor. Conner checked in the tiny lavatory compartment and inside the cabin. His heart raced.

The boy couldn't have jumped overboard. They would have heard something. Conner's mind reeled, but he wouldn't let himself give voice to his fear. Those things couldn't have taken the boy. He had been safe down below. How could they . . . ?

No, he pleaded silently. *Not him! He was*

just a kid.

He went back on deck. His eyes were wide, but he didn't know how to tell the others.

"Conner?" Helen frowned. "What's wrong?"

Conner shook his head. "The kid's gone."

27

Mitch navigated into the small harbor as Conner and Helen tore the boat apart looking for the mute kid. Mitch shook his head. The lawyer was starting to lose it. He had obviously formed some kind of attachment to the kid. Maybe that was just part of being a father or because Conner's own son had died or something.

Mitch, on the other hand, felt oddly detached from the whole situation. Sure, he felt bad, but it wasn't like they could have done anything to prevent it. And it wasn't like they could do anything about it now.

Besides, he had never really gotten over his suspicion that the kid might be connected to the aliens somehow. The lawyer said he had found him wandering around in a cemetery, which was odd enough. But the kid just seemed a little too familiar with the creatures. Maybe he jumped overboard sometime during the night. There had been a lot of confusion. Anything could have happened.

Several boats were tethered to the dock. A handful of outboard fishing skiffs and an old pontoon boat. Mitch pulled into an open slip and Devon tied them off.

Mitch checked the weapons he had taken from Earl's Sporting Goods, making sure each one was loaded. He put the three handguns in his backpack and stuck the rifles and two shotguns in a large canvas bag he had found inside the cabin.

Conner was sitting at the table, shaking his head. "He was just a kid."

Mitch gathered his things. "Look, dude, I'm sorry about the kid, okay? But there's nothing we can do for him now. We got to take care of ourselves."

The lawyer's eyes turned fierce. His face flushed red. He got up and blocked the doorway. "He didn't even want to get *on* the boat. He tried to warn us. It was *your* idea to go on the lake in the first place!"

Mitch's fists tightened. "Don't blame *me* for this!"

Conner didn't back down. "You nearly got us all killed!"

"Don't pin that kid's death on me!" Mitch slammed his fist into the lawyer's chest, knocking him backward onto the deck.

Conner tumbled into the toolbox next to the engine compartment. He scooped up a wrench from the tray and rolled back to his feet . . .

And came face to face with the barrel of Mitch's gun.

"Come on!" Mitch hissed through his teeth. *"Do it!"*

"Stop it!" Helen thrust herself between them. "We can't afford to lose it now! It's *nobody's* fault!" She touched Mitch's hand, and her voice softened. "It's no one's fault."

For a moment Mitch had wanted nothing more than to send a bullet through that lawyer's smug face. And for that brief instant, he would have. But then he felt Helen's hand on his. It reminded him of his mother's gentle touch. She had been the buffer between Mitch and his father. Always the one to defuse their tension.

Now Mitch's own anger drained from him. Slowly, he lowered his gun.

"Just stay out of my face," he said.

Conner didn't say a word. His eyes were glazed over. He dropped the wrench and turned away. He stood at the back of the boat, staring out at the water while the others unloaded their supplies.

Mitch walked up the dock and surveyed the area. It consisted mostly of small stores and cafés. But everything looked dingy and unkempt. Like the whole town had been abandoned weeks ago.

The first thing they needed to do was to figure out where they were. Had they gone north to Wisconsin? south to Indiana? Or had they crossed the lake completely to Michigan?

He spotted a small convenience store with a gas pump. Inside was a public phone with a Yellow Pages underneath. Mitch glanced at the cover. Indiana. That hardly seemed possible. He pulled a state map from the rack next to the cash register, shoved it into his pocket, and went back out.

"We're somewhere in Indiana," he announced to Helen and Devon, who were walking up the dock. He looked around and shook his head. "Sheeesh! Talk about a ghost town."

Helen rubbed her arms. "So what's the plan now?"

Mitch bit his cheek for a moment. Plan? The original plan hadn't really changed, as far as he was concerned. They still needed to search for other survivors. Maybe they'd find a larger population of people farther south. Or east. It was anybody's guess.

"I dunno," he said finally. "I guess we find some more food and keep moving. Keep looking for . . . other survivors."

"Where?"

Mitch rubbed his jaw. "Maybe east? Find out what happened to the East Coast."

Helen cast a glance back at the boat. "We're not going to leave him there, are we?"

Mitch shrugged. "You want him along, you go get him. I'm going to find us a ride." He turned and headed into town.

"Hey, man, I'm comin' with you," Devon said.

Conner stood on the deck, staring out at the small harbor. His mind was still a fog of shock and regret. And denial. He kept hoping the boy would pop out of some hidden compartment on the boat and everything would be okay. He rubbed his forehead, going over all the things he could have done differently. Every choice he had made during the last twenty-four hours had been the wrong one.

He recalled the boy's expression on the dock. He had desperately not wanted to get on the boat. He'd tried to resist, but Conner had picked him up and carried him on board. The kid was tired, so Conner sent him below. It was the safest place on the boat. He should have been safe there.

He should have been safe.

"We're in Indiana." Helen's voice drew him from his thoughts.

Conner looked up. "He didn't want to get on the boat."

Helen shook her head. "It wasn't anyone's fault. I saw those things. How they took Devon's friend. There's nothing we could've done, even if we had known about it. We can't stop them."

"But I *forced* him to get on board."

"What were you supposed to do? Leave him there? We all thought it was a good idea at the time."

"I was supposed to watch out for him."

"You didn't do anything wrong."

"I was supposed to take care of him."

"Conner." Helen's tone was gentle but firm. "Sometimes you can do everything right and bad things still happen. That's not your fault. It's just . . . life."

"Life?" Conner looked away. He had always thought of himself as stoic. Now he wasn't so sure. "Not for him."

"But we need to keep going. Mitch thinks we should head east."

"Does it really matter?"

"Look." Helen's gentle tone was quickly evaporating. "We need each other. You can't just give up now. There's got to be an answer out there somewhere. We just need to find it."

Conner rubbed his eyes. Part of him knew she was right. There might be a time to mourn. But not now. Now they had to get moving. He picked up his bag and climbed onto the dock, casting a glance back at the water.

"Sorry, kid."

Mitch and Devon walked up the main street away from the marina. There were only a few older cars and a faded blue Ford pickup along the street.

"Man —" Devon shook his head — "it's like Mayberry. Didn't anybody drive anything new in this town?"

But Mitch was looking for an SUV or a van, something to carry the four of them and whatever supplies they could find. And preferably something with four-wheel drive. Just in case.

After a few blocks they looked down a wide dead-end street with a few houses along it, ending at a large open field. Devon pointed to an old Jeep Cherokee parked beside the white clapboard house at the end of the street.

Mitch sighed. "I guess it'll do for now."

He tried the door handle. It clicked and

opened. He rummaged around but couldn't find any keys. Then he cast a sideways glance at Devon.

"You wouldn't know how to . . . ?"

"What?" Devon wrinkled his forehead. "You think just 'cause I'm a black kid from Chicago, I know how to hot-wire a car?"

"A black kid from Chicago with a gun in his pants," Mitch sneered, nodding at Devon's forearm. "And I suppose that's a Cub Scout tattoo."

Devon looked away. "We usually just steal the keys," he muttered.

"Nice." Mitch peered at the house. "I guess I'll see if anyone's home."

The side door was unlocked. Mitch walked in and looked around the cramped kitchen. The shades were drawn. The place smelled of urine. The cabinet doors were either hanging open or missing altogether. Piles of dirty dishes were stacked in the sink, and several food-crusted pans cluttered the stove. Mitch scanned the room for a set of keys.

Devon stepped inside and swore. "Looks like Aunt Bee went on strike."

"Look for the keys," Mitch said.

A living room opened off the dining area. The shades were drawn, but the odor was stronger. Mitch was going to open the

shades when he heard a voice behind him.
"I wasn't exactly expecting guests."

28

Conner and Helen walked up the main street. There was no sign of Mitch or Devon anywhere.

"I saw them head up this way," Helen said. "They couldn't have gotten too far."

She started to call out for them, but Conner put his hand on her arm.

"Let's not make too much noise just yet," he said. He dug through his bag and pulled out the two-way radio. He switched it on, hoping Mitch still had his with him.

"Mitch," he said. A sudden wave of embarrassment passed over him as he recalled their argument earlier. He may have overreacted, blaming Mitch for the boy's disappearance. But for his part, Mitch had nearly shot him in the head. He might not be in the mood to talk.

Static hissed through the radio. Conner tried twice more with the same results.

Helen looked at him, her eyes widening.

"You don't think . . . ?"

Conner shrugged it off. "He probably doesn't have it turned on."

He motioned to one of the storefronts along the street — a mom-and-pop grocery store. Inside, they found the shelves nearly empty. Food packaging, wrappers, bottles, and cereal boxes lay strewn through the aisles.

"This isn't looted," Conner said. "It looks like someone's been coming here to eat."

"You mean there might be others in town?"

"Or there were earlier." He frowned. "That's an awful lot of food for just one person."

Suddenly, Helen touched his arm. A gray Cherokee pulled up at the curb. Conner could see Mitch and Devon inside along with a third man at the wheel.

They all got out.

"Howdy!" The stranger grinned. He was lanky, dressed in layered shirts and baggy jeans. Unruly brown hair hung down to his shoulders, and a wispy goatee lined his chin. He stuck out his hand. "Name's Ray Cahill."

Conner blinked at the overpowering body odor. "Uhh . . . Conner Hayden."

"Helen Krause," Helen said, holding a

hand under her nose.

Mitch curled up an eyebrow and stuck a thumb over his shoulder. "We came across him a few blocks away."

"They broke into my house." Ray chuckled. "I don't mind tellin' you I was a bit surprised. I figured it was the end of the world, y'know? I thought I was the last man on earth. But I'm glad to finally see some real live human beings."

"You're all alone here?"

"Yep. Except for, y'know . . . the aliens."

"You've seen them too?"

Ray nodded. "They show up every once in a while."

Conner frowned. "They've never attacked you? tried to abduct you?

"Attack? Naw. They pretty much keep to themselves. They show up at night, mostly. I seen 'em watching me through the windows. That's why I originally kept moving from house to house. But they never did anything to me."

"Did they ever try to communicate with you?"

Ray shook his head. "I heard 'em whispering to each other, but I couldn't understand what they're saying."

Conner paused a moment. "What about hallucinations?"

"Hallucinations?"

"Yeah, have you ever seen anything you knew wasn't there? Or couldn't be there?"

"Well . . . yeah." Ray scratched the back of his neck. "I thought maybe I was goin' crazy. Y'know, insane or something."

Conner shook his head. "We've had similar experiences. And wondered the same thing. They must be able to scan our thoughts somehow and create images from our memories."

Ray breathed a sigh. "Well, that explains an awful lot."

Conner nodded toward the store. "You've been getting your food from here?"

Ray put his hands up. "I know what you're thinking, but it ain't really like stealing. I mean, I *had* to eat, y'know."

"It's not that," Conner said. "It's just . . . exactly how long have you been here?"

"Oh, uhhhh . . ." Ray's eyes rolled up. His lips moved silently.

Conner and the others exchanged glances. Their frowns deepened.

After a moment, Ray snorted. "Oh, I don't know. I lost count. Maybe six or seven weeks."

"Six or seven *weeks?*" Helen raised her eyebrows.

"Maybe more." Ray shrugged. "What's

wrong?"

Conner narrowed his eyes. This guy was obviously not firing on all cylinders. "You, uh . . . you sure it's been that long?"

"Well, I kept a calendar for a few weeks. Thought I'd need to keep track of time. After a while, I figured, what's the use?"

"Dude," Mitch said. "This all just happened yesterday."

"Yesterday!" Ray started to laugh, but his grin quickly faded. "What are you talking about?"

"The storm," Conner said. "Did you see it? The cloud with all the lights in it?"

"Sure did. But I hate to tell you, that first showed up a couple of months ago." Ray snorted again and shook his head. "Where've you folks been all this time?"

29

They all stood in silence. Conner shook his head, trying to process this new information. The whole experience was getting more and more bizarre. The last thing he recalled before the storm — the night before last — was having supper with Rachel. Then he woke up the next morning. At least he'd *assumed* it was the next morning. He never actually checked what day it was. Or what month. He had just made an assumption. They all had.

Devon threw his hands in the air. "Man, this is *not* happening to me!"

Mitch just leaned against the Cherokee, his head lowered.

Helen shook her head. "I don't get it. What's going on?"

"The food." Conner rubbed his jaw and nodded to himself. "Maybe that's why all the food is stale. And the meat in my refrigerator was spoiled."

"So where have we been for seven weeks?" Mitch said. "On the mother ship somewhere?"

"I don't know. But maybe that's how they're able to know so much about us," Conner offered. His head was reeling at the thought. But nothing else made sense.

"I can't . . ." Helen's voice cracked. "I can't take much more of this. . . ."

"Remember what I was saying on the boat?" Conner said. "This whole thing has been like a big experiment. It's like they're testing us. Putting different stimuli in our paths to see how we react. Or how we'd work together. Maybe that's what this is all about."

Mitch folded his arms. "Like rats in a maze?"

"Exactly," Conner said. It was all about piecing together the evidence. Following the trail. Finding the truth. "Like lab rats."

"Dude, I know what they do to lab rats." Mitch shook his head. "I don't think I like being one."

"I know," Conner said. "There's still a lot that doesn't make sense."

They piled into Ray's Cherokee and drove back to his house. He said they were in Thorton, Indiana, a small, unincorporated town on the Lake Michigan shore.

Mitch was looking at a map, shaking his head. "Looks like we almost came clear across the lake."

"I grew up here," Ray was saying. "I moved to Kentucky for a couple years when I was twenty. And then a year in California. A couple years in Washington. Oh, and a year in Arizona." He shook his head and chuckled. "Hmm, Arizona was great. . . . But I just moved back in with my folks about six months ago. Well —" he scratched his head — "six months before this all happened."

Conner tried to pry more useful information from him. "But you haven't seen anyone else this whole time?"

"Nope."

"Did you ever leave town? Did you ever go out and *look* for people?"

"Yeah, I drove around a bit. I spent the first week or so sitting out on the interstate during the day. But no one ever showed up. So I figured, if I'm gonna spend the rest of my life alone, I might as well have fun. Y'know? Plus I figured I'd have a better chance of someone seeing me if I stayed put."

"And the aliens," Conner said. "How often do you see them?"

Ray shrugged. "Once every few nights.

They really freaked me out at first so I got a couple shotguns. But they never did anything, so I guess I just learned to ignore them."

Devon grunted. "Well, the ones in Chicago ain't so friendly."

Conner pressed further. "Do you ever see where they come from?"

Ray glanced in his rearview mirror. "They come out of the lake. Best I can figure, they stay there during the day. I see 'em walking up from the beach when the fog rolls in."

"And you say they never attack you?"

"Nope," Ray said. "But the whole town kinda looks like a bad zombie movie. They just wander around. I think maybe they're just exploring. Looking around, y'know? Checking out the buildings and stuff."

Helen shuddered. "Well if it's all the same to everyone else, I just as soon not stick around for that. I think we should keep moving."

"Where to?" Ray said, frowning.

"East," Mitch said. "I think we should head to Washington. If anyone survived whatever happened, it'd be those folks. All those guys have bunkers to hide out in, in case of nuclear war or something."

No one disagreed. No one seemed able to offer a better plan. Conner had to admit it wasn't bad logic, though he didn't think they'd find anyone there either. He decided not to share those feelings. No need to be the pessimist.

They pulled up to Ray's house and went inside. Helen's eyes widened when she saw the mess. Ray apologized profusely and set about clearing away the clutter and opening the shades and windows.

Conner suggested they take the morning to rest. They had all been up for over twenty-four hours now, and he was exhausted.

Mitch said they should sleep in shifts and offered to keep watch first.

Helen lay down on a sofa in the back den, off the kitchen. Devon fell into a stained recliner in the living room. Conner, unable to stand the odor inside the house, found a padded bench swing on the front porch. He fell into it and yawned.

Mitch and Ray settled into a pair of lawn chairs on the other end of the porch with their guns.

Conner watched Mitch for a moment. "By the way, I'm sorry about losing it earlier. Blaming you for what happened to the kid. I don't normally overreact like that. It's just, this whole thing has been a nightmare for everyone."

"No problem." Mitch shrugged it off. "Sorry for almost blowing your head off."

Conner chuckled and leaned back. He heard Ray ask something about what kid, and Mitch began a brief explanation of their encounters thus far. Their voices faded to a muddled blah, blah, blah, as Conner felt himself swinging gently and drifting off to sleep.

It was the first time he had a chance to actually lie down and close his eyes. He hadn't gotten any sleep on the boat. A soft breeze wafted over the porch. Conner was soon on the verge of slumber. That point at which there remained a faint awareness of the things around him, yet where he was far too relaxed to react. And just at that point, he heard something.

A thump, thump of footsteps on a wooden floor. But not footsteps.

In the fog of his half sleep, Conner tried to pinpoint the sound. It was one he had heard before, though not in a long while.

Not footsteps . . . a ball.

Bouncing down the stairs.

30

Conner's eyes snapped open.

He was no longer on the swing. Or the porch. Or in Thorton, Indiana, for that matter. He was . . .

He was home.

Not his condo. That had never really felt like *home* in the two years he had lived there. No, this was *their* home in Lake Forest. The home he and Marta had purchased together. His chest ached. It was the home he had grown to despise of late. And the home he had come to miss even more.

He was standing in the breakfast nook. Sunlight poured in through the bay window. Papers were strewn across the table. The sun was so bright.

And noise. He could hear noises echoing through the rooms. Layer upon layer of sound. He strained to listen and immediately discovered he knew these sounds. He had heard them before. Laughter and weeping and bedtime stories and arguments and lovemaking and singing. The sounds of life. All happening at once. All together. All still a gentle cacophony.

Music. Marta loved music. Amid the collage of sounds, Conner could hear her familiar voice. Sweet and soft. Singing to herself as she cooked. She used to fill the whole house with her singing. It was soothing in a way, and he remembered he had forgotten how much he loved her voice.

And there was Rachel's laughter. Conner grinned at her jittery giggles flowing through the hallway. She would laugh like that when he'd tickle her on the backs of her legs. He could hear seven years of piano lessons. "Chopsticks" and Chopin. Beethoven and "The Entertainer." He spread his arms and closed his eyes and let it flow over him and through him.

Then came a tiny Tarzan yell.

Conner's eyes snapped open again. His lips moved. *Matthew?*

Tarzan. Spider-Man. Batman. All rolled into one. Swinging on the tree rope, flopping on the trampoline, jumping on the sofa. Bouncing basketballs and kicking soccer balls through the house. And always, always making noise. Conner's eyes stung. Matthew played with such gusto.

Watch this, Daddy!
Look what I can do!
Didja see that?
Didja see me?
And then . . .

Then the sounds slowly faded. Conner strained to keep them. He spun in the room, reaching out as if to gather them back. "Please!" he pleaded. "Don't go! Not yet . . ."

He missed it. He missed all of it and he longed now more than anything to have it back. If just for a minute.

Thump! Thump! Thump!

The sound came again. A singular beating. A ball, bouncing down the steps. Followed by footsteps pounding in the upstairs hall. Now down the stairs.

Conner rushed into the front hallway. A soccer ball rolled past and a tousled form tumbled after, laughing. Into Conner's front room office they went, the ball and the boy. Conner was forever shooing Matthew out. He hurried down the hall to the doorway. He would catch him at last. He would finally catch him. And maybe then find the answer.

Conner looked into the room. Matthew's back was toward him, the ball tucked under his arm. He stared out the window.

Conner's heart raced. He could hear it pounding in his ears. He could feel his whole body throbbing.

"Matthew!" His voice was a hoarse whisper. He didn't want to scare him.

Matthew didn't move. He raised a finger and pressed it to the glass.

Conner took a step into the room. "Matthew? It's me. It's Daddy."

Matthew's finger tapped at the glass. He whispered something. Conner leaned forward. He couldn't make it out.

Conner knew the vision wasn't real, yet here he was. He knew it was a hallucination, yet he couldn't keep himself from being drawn further in. He had to know. He had to find out.

"What?" he said, taking another hesitant step. "What did you say?"

He squeezed back tears. He just needed to know.

Matthew tapped the glass again and turned around.

Conner fell back. His mouth opened to scream, but his breath was sucked from his lungs.

Matthew's blond hair tumbled down onto his forehead. Beneath his forehead, only shallow indentations of flesh marked the place where his eyes should have been. Only two flittering nostril slits opened on a pallid bump. And his mouth. He had no mouth. Only smooth flesh.

Conner shook his head. "No!" He tried to scream but he had no strength to move. Hardly even to breathe.

A tiny slit then appeared in the flesh where Matthew's mouth would be, like the skin unzipping a small opening. It moved more like a doll's than a living mouth.

A thin voice whispered, *"They're coming."*

31

Conner opened his eyes. The bright morning sunlight of his dream dissolved into gray shadows. Someone was standing over him. Conner swore and tumbled out of the swing onto the porch floor, flailing his arms in front of him. He felt his fist connect with something solid. He heard a voice swear. Then meaty hands gripped his wrists and pinned them to the floor.

"Dude!" Mitch's face appeared as Conner's eyes adjusted to the dim light. "It's me."

Conner stopped struggling. "What happened?"

Mitch released Conner's wrists and stood up, shaking his head. "I don't know. I must've fallen asleep or something. One minute I'm talking to Ray, and the next thing I know I'm laying on the floor and it's dark."

Conner struggled to his feet, his heart still

racing. "We need to get going!" He saw Ray standing at the front steps, staring down the street. "Ray, we have to leave."

Ray turned around with a dazed look on his face. "They're coming."

A white carpet of mist was rolling up from the lake. It curled around houses and cars as it crept up the dead-end street. Its leading edge billowed and churned, reaching out slow, slender tendrils as if pulling itself along.

And inside the mist, tall, gaunt silhouettes were moving. Some strode upright; others crouched low, nearly crawling on all fours. The mist curled around their limbs and torsos like a cloak roiling in the wind.

Conner's chest pounded. His mouth went dry. "Get inside!"

Ray just shook his head slowly. "There's so many of them tonight."

They went inside. Mitch set about locking the doors and windows and drawing all the curtains. Conner found Helen and Devon still asleep and woke them.

Helen looked dazed at first but grew wide-eyed when she saw it was already dark. "I said we should leave! I told you we shouldn't stay!"

Devon peered through the curtains out the front window. "I do *not* want to go through another night like last night."

Conner found Ray in the corner. "We need to turn on all the lights."

"Lights?" Ray sputtered. "I haven't had electricity in three weeks. All I got are a few candles."

Devon threw up his hands. "Oh, that's great! Man, that's just great!"

Helen grabbed Conner's arm and whispered, "We have to leave."

Suddenly, a light snapped on in the kitchen. Mitch had his bag in one hand and the boat's flashlight in the other. "I say we make a run for the Cherokee."

Ray was shaking his head again. "I don't see what all the fuss is about. They do this every few nights. I told you, I've been here for six or seven weeks. All they do is walk around and —"

There was a loud thump on the front porch followed by soft clicking like claws on wood. A moment later, more scraping sounds came from the back entrance.

"Are all the doors locked?" Conner said.

"Locked?" Devon said. "Man, I'm tellin' you it don't matter. They'll come right through the walls if they want to."

Helen crouched down in the hallway, shaking her head. "We're not safe here. We have to leave!"

Conner held out his hands. "Look, everybody just *calm down.*"

A heavy bump rattled the side wall. More claws skittered, this time across the roof.

Ray backed away from the door into the middle of the living room, where Mitch was standing with the flashlight. "They, uh . . . they've never done this before."

Something scraped against the front window. Like steel against glass. It moved down to the windowsill where it started picking at the wood.

The same sounds came from one of the windows in the kitchen. And more scraping at the front door.

Helen covered her ears. "No! Make it stop!"

Mitch swung the flashlight from window to door as each new sound started. Another thump shook the outside wall, then a slow, steady pounding. More claws skittered across the shingles.

Each new sound built upon the last as the din grew steadily louder. Devon erupted in a string of curses and pulled out his gun. He started blasting at the windows and the front door.

Conner dove to the floor. "Stop!"

But Devon was screaming at the top of his lungs. Mitch swung the flashlight beam from window to window. Conner thought he may have been firing his gun too. The noise was deafening.

"Stop! Stop!" Conner shouted. Bits of wood and glass flew across the floor. He tried to crawl for cover. Smoke from gunfire filled the room. The sharp sulfur odor stung in Conner's nostrils. Helen screamed. Devon shouted. The steady thunder of gunshots shook the house.

Then everything stopped. Conner could hear the click-click-click of the triggers; both guns were empty. A moment later, Devon stopped shouting. Then the only sounds were panting and gasping for breath. Conner peeked out from under the kitchen table, his ears still ringing.

Mitch and Devon stood in the middle of the living room with their guns still drawn. Smoke coiled and swirled in the beam of the flashlight. Ray crouched behind the recliner. Helen remained huddled somewhere in the dark hallway, her arms covering her head.

Silence.

Conner crawled out from under the table. Chunks of glass and wood and plaster covered the floor and bit into the palms of his hands. The curtains were shredded and riddled with bullet holes. The front door was chipped and pocked. But there was no more pounding outside. No claws skittering across the porch or on the roof.

Nothing.

Conner stood up. His knees shook. His hands trembled. They all stood, silent in the smoky glow of the flashlight. Listening.

Mitch closed his eyes, his chest heaving.

Ray crawled out from behind the chair. He stood up slowly and made his way to the front window. Lifting the tattered curtain aside, he peeked out into the night. "It's okay." He craned his neck. Then he breathed a sigh and shook his head. "I think they're g—"

Two long, gray appendages crashed through the wall behind him, sending shards of wood and chunks of plaster flying across the room. Devon and Mitch tumbled backward onto the floor and couch.

Gnarled, skeletal hands unfolded from dark forearms. Multijointed fingers spread open and clutched Ray's chest. The flashlight shone on his pale face. He let out a high-pitched shriek as his skin grew discolored. A creeping purple rash spread up from his neck over his face. He struggled to pry himself loose, but the elongated fingers interlocked and wrenched him back through the plaster, lattice, and clapboards and out into the darkness.

Conner froze.

Ray's screams echoed in the mist, growing more and more faint.

Then the silence returned.

32

Mitch blinked and scrambled for his bag. He still had a box of bullets inside. His fingers trembled as he hurried to reload the gun in the glow of the flashlight. The creatures could be back any moment. They couldn't waste any time.

"We need to go!" His voice was shaky.

Conner's voice came from the darkened kitchen. "They just . . . *took* him!"

Mitch dropped a bullet and swore. "We need to *go!*"

"They just . . . broke right through the wall and . . ."

"Man, I *told* you that!" Devon got to his feet. "You can't hide from those things. That's just what they did to Terrell."

"But why only him? Why didn't they attack all of us?"

Mitch finished loading his gun and stuck it in his belt. "Everybody shut up and help me find the keys!"

He swept the flashlight around the floor and counters. He finally spotted the key ring next to the stove and snatched it up.

"Everybody take a gun." Mitch unzipped the bag with the handguns he had taken from the store in Lake Forest. At the time he thought three would be enough. Now he wished he had cleaned the place out. He slung one of the shotguns over his shoulder and handed the other to Devon along with one of the handguns.

"Now that's what I'm talkin' about." Devon nodded.

Mitch held out the second handgun to Conner, who started to protest.

"Just take it," Mitch grunted, shoving it in his chest.

He swung the light back around and found Helen standing in the darkened hallway. She was still trembling. He handed her the third gun. She took it but shook her head. "These aren't going to do us any good."

"If we can't kill them, maybe we can slow them down," Mitch said. "Maybe that's why they stopped attacking the house."

"They stopped because they took Ray," Helen said. "Not because of the guns."

Mitch zipped up the bag of ammo. "You don't know that."

Devon pointed to the hole in the wall. "Did you see his face? That same purple rash was all over him when they grabbed him!"

Conner's voice came from the dark. "It was like they just wanted *him.*"

"We don't know that!" Mitch was getting fed up. "We're wasting time."

He opened the side door slowly and listened. Nothing. A moment later he slipped outside, followed by Devon. Mitch assumed Conner and Helen were following too but frankly couldn't have cared less at that point. Either way, *he* was going to get out of here.

Silence engulfed them. The mist still lingered, hugging the ground. Nothing moved. No shadows, no sign of any life.

They moved quickly down the gravel driveway to the Cherokee. Mitch slipped inside and started it up. It chugged to life as the others piled in, and a moment later, he tore out of the yard, onto the street, out of town.

He handed the map to Conner, sitting next to him. "See if you can figure out where we are."

Conner unfolded the map, peering at it with the flashlight. "Okay . . . Thorton . . . Thorton . . . Here it is."

Mitch came across a two-lane highway and swung left. "We're on Highway 12, headed east. I think."

"Twelve, twelve . . ." Conner studied the map for a minute, muttering to himself. Then he flipped it over.

The fog was growing thicker. The headlights cut into it, casting a sickly glow. Mitch could see only a few yards ahead. He swore and slowed down. "I can't see," he mumbled. It reminded him of being out on the lake the night before. Though at least on the lake he didn't have to worry about driving off the road or crashing into a tree.

"Uh . . . here it is," Conner said. "Yeah, stay on this until you hit 35, and that gets you to the interstate."

"East," Mitch said. "We still want to head east, right? To Washington?"

Conner sat back and rubbed his neck. "I guess so. I guess that makes sense."

"How much gas do we have?" Helen leaned forward.

Mitch glanced down. "A quarter tank. We should find someplace to fill up before too long."

"There's no electricity back there," Helen said. "We'll need to find someplace with power, right?"

"Not necessarily," Mitch said. "We could

siphon it out of another vehicle if we need to. It depends how much of the area is blacked out."

Conner frowned. "Ray said he'd been without electricity for a few weeks already."

"We still had power in Chicago," Helen said. "Just yesterday."

"The power stations for a bigger city can probably run longer without anyone operating them," Mitch said. "But what about the nuclear plants. If no one's there to run them . . ."

"Great," Devon mumbled. "Now we gotta worry about a nuclear meltdown, too."

Conner shook his head. "Somehow I think that's the least of our worries." He looked at the others. "What if we've been thinking about this the wrong way?"

Mitch narrowed his eyes. "What d'you mean?"

"We've been under the assumption this whole time that everyone has disappeared."

Mitch snorted. "Yeah, I guess it was, y'know, all the empty streets and buildings."

"I mean, what if *we're* the ones who've been abducted?"

Mitch frowned. "You mean for those six or seven missing weeks?"

"No, I mean now. What if we're not really in Indiana at all?"

Mitch cast a glance back at Helen and Devon. They both looked as confused as he felt. "Dude, did you hit your head or something?"

"No, remember?" Conner leaned forward. "We talked about how we felt like rats in a maze? Like everything they're doing to us is just to see how we react? What if this is all some kind of laboratory experiment. Like a virtual reality. Maybe they have us somewhere, hooked up to some computer to make us *think* we're really on earth."

Helen just shook her head.

"Think about it," Conner went on. "What makes more sense? That some aliens could make an entire population vanish without a trace? Or that they just abducted a few of us and made us *think* everyone else has disappeared?"

Mitch raised an eyebrow. "So I'm not really driving anywhere?"

Conner shrugged. "What *is* reality? It's just our perception of the world. Just electrical impulses interpreted by our brains. All the things we see or hear or touch are ultimately just electrical signals."

"So if I let go of the wheel . . ."

"It's just a theory," Conner said. "But think about our hallucinations. They *seemed* so real. Not just visually but the sounds and odors too."

Helen nodded. "I touched Kyle. I could feel him."

"So what?" Mitch shrugged. "What do we do with that? How can you prove it?"

Conner sat back and shook his head. "I'm not sure just yet."

They came to Highway 35 and turned right. It was a four-lane highway, heading south. Mitch felt a little more comfortable driving on the wider road in the fog and picked up his speed.

"Keep an eye out for a gas station or something," he said. "I don't want to get stranded out here in the middle of the night."

Before long, Helen and Devon had drifted off. Conner was staring out the window, apparently lost in thought.

Mitch was no longer in the mood for conversation. He peered into the oncoming fog, trying to focus on the road ahead. But his thoughts turned to Linda. He had tried so hard not to think about her over the last two days. He couldn't afford to. Not with all that was going on. He refused to lose his head, or give up hope that he'd see her again. But now he wondered if she was even still alive.

He'd had plenty of girlfriends before her,

and none of them exactly virtuous. But Linda was different. Self-confident. Independent. She had her head on straight. And her voice . . .

Her voice was the sort of soft, soothing tone that his mother had. . . .

Mitch blinked and glanced over at the lawyer. He was staring out the window. No doubt working on his theory. Mitch sniffed. He'd gotten accustomed to giving the guy a hard time about everything. And this new idea was a little too crazy for Mitch to take seriously.

Although, his hallucination had *seemed* real. He had actually *felt* his mother's hand touch him during his episode on the boat. It felt so real. Exactly like when he was a kid. He bit his lip. He thought he had forgotten that. He had tried so hard to forget. . . .

"Hey, that looked like a gas station back there." Conner perked up.

"You sure?"

Conner nodded. "Pretty sure, yeah. It looked like there was a truck or something parked there, anyway. If we need to siphon some gas."

Mitch turned the Cherokee around and headed back. A shadowy building loomed up in the fog. He pulled in. It was a muffler and brake shop. No gas pumps, but there was a pickup truck parked in the lot. Mitch pulled to a stop and tapped the wheel.

They had a little less than a quarter tank. They could probably make it another hour or so. But still, they shouldn't pass up an opportunity. It was the first building they had seen in a while.

Mitch got out and inspected the truck. It was unlocked, but the keys weren't in it, so he couldn't read the gas gauge.

He shrugged. "It's worth a shot. I need a hose or something."

He grabbed the flashlight from the Cherokee and went inside.

"I'll yell if I see anything," Conner called after him.

The door was unlocked. Mitch tried the lights. Nothing. He searched through the front office area and then moved back into the garage. There had to be something he could use. He shined the light across the shelves and worktables and soon spotted a hose connected to an air compressor.

"Good enough," he said to himself.

He found a utility knife on the worktable, sliced off both ends of the hose, and coiled it up. Then he turned to leave but stopped in his tracks.

There was a light rustling sound in the

darkness. Mitch jumped back, nearly dropping the flashlight. He swung the beam across the garage. He had definitely heard something move in the dark. Skitter across the floor. He pulled the gun from his belt.

There was a soft thud. Mitch spun around. The shelving unit along the back wall jiggled slightly. An empty oilcan toppled to the cement and rolled toward him.

A door slammed. Mitch swept the light further. It shone on the restroom door in the back corner. Closed up tight. His heart pounded against his ribs. His throat went dry.

Part of him screamed for him to run. To get out of there. But part of him was fed up. He'd had enough. Enough being scared. Enough running away. It was time to put a bullet squarely into one of these alien heads.

33

Mitch went to the door. Shined the light around the edges. He held his breath and listened.

A dim light leaked out through the bottom, and a soft sound came from behind it. Sporadic and wavering. Almost like . . . no, *exactly* like the sound of someone singing.

Mitch backed up and scowled. Singing?

Soft and distant and slightly out of tune. But someone was definitely singing inside the bathroom. For a moment he thought to kick the door in. Then he gathered his courage and turned the knob.

The door swung open. It was no bathroom at all but a large, dimly lit bedroom. A man sat in a chair at the bedside, his back toward Mitch. But Mitch recognized him immediately. This was his parents' bedroom. That was his father.

Mitch shook his head slowly. His lip trembled but he clenched his jaw against it.

"Why are you doing this?"

His father's song was soft and gentle. Mitch had heard it a thousand times in church sitting between his parents. He had grown to hate it.

"What a Friend we have in Jesus,
All our sins and griefs to bear!
What a privilege to carry
Everything to God in prayer!"

"Stop it," Mitch said. His voice quivered slightly. "Stop singing to her."

"Oh what peace we often forfeit,
Oh what needless pain we bear . . ."

Mitch grimaced. "You hear me?"

"All because we do not carry
Everything to God in prayer!"

"You think that helps her? You think that makes the pain go away?"

His father paused for a moment, turning his head slightly as if only to acknowledge Mitch's presence. But he didn't make eye contact. He never did. The congressman had devoted his life to his political career. To his reputation. He could talk for hours with voters and community leaders but could never manage more than a few curt sentences to his son.

> "Have we trials and temptations?
> Is there trouble anywhere?"

Mitch could see his mother squirm beneath the sheet. The pain made her ever restless. Toward the end she couldn't even sleep. And her breathing! The constant rattling of her lungs. He remembered how she would groan during the night. He would lay in the dark, covering his ears as she gagged and vomited.

But his father couldn't see it. Or wouldn't. He just kept singing. When it was obvious the painkillers were no longer working, he would just sing more softly. Sometimes he would read that Bible of his, as if it were some sort of balm. Some magic elixir. But Mitch knew the man's religion was little more than window dressing for his political aspirations. And Mitch was forced to conform for the sake of his father's reputation.

> "We should never be discouraged;
> Take it to the Lord in prayer."

Prayer? Mitch had prayed every night. For six months he prayed for her to get better.

Finally he prayed that she would just die. But still she lingered, suffering. And no one would do anything to ease her pain. No one seemed willing to help her.

Mitch cursed his father. "Do you think He's listening? Do you think He even cares about any of us? We're on our own down here, Dad. We're all alone. We have to find our own way."

His father stopped singing and straightened up in the chair. "I can take a lot of disrespect from you, Mitch."

Mitch frowned. That wasn't his father's voice.

The man stood and turned around.

Mitch's eyes widened and he backed away from the door.

This was not his father.

Smooth flesh covered over the space where his eyes should have been. And his mouth looked like an elongated incision in the pale flesh, spreading from one cheek to the other. It peeled back to reveal multiple rows of narrow, pointed teeth. His jaw opened to a curling, ink black tongue.

A bass voice rumbled at Mitch. "But I *will not* abide you blaspheming the Lord!"

The creature wore his father's sweater and corduroy pants. It had his father's hair.

Mitch felt a frigid blast of air, paralyzing him.

The thing strode toward him. "Now get out! And leave us alone!"

The door slammed shut.

34

Conner could see Mitch's flashlight sweeping back and forth inside the garage. He wondered now, was it even worth stopping in the middle of nowhere? In the middle of the night? He ran his fingers along the barrel of the gun and made sure the safety was off, for the seventh time.

What was taking Mitch so long?

The fog pressed in on him. Conner shuddered. Sure, he had a gun, but he felt helpless without the flashlight. He even considered waking Helen and Devon but thought better of it. They at least should rest. For Conner's part, he was wide awake. He recalled his earlier dream and didn't think he would ever sleep again.

Conner tensed at the sound of a slamming door inside the building. He could still see a light through the windows of the garage door. "Mitch?" he called, but not too loud. "Are you okay?"

A minute later, Mitch returned, walking stiff and upright, like a zombie in a campy movie. But he was carrying what looked like a coil of hose and a gas can.

"Everything okay?" Conner said as Mitch approached.

Mitch didn't answer. Didn't even look at him. He walked around to the side of the truck, unscrewed the gas cap, and fed one end of the hose into the tank. Then he blinked and shook his head. It looked to Conner as if he had just awakened from a trance.

"Are you all right?"

Mitch glanced at him and offered a quick nod. Then he bent his ear down to the gas tank and jiggled the hose. After a moment, he straightened up. His frown had deepened.

"What is it?" Conner was growing weary of the one-sided conversation.

Mitch stared at the truck. "It's empty."

"What?"

He pulled the hose back out. "Completely dry."

"Dry? Isn't that a little strange?"

Mitch snorted. "Dude, that's like the *least* strange thing that's happened to us. We'll just have to keep going."

"There wasn't any gas inside?"

"Go look for yourself if you want to." Mitch coiled the hose and stowed it in the back of the Cherokee along with the gas can. As he circled back to the driver's door, Conner met him with an open palm.

"I'll drive."

Mitch frowned. "I'm not tired."

"Neither am I."

Mitch rolled his eyes, dumped the keys into Conner's hand, and went around to the other door. He sank into the passenger seat and leaned his head back.

Conner pulled onto the highway. Helen and Devon were still asleep. But Conner could sense something was wrong with Mitch. Something had happened inside the garage. Something wasn't right.

After a minute, he ventured a conversation. "What's wrong? What happened in there?"

Mitch just grunted. "Nothing."

Conner wasn't buying. He had used that act too many times himself. "Come on, Mitch. If something happened to you in there, let me know. We can try to help you."

Mitch laughed; not one of his snide chuckles — he *laughed.* "Dude, there is no one on this planet who can help me anymore."

"That's not true. Look, if something happened to you, it could be important to help us find out what's going on."

Mitch's laughter died away. He shook his head and rubbed his eyes.

Conner persisted. "Did you see something?"

Mitch snorted and leaned back again.

"You *did* see something." Conner nodded. "What was it? Another hallucination? Was it your mother again?"

"It was nothing important."

"Everything is important here. Any clue could help us figure out what's going on."

Mitch sighed, long and loud. "I'm going crazy is what's going on."

"You're not going crazy, Mitch. We've all had hallucinations. What did you see? Your mother again?"

Mitch just stared at the dashboard.

"Mitch? Was it her again? Did she try to talk to — ?"

"It wasn't my mother this time!" Mitch huffed. His lips tightened a moment. Then his voice softened. "It was my dad."

"Your dad?" Conner frowned. "What'd he do? Did he say anything?"

Mitch shook his head. "Only it wasn't my dad. It . . ." He hesitated. Conner could tell he was searching for words. "It . . . was one of them, I think."

Conner bit his lip. A sick feeling swelled

in his stomach. "What?"

"It . . . he looked like one of those things. He didn't have a face."

Conner's foot drew off the gas pedal. The image of Matthew's eyeless, alien face flashed back into his head. "Mitch, I saw the same kind of thing when I was dreaming of Matthew before. He looked the same way." His frown deepened. There were no such things as coincidences here. "What did he do? Your father. Did he say anything?"

"No." Mitch's voice grew tense. "He just yelled at me. Just like when I was a kid."

Conner could see him struggling to put his thoughts into words. What had happened to him? Something with his father? A childhood trauma? He said his mother had died when he was a teenager. But there was something more. Something else was bothering him.

"So what happened between you and your father?" Conner prodded him. "You said you'd had a fight or something but he had called you recently."

"He called the night all this started. He'd been trying to get ahold of me, but I didn't want to talk to him. I didn't know what to say."

"What'd he want?"

"He said he just wanted to . . . to patch

things up between us."

"Did you?"

"No. I was on my way to pick up my girlfriend. I was going to propose. And I was running late, so I didn't have time to talk. And I didn't really *want* to talk."

Conner fell silent for a moment. Something wasn't adding up. "So what was this fight about? When you left home?"

Mitch shook his head. "It doesn't matter anymore."

"Sure it does. They're using this to get to you. They're trying to mess with your head. Just tell me what happened, and maybe we can figure out how to stop it."

Mitch was quiet for a moment. Conner peered at him in the darkness. He was usually pretty good at reading body language. He could tell when someone was ready to reveal the truth or if they were hiding it. Mitch fidgeted in his seat. Conner could see he wanted to tell him more. He had probably wanted to tell somebody for a long time.

They drove in silence through the fog. Outside, eddies of mist rushed toward them, glowing in the headlights, swirling past them like ghosts. Conner remained silent. He knew how to get people to talk. But there were occasions when the best tool was just to be still and give them a little time. Sometimes the words would begin to emerge on their own. He let the silence do its work.

At length, Mitch spoke again. "Did you ever have to watch someone you love suffer? I mean, go for months in pain?"

Conner hesitated. "No."

Mitch nodded and stared out the window a moment longer. "My mother died slowly. Pancreatic cancer. It spread to her lungs and brain. There wasn't anything they could do."

"How long did she suffer?"

"She was sick for over a year, but the last few months were the worst." Mitch shook his head. "I was fourteen. I'd sit in her room. Y'know, praying for her. Until my father would come and kick me out. He wouldn't let me near her."

"He didn't want you to have to watch her suffer."

"Maybe. I didn't get it at the time. I wanted to be by her, but I couldn't stand to see her like that. She was in . . . a lot of pain."

"And you resented him for that? kicking you out of the room?"

Mitch shook his head. "My old man was real religious. He'd kick *me* out. But *he'd* sit there by her bed and sing these hymns and read his Bible to her. She'd be groaning in pain, and he was like a robot. Like his singing was going to make her feel better or something. At least I kept quiet. She hardly even knew I was there."

Conner thought he was beginning to understand. "So you got tired of the hypocrisy?"

Mitch shrugged. "He was in politics. A congressman. When the dude wasn't campaigning, he was getting ready for the next election. I hardly even knew him. My mother was the one who raised me. She tried to teach me history and stuff. She said I could grow up and run for congress like my old man." His jaw tightened. "But I never wanted to be anything like him."

Conner nodded. "That's not all that uncommon with kids of high-profile parents."

Mitch drew in a breath. "After she died, things just got worse between us. It was like I didn't even exist. He talked to me even less than he had before. When I turned eighteen, I let him have it. Both barrels. I told him what he could do with his politics and his religion. And his God."

"And you hadn't talked to him until he called you?"

Mitch chuckled, and it grew into a hollow laughter. "In twenty-four years, the first time the man ever said he loved me was when he called that night."

Conner fell silent. Over the last several minutes he had been cultivating a righteous anger toward Mitch's father. He had always been disgusted with the purveyors of politics and morality, forever barking down commandments to others but rarely living up to them. And Mitch's father seemed like a classic example. But in Mitch's bitter laugh, Conner suddenly felt the story turn on him. Like a mirror, he saw *himself* now, hypocritical and self-righteous. And Rachel was the one bitter and laughing.

He couldn't recall the last time he had told her he loved her. And Marta's words echoed in his mind.

"She wants to be with you. . . ."

His indignation had run its course. It left him feeling hollow and cheated.

Mitch's voice drew him from his thoughts. "I never thought I'd ever hear him say that. I never thought he'd forgive me."

Conner frowned. "Forgive you? For wha—?"

The Cherokee lurched slightly. The engine sputtered. Mitch swore and sat up.

Conner checked the fuel gauge. It was well

past empty. He peered back out the window. "No . . . not now."

35

Conner scanned the fog for any sign of a gas station or any building with vehicles. The Cherokee sputtered again. Conner let off the gas. Mitch was scanning the roadside as well.

"We had a quarter tank. We can't be out already."

Conner shrugged. "We haven't been driving that long."

"Dude, we cannot get stranded out here!"

Helen and Devon stirred in the backseat as the engine sputtered again. "What's going on?" Helen mumbled.

Devon swore. "Outta gas? How can we run outta gas?"

"We've been looking. We haven't seen any place to stop."

Helen leaned forward. "There's gotta be someplace nearby."

Conner shook his head. "We stopped someplace about twenty minutes ago, but there wasn't any gas. We even tried to siphon some from a truck parked outside, but its tank was empty."

Mitch was growing agitated. "We haven't seen anything but trees and empty fields this whole time."

"I thought we were close to the interstate?" Helen said. "Wasn't there a gas station when we got on?"

"We haven't seen the interstate yet," Conner said. "But this fog's been so thick, we can't see much of anything."

The Cherokee sputtered once more, and the engine finally stalled.

"There!" Mitch pointed ahead. "I see something! There's a building up there. And I see some cars!"

Conner spotted the boxy shape of a building in the fog and turned into the driveway. The Cherokee rolled to a stop in the middle of a gravel parking lot.

They got out and listened. The fog seemed to press in on them from all around. The building itself looked to be a small roadside bar. No gas pumps. No lights. But three cars were parked near the entrance: a station wagon, a pickup, and a compact.

Mitch retrieved the hose and gas can from the back and went to the station wagon. He fed the hose into the tank. They could hear a dull, hollow thud.

Mitch looked up. His expression was grim.

"That's dry too?" Conner shook his head. "Doesn't anybody in this state keep gas in their cars?"

Mitch tried the pickup and the compact as well with the same results.

"Oh, that's great, man!" Devon pounded the hood. "That's great! We got no gas and we're stuck out in the middle of nowhere! What are we supposed to do? Walk?"

Conner inspected the bar more closely. The windows were broken out. Shards of glass lay strewn along the ledges. The door hung ajar. He shook his head. "Looks like we're not the first ones here."

Mitch flipped on the flashlight and pointed it through one of the windows. "The place is trashed."

"What do we do now?" Helen asked.

Conner stood with his hands on his hips and looked around. "There's got to be other places around. Maybe houses. I say we wait until dawn and see if the fog lifts."

Mitch spread the map out on the hood and shined the flashlight on it. "I can't believe we missed the interstate."

"We couldn't have missed it," Conner said. "We would've seen something."

Mitch shook his head. "You said this road

connected right to the interstate."

"I have a law degree; I know how to read a map."

Mitch traced his finger along the map. "Dude, it was just a few miles."

"And you were driving first," Conner shot back. "Why didn't you see anything?"

"Will you two stop fighting!" Helen grabbed the flashlight from Mitch. "I thought I heard something."

She swung the light around the parking lot. Their visibility wasn't much more than a dozen yards or so.

Conner peered into the fog. "What'd you hear?"

Helen shook her head. "I . . . I don't know. . . . There it is!"

Conner strained to listen. At first, all he heard was his own breathing, then Helen's. But then he caught something else.

Voices. Whispering in the mist.

36

They all stood back to back, guns drawn. Conner's chest pounded, and his palms grew moist. He could hear the voices more clearly now, though he couldn't make out what they were saying. Just like on the lake, they were whispering to each other. Conner swallowed. His throat was so dry. . . .

Mitch whispered, "I don't see anything."

"I do." Helen's voice quivered.

Then Conner saw them as well. Vague silhouettes, tall and thin, encircled them. Some stood upright, some slightly bent, swaying in the fog. Others crouched low.

"I've had enough of this!" Mitch shouted.

The night erupted with the thunder of gunshots. Mitch shouted a string of profanities, and Devon as well. Conner could hear Helen screaming. Not out of fear but anger. A mad, high-pitched tirade. And more gunfire.

Conner felt a sudden surge of emotion in

his chest. Anger and hate welled up as adrenaline released into his bloodstream. He brought the sight up onto one of the creatures and fired.

A flash of light erupted from the end of the barrel. The blast kicked back into his wrist and arm. Gripping the gun with both hands, Conner squeezed the trigger again, pumping the remaining rounds into the creature. He didn't even know how many rounds he had fired. He just kept shooting. And screaming.

Then it stopped. Conner kept squeezing the trigger but felt only the impotent click of an empty chamber. As the smoke cleared, the ring of creatures remained. Conner's shoulders slumped. It hadn't even fazed them.

"Get back in the Jeep!" Mitch yelled. The extra ammunition was inside the Cherokee, and it was the last source of refuge they had. The last barrier between them and the creatures.

They jumped inside and locked the doors. Mitch rummaged though his bag for extra bullets.

Devon's face was pressed to the glass. "They're coming!"

Out of the mist, the figures approached the car. Faceless gray heads lowered as if to look through the glass at them. Conner now saw the gray, mottled, and leathery skin up close. These were no phantoms. These were things of flesh and form.

Something thumped on the roof. It dented inward. Another thump dented the hood. The pounding against the Jeep grew louder and fiercer.

One of the heads bent down and seemed to peer through the window next to Conner. He could see only tiny nostril slits undulating in the featureless face, as if smelling them. Was that it? Were they operating only by smell?

Out of nowhere, thin, dark lines appeared in the pallid flesh above the nostrils. As if some invisible knife were cutting through the coarse, beaded skin. Then the skin pulled itself open to reveal two milky orbs.

The eyes made contact with Conner, and immediately the rash on his wrist prickled with heat. Conner winced and clutched his arm.

The creature's head jerked and swiveled with insect-like movements, as if inspecting the other occupants of the vehicle.

Helen screamed as a second pair of white, vacant eyes looked through her window as well. Then more of them appeared through the back.

Devon cried out and clutched his neck.

They were completely enveloped now. All the windows seemed filled with gray limbs and torsos and soulless, white-eyed faces. Staring. Pounding. Clawing. The attack continued with the sound of claws on the metal of the roof and hood. Thumping against the glass.

The window next to Conner cracked as the alien pressed against it. The creature seemed to lock its gaze directly on him. Now another razor slit appeared in the skin beneath its nostrils. It widened from one side to the other. The leathery skin peeled back, far beyond what any human mouth would be capable of, folding over itself to reveal dozens of narrow, dark teeth.

Conner tried to scream, but his throat was frozen. He could neither cry out nor move as the hideous face took shape before his eyes. A deep growl emanated from the creature and grew in volume. The grotesque jaws parted, revealing even more teeth and a thick, black tongue. Inklike saliva dripped and pooled inside the gaping mouth.

The Jeep wobbled and shook as the creatures mauled it, pounded it, and climbed onto it. The roof dented sharply. Helen screamed. Mitch struggled to load his gun in the dark. Devon shouted incoherent curses at the top of his lungs.

The rear window shattered. The barrage of inhuman croaks and growls grew louder.

The hellish face pressed against Conner's window, cracking it further. Lines spread out like a web.

Conner closed his eyes.

Then, through the screaming and pounding, there was another sound, thunderous and deep — like the blast of a foghorn. The sheer volume of it shook the Jeep.

The creatures halted their attack and howled as a sudden white light enveloped them, blazing down through the fog. Brilliant and intense, it came from somewhere above and in front of them. The creatures scurried from the windows and tumbled off the roof as a second, deafening horn blast shook the ground.

37

The blast echoed off into the distance.

The entire Jeep was flooded with the intense light. Conner shielded his eyes. They all sat in shock, unable to see anything but the brilliant glow in front of them. Helen was sobbing softly and gasping for breath. Mitch wrapped his arm across his face.

Now Conner heard something else: a deep, sustained rumble — like the roar of a jet engine — that grew steadily louder. He squinted into the light and saw something moving inside the glow. A lone figure, obscured by the glare, descended and came toward them.

Footsteps crunched on the gravel and a hand knocked on the glass.

"You all right in there?" said a muffled voice. "It's okay. They're gone for now."

Conner tried to open the door, but it was stuck. The damage to the Jeep had jammed it. He kicked against it and managed to push it far enough to squeeze out. Conner could hear the source of the rumble better now. It was some sort of tractor engine.

He squinted in the light and found himself looking up at a rather unassuming figure clad in denim bib overalls and a plaid shirt. He was tall and gaunt, with unruly gray hair and wire-rimmed glasses.

"You all right?"

Conner nodded. A wave of relief flooded over him. "Mister, you saved our lives."

The man chuckled and held out a hand. "Name's Bristol. Howard Bristol." He stuck a thumb over his shoulder. "I live just up yonder there. Saw your headlights in the fog and heard some gunshots. Figured somebody needed some help."

The others squeezed out of the Cherokee, looking dazed. Howard raised his eyebrows. "Four of you! Good gracious. Well, I can't tell you how glad I am to see you!"

Mitch rubbed his head. "The feeling is more than mutual."

Conner's eyes adjusted to the light enough to see its source: an enormous tractor or harvester of some sort. Two rows of floodlights were mounted across the top of the reaping apparatus on the front, and a huge bullhorn speaker was attached to the hood.

"What is this?" Conner said.

Howard glanced back. "Oh, that's just my harvester. Well, plus some modifications. You know, they don't like the light. And they seem to hate loud noise even more." He chuckled. "I need to run 'em off from time to time."

Helen walked up. "What are they? What are those things?"

Howard held up his hand. "Best we get back to my place and talk, though. They don't ever go very far, and they'll be back before too long."

Conner surveyed the Jeep. It was dented and crushed. Numerous long gashes — as if from claws — cut across the crumpled roof and front fenders.

Howard climbed a set of steel rungs to the cab of the tractor. He motioned for the others to join him. They all climbed up as well. Helen squeezed into the cab behind Howard. He pointed to a grated ledge along the side. "Grab hold of something. I'll get us turned around."

Conner, Mitch, and Devon stood on the grating and held on to whatever they could find. Howard shifted the massive tractor into gear. It lurched forward and rumbled off.

From his vantage point, Conner examined the field. The lights illumined a fifty- or sixty-foot diameter around the harvester. He could see the tracks the vehicle had made on its way to them. Howard was obviously following the same trail back.

They rolled up a broad incline until it crested. Conner gasped as he looked down on a ring of what appeared to be stadium lights, pointing outward, encircling a farmhouse, a barn, and a few small outbuildings. A bevy of lights was set up inside the circle as well. They lit up the fog like a small town.

They rolled into the compound, and Howard shut the tractor off. As they climbed down, Conner looked around. Bars of lights were rigged up on every building. In the center of the compound was a large pole with what appeared to be an air-raid siren mounted at the top. He could hear several gas generators running. Power lines crisscrossed the ground.

"Watch your step," Howard said as he led them across the yard into the main house.

They found themselves in a large kitchen lit by more than a dozen candles. Howard stamped the dirt off his boots. "Y'all must be starving."

Conner was thirsty more than anything else. The others indicated the same.

Howard motioned to the cupboard next to the sink. "Go ahead and help yourselves.

My fridge hasn't worked since the power went out. And I've needed every generator I could get my hands on just to keep the lights running."

They poured themselves several glasses of water each. Howard brought some snack crackers and bread from a pantry, along with a jar of peanut butter.

"It ain't nothing fancy," he said. "But I'm stocked up pretty well."

Conner was still shaken from the experience in the Jeep. The discoloration on his wrist had now spread a few inches up his forearm. What was particularly disconcerting was the intensity of the pain he'd felt as the creature made eye contact. It was as if they were controlling that as well.

Howard inspected the marks on Conner and Devon. "I have no idea what that is," he said. "Although I never had the occasion of one of them suckers touching me."

As they sat down around the table, they related their account to the old man: their encounters with the creatures, their hallucinations, and Conner's seizures.

Howard listened to it all quietly.

"Do you know what's going on?" Helen leaned over the table. "What those things are?"

"Ma'am, all I know is the obvious. Those

things out there ain't of this world." Howard pointed at the back door. "They got a ship or something out in the woods. That's where they seem to congregate."

Mitch frowned. "They may have one at the bottom of Lake Michigan, too."

"I wouldn't doubt it." Howard nodded. "If what you say is true, seems like they're just as dangerous in the water as on land."

"But they do have a weakness," Conner said. "They don't like bright light and, apparently, loud noises."

"That's true," Howard said. "I've been able to keep 'em away at night. And they don't seem to be too active during the day."

Conner nodded to the window. "How many generators have you got keeping this place lit up?"

"Oh . . ." Howard squinted. "I got six running and two spares. But I've had to use every drop of gas in a twenty-mile radius to keep 'em running."

Mitch nodded. "So that's why all the gas tanks in the cars we found were dry."

"Yeah-boy," Howard said. "I siphoned those off a long time ago."

Everyone grew silent at that comment.

"Wait a minute, wait a minute," Conner said after a moment. "Exactly how long have you been out here?"

Howard raised his eyebrows and drew in a deep breath. "Mmmm . . ." His eyes traced a path across the room. "Can't rightly say anymore. Seems like years."

"Years?" Helen gasped.

Conner found himself staring at the old man and shaking his head. "That can't be. . . ."

Howard just chuckled and leaned back. "I know you're thinking this all started only a few days ago. But, son, I think these creatures have been around a lot longer than you realize."

Conner narrowed his eyes. "How long?"

Howard shrugged. "No way to be sure. Maybe just a few years. Maybe longer." He laughed nervously. "Maybe a *lot* longer. But if they can make you see things that *aren't* there, who's to say they can't keep you from seeing things that *are?*"

Mitch furrowed his brow. "You mean they could've been hiding here for . . ."

"Not necessarily hiding," Howard said. "Just preventing us from seeing them as they really are."

"How?"

Howard shrugged again. "Maybe their technology. Maybe it's some kind of biological trait."

Conner sat up. In a bizarre way this was

making some sense. His unsettling experiences on the day of the storm. The people watching him. Their white eyes. The faceless maintenance man. What if these were inadvertent glimpses behind some kind of alien curtain? He shuddered to think that these creatures had been walking among them for years. Centuries perhaps. Maybe longer.

"They could have been living among us since ancient times," he said. "Blinding us to their appearance. They could make themselves appear like . . . anyone."

Helen shook her head. "I don't get it. That doesn't explain why everyone disappeared. Or how you could be living out here for years while it's only been a few days for us. How is that possible?"

"I'm not claiming to have all the answers." Howard drummed his fingers on the table. "All I'm saying is that it's possible you and I could be living in the same world but having two entirely different experiences. There's no telling what they're making people feel or see. Or believe they're experiencing."

"Well, the question is, what are they up to? What do they want?" Conner said.

Devon had been quiet until now. Finally he snorted. "This is getting too crazy. Y'all are talking like you believe this dude. This is all just crazy!"

"I don't know what to believe," Mitch said. "But I *do* know that back there in the Jeep, I was sure we were all going to die until Howard showed up. And that for the first time since this whole thing started, I finally feel a little safe."

Howard smiled and shook his head. "Well, I don't claim to be no expert. But I think as long as we can keep these lights burning at night, we should be all right until we can figure out what to do next. Gas is getting low, though, so if you don't mind, I could use some help scrounging up a little more in the morning."

38

Morning came and the fog lifted; however, the gray blanket of clouds that had rolled in two days earlier still hung low and oppressive.

Conner stepped onto the back porch and looked over the yard. He had actually slept last night. And slept well. If he had dreamed anything, he couldn't remember it.

Howard had a few spare bedrooms in the old farmhouse. Complete with actual beds. Conner had slept deeper than he had in a long time and had awakened feeling refreshed, aside from still being chronically thirsty. After several glasses of water, some bread, and a cup of coffee, he felt ready to tackle all the bizarre theories of their experience with a fresh mind. The old farmer had even managed to rig up a water heater and provided them all with hot showers.

Howard was walking up from the barn. "I

ain't seen the sun in I don't know how long."

Conner peered at the clouds. "You think they're controlling the weather, too?"

"Shoot, I wouldn't put anything past them. I figure they're trying to make our planet to be more like their own. Maybe they lived underground or underwater on their world. Can't stand the sunlight."

"You think that's it? They're colonizing? invading other planets to populate?"

Howard chuckled. "Sounds like a bad science fiction movie or something. But it's a thought." His face turned serious as he climbed the steps. He lowered his voice. "I don't want to get the others worried or anything. . . . I've been planting a garden for food, but I haven't been able to grow a thing this last year. I don't even get weeds. I don't know if it's the lack of sunlight or maybe something they're doing to the soil. . . ."

Conner frowned. "Maybe some kind of contamination?"

Howard shrugged. "Don't know. But it makes me worried about the quality of my well water. It don't taste any different, but if they're doing something to the soil . . ."

"Is there a test you can run? At least to check for bacteria or contamination?"

"Nothing I got here." Howard smiled. "I'll put it on the shopping list."

Conner looked at his wrist again. Up until now, he had been so concerned with escaping these creatures, he didn't have the luxury of worrying about the rash — if in fact it *was* a rash. Now he had a multitude of questions. Was it chemical or biological in nature? How far was it going to spread? What other effect was it having on him? He had hoped it was just something innocuous, like a chemical burn or an allergic reaction to the creature's physiology. Now that it was clearly spreading — along with the experience in the Jeep last night — he was thinking there might be some biological agent at work.

Howard had provided some fresh gauze and antibacterial ointment. Conner was grateful, but Devon rejected it. The kid seemed to be withdrawing further into himself, becoming increasingly sulky. Conner wondered if it had something to do with the rash, if maybe it was some kind of method the creatures used to influence the moods and emotions of their victims. Or it could just be the stress of their predicament. The kid was only sixteen, after all.

Conner would need to focus on this more, but he wasn't a doctor. He had no idea where to go for answers.

"Do you know if there's a library nearby? Or any school that might have one?"

Howard nodded. "There's a library in town. About twenty miles up the road. We can stop by there on our gasoline run."

Mitch stepped out on the porch and stretched with an expansive yawn. "Man, I slept good."

Howard chuckled and slapped him on the shoulder. "Grab some breakfast, Hoss. We need to get going soon. Daylight's wasting."

39

Helen sat on the bed, drying her hair with a towel. She closed her eyes and sighed. It felt wonderful to get a good night's sleep, a hot shower, and a change of clothes.

She had slept fitfully at Ray's house and even more so in the Jeep. She had dreamed of Kyle . . . only it wasn't Kyle, but a faceless doppelgänger haunting her dreams. Always accusing her, always insinuating this whole thing was somehow her fault. She tried to shake it off. They were only dreams. Some kind of twisted, sadistic mind game these aliens were playing with her. With all of them. And she had to keep those thoughts out of her head. She had to focus on positive things.

She got dressed and went down for some breakfast. As she passed by one of the other bedrooms, she spotted Devon sitting on the bed, staring at the floor.

She paused in the doorway. "You okay?"

Devon shook his head slowly. "No, I ain't okay. None of this is okay."

"I know, but you can't give up hope. We're still alive. We've made it *this* far."

He pulled down the collar of his T-shirt, and Helen gasped. The skin over his collarbone and upper chest was covered with purple blotches. The rash, or infection, on his neck was definitely spreading.

Helen frowned. "Does it hurt?"

"Not too much," Devon said. "But last night, when those things were attacking us . . . it started to burn. Bad. Like they were doing something to me. Then this morning it started to spread all over."

Helen could see fear in the boy's eyes. He was obviously scared to death about what was happening to him. But she wasn't sure what she could do. He was too old to offer some simple word of comfort. He'd see through that in a minute. But she couldn't bear to share the truth: that she didn't have the faintest idea what it was or what was going to happen to him.

"I know you're frightened." She sat down next to him. "I wish I could tell you there's nothing to worry about. But we just don't know what we're dealing with."

Devon touched his skin lightly. "It feels cold, but it hurts like it's a burn."

Helen touched his neck. It was indeed cold, almost as if he'd had ice on it. "Conner mentioned something about trying to find some medical books, see if there's information on anything like this."

"*Medical books?* He ain't no doctor." Devon wrinkled his forehead. "What's he gonna be able to do?"

"I don't know. Maybe nothing. But it's worth trying, isn't it?"

"You think it'll do any good?"

Helen forced a smile. "I'm not ready to give up hope just yet."

Devon grunted. "Hope?"

"Yes. Hope, Devon. Hope of seeing your family again. And your friends."

"Trouble is, other than Terrell, I don't have too many friends. And no family to speak of."

"What about your mom and dad?"

Devon grunted again. "My old man was killed in prison, and my mom's an alcoholic. You ever live with a drunk?"

Helen's gaze fell. "No. I can't say that I have."

"Well, let's just say if I had a choice of going to be with her or staying here . . . I think I could get used to this place."

"Did you ever try to get her any help?"

Devon looked at her with what almost

looked like amusement in his eyes. "Help? She gotta *want* help. And my mom never wanted nothing from me."

"So Terrell is the only family you really had?"

"You do what you gotta do to survive, right? We always watched each other's back, ever since grade school. We were always there for each other." He shook his head slowly. "And now he's gone."

Helen fell silent for a little while. "Look, we probably never would have met if it wasn't for this whole mess. So now you have us. Me and Conner and Mitch. And even old Howard. We'll watch your back now. Right?"

Devon snorted. "Bunch of crazy white folks."

Helen chuckled and went down to the kitchen, where Conner, Mitch, and Howard were talking.

"Morning," Howard said. "We're getting ready to go for some gas and supplies. You and Devon feel okay about holdin' down the fort for a few hours?"

Helen raised her eyebrows. "Uh . . . well . . ."

"You'll be okay," he said. "They never come out during the day."

"Ray Cahill had the same confidence in

them. Then we showed up, and they abducted him."

Howard nodded. "But that was at night, too, wasn't it?"

"Well . . . yeah."

"So, we'll be back in a few hours. We're just headed up the road twenty-three miles. We'll be back before you know it."

Helen explained her concerns about Devon as well, about the spread of his rash and his increasing despondency. She didn't think he'd be of much help if anything happened to them.

Howard showed her how to start up the generators and switch on the outer lights just in case. He also showed her how to run the tornado siren he had rigged up. Helen wrote everything down.

Twenty minutes later, Howard, Mitch, and Conner were headed down the long, gravel drive in Howard's old milk truck.

Helen sat on the back porch and watched them pull away. Then she soaked up the immense solitude of the farm. Everything was so quiet. There wasn't even a breeze to rustle the trees any longer. Beyond the barn, a wide field stretched back several hundred feet to the threshold of a forest. Gnarled, bare branches reached upward in row after row . . . too dense to see anything through.

Helen peered at the forest and shuddered. Howard had said the creatures had made a base back in there. Or perhaps had a ship. Maybe the answers to all of their questions lay there as well, but after her experience in the Jeep, Helen was none too eager to investigate.

After the three men had gone, Devon came downstairs and joined Helen on the back porch. "Where'd everybody go?"

"Howard took Conner and Mitch with him to get some more gas for the generators."

"How long are they gonna be gone?"

Helen shrugged. "Not long — just a couple hours."

Devon strode to the edge of the porch and stared out at the field and forest. "He says they have a ship in there?"

Helen nodded.

Devon gazed at the forest a long while. Then he turned around. "I think they have Terrell back in there."

The statement was so frank and matter-of-fact that it took Helen by surprise. "What? Why do you say that?"

Devon turned back to the trees and nodded to himself. "I saw him."

Helen blinked and shook her head. "You *saw* him? When was that?"

"This morning."

"Why didn't you say something earlier?"

He shrugged. "I figured you'd think I was crazy. I had a dream about him last night. Then I woke up just when it was getting light out and I looked out the bathroom window. And I saw him. He was standing at the back of the barn, waving to me. Then he walked toward the forest."

"No," Helen said. "They're doing that to you. They're just making you *think* you see him. That's just what's been happening to us. They're messing with our heads."

"How do you know that? Maybe it's Terrell who's trying to communicate."

"Because they . . . they're just . . ." Helen tried to think of a logical answer but was unable to. "They can manipulate us too easily."

Devon shook his head. "Well, I think it was Terrell. I think he's trying to show me the way back."

Helen stood up. "Don't you even *think* about going out there!"

"What are you, my mama now? I'll go if I feel like it."

"Look, Devon —" Helen tried to calm her voice. She was getting shrill — "let's just wait until the others get back. Then maybe we can all go. There's strength in numbers, right?"

"No." Devon's expression turned dark. "I've been following you people for two days 'cause I was too scared to be alone. I don't care anymore. I think y'all are just afraid to do anything. What are you gonna do, stay here the rest of your lives like Howard?"

"No, but that doesn't mean we should go off and get ourselves captured."

"I need some answers!"

Helen tried to calm him down. "Look, I'll go with you a little ways, okay? Can you compromise a little? I just don't want you going all alone."

Devon thought for a moment. Then he nodded.

Five minutes later, Helen found herself following Devon across the field. She shook her head. What was she doing? Had she gone completely nuts? This was by far the most idiotic thing she had ever done.

She stopped halfway across the field. "Okay, that's close enough."

Devon turned and scowled at her. "We can't even see anything from here. Let's just get to the edge of the trees."

"No!"

Devon took her hand. "Please? I just want to see if I can see anything through the trees." He pulled her gently.

Helen clenched her jaw and took a few more steps. They were within fifteen yards of the forest now. She stared at the black trees. "Something's wrong. The branches are all bare. Yesterday, back in Thorton, the trees still had their leaves on. They're all off now." She pulled her hand away.

Devon took a few more steps, peering at the trees. "So, it's easier to see through them now. Let's just get a little closer."

Helen ran to stop him. She caught his arm. "No! That's far enough."

Devon turned to face her. "What are you, my mama now?"

With each word, his voice seemed to grow more unnatural. His head turned. His eyes had gone white. His lips pulled back to reveal a row of teeth. Inhuman teeth. Teeth she had seen before. Eyes she had seen before.

Helen screamed and stumbled backward, falling into the dirt.

Devon reached out for her. Clutched her arm. His fingers seemed to burn through her shirt, searing her flesh. His voice was deep and inhuman. "Just a little farther . . ."

Helen pulled out of his grasp and scrambled back to her feet. She ran. Tripping and stumbling across the field, she ran back to the house, screaming.

40

Conner peered out the window at the drab, gray countryside shuffling past. Nothing but acre upon acre of empty fields, marked only by patches of barren trees and an occasional farmhouse or a cluster of lackluster rural dwellings. Then more empty fields.

What a miserable place.

Howard was talking up a storm. Making up for years of solitude, Conner guessed. He had apparently given himself to maintaining his daily rituals. Showering, shaving, keeping a garden. He had to do it, he said, to keep his sanity. To hold on to some semblance of normalcy in his world otherwise turned upside down. He was vague on the details of exactly how long he had been alone, but Conner got the feeling it was several years.

Years.

Conner's mind reeled at that thought. How long had this been going on before that? How long had this alien civilization coexisted with them? He had always considered man the dominant species on the planet. That was no longer the case, and his hubris was painfully obvious now. But how deep did this illusion run? How much of his life had been shrouded by the delusion created by these creatures? And how many other people were in the same situation? What about Marta and Rachel? Had they even existed, or were they merely part of the fantasy these creatures were creating? If they were real, where were they now? Were they alone somewhere too, being subjected to their own kind of hell? Had his whole life simply been an unending series of illusions?

Conner rubbed his eyes. This was more than he could handle right now. His mind would take this scenario to endless levels of speculation if he let it. Right now he had to focus on what to do next. And that at least consisted of finding out what this infection was.

They pulled into a small town. Conner didn't catch the name on the road sign. It didn't really matter anyway.

"We got a whole new town of gas to siphon," Howard said. He almost looked like a kid on Christmas morning.

There were a couple of gas stations in the

community, but Howard was unable to pump the gasoline from the underground tanks. So for now, they had to be content with siphoning gas from cars, one at a time, and pouring them into the milk tank on the truck.

They started at one end of town and canvassed three blocks. Howard had a small hand pump he had rigged up to make the job a little easier. He'd pull the truck up to the driveway while Conner and Mitch siphoned gas from any vehicle parked there. They worked with a set of three five-gallon gas cans. Mitch would fill one; then Conner switched it out with another and handed it up to Howard, who poured it into the truck. This kept a pretty steady stream of gas flowing into the milk truck. But it was slow going. After two hours, they had checked some fifteen houses by Conner's count and had siphoned nearly two hundred gallons of gas.

Howard kept track of which houses they had visited, in a small notebook tucked into his sun visor. He was all smiles. "This would've taken me a whole day! What say we see if we can get the rest of this street?"

Conner looked at his watch. "We told Helen we'd be back in two or three hours. I don't want her getting worried. Besides, I was hoping to find that library."

Howard nodded up the street. "I think it's up that way a few blocks. Why don't you go have a look-see. Me and Hoss here'll finish up the gas on this block."

Mitch shrugged. Conner could tell he wasn't too amused by the nickname Howard had given him. But he waved Conner on. "We'll pick you up in a half hour or so."

Conner nodded and took a flashlight from the truck. He recalled seeing a bike parked next to a garage a few doors down. He took it and set off.

After a few blocks, Conner came upon the small community library. The doors were unlocked, so he made his way inside. A musty odor filled the building — the scent of paper and mold. The place felt like it had been abandoned for years. Gray daylight poured in through the row of windows along the back. But the interior of the building was quite dark.

Conner flipped on the flashlight. The card catalog was computerized and so was useless. He would have to search the aisles one at a time, scanning the book titles.

He quickly found the nonfiction section and skipped past history, modern architecture, and how-tos. The third aisle contained health and wellness–type books. Conner slowed down and scanned more closely.

After several minutes of searching, he settled on a half dozen books on human physiology and modern medicine and stacked them on one of the carts.

He rolled the cart to a table next to the row of windows and started to peruse one of the medical books. He still had some time before Howard and Mitch showed up.

He searched the indexes for rashes and diseases but couldn't find a description of anything that matched his condition. Eventually he gave up and flipped through a lexicon of diseases he had found. There were pictures of several conditions that looked similar, however nothing that matched completely. He examined his arm again. The discoloration had nearly doubled in size, spreading up his forearm and onto the back of his hand.

It was cold to the touch, almost as if he was losing circulation. He pressed the skin for a moment and released. His flesh turned white where he had pressed it. A few moments later, the purple color returned. It looked so much like a bruise yet seemed to be spreading like a rash.

He had flipped through a few more pages when he winced at a sudden flash of pain. His arm stung, just as it had —

Conner sat up, his muscles tense. *Just as*

it had the night before. He jumped up from the table and swept the flashlight into the shadows of the library.

Nothing moved among the rows of shelves. Still, Conner could feel a presence with him in the library. Something in the shadows. Unseen. Watching him. Outside, a gust of wind moaned past the windows. His arm stung again with a sharp chill.

He gathered up the books and slipped back along the darkened center aisle toward the front doors. Halfway down, his arm jolted again. It was so severe this time that he dropped the flashlight and books and doubled over. The wind moaned again. The whole building seemed to shudder. Conner straightened up, clutching his arm, and froze.

A tall, gray figure blocked the aisle before him. It stood upright, shoulders back, head forward with its thin arms bent slightly — a posture that gave Conner the impression of readiness. Alertness. Yet its face was blank gray flesh except for its two small nostrils.

Conner's heart raced and he struggled to control his breathing. He backed up a step and the creature moved toward him, mirroring his movements.

Conner stammered, "What do you want?"

The creature stopped. Its head tilted. Its

nostrils undulated.

Conner raised his arm. "What is this? What are you doing to me?"

The creature's head swiveled slightly, as if following the sound of Conner's movement. It raised its arm and spread out its spider-like hand.

Conner slowly moved to one side. The creature mimicked him, blocking his path.

"Why are you doing this to us?"

In a swift, smooth motion, the creature lunged forward. Its gray head leaned in just inches from Conner's face. Conner tensed, unable to run. A septic stench stung in his nostrils. The creature's head angled slightly, drawing in air through its nostrils, as if smelling Conner, identifying him by his odor. Then a mouth slit formed in its gray flesh and peeled open. Gaping jaws parted. Black saliva dripped. A cold breath wafted across Conner's skin.

Soon.

The word came less from the creature's mouth than from its head. Conner jerked backward, unsure of whether he had *heard* the voice or merely *thought* it.

With a deep, gargled hiss, the creature slipped down one of the side aisles and disappeared from view. Conner's breath came in tight gasps, pupils dilated, heart racing.

For a moment he stood there. Frozen.

Then he sprinted for the doors.

41

Mitch watched the last drops of gas trickle from the green Chevy Blazer into his gas can. It looked like the last vehicle on the block. They had been on a lucky streak for the final few houses. Each one had a vehicle nearly full of gas. By Mitch's estimate, they had gotten an additional seventy-five gallons.

He handed the gas can up to Howard, who poured it into the milk tank.

"That oughta keep us running for a couple weeks," Howard said. "Maybe next time, we can load up one of my generators and bring it along. They're too heavy for me to get on the trailer by myself. Then we'll see if we can't get those gas station pumps working. That'd save a lot of time."

Next time?

Mitch bristled at the thought. How long did this guy think they were planning on staying? He was certainly thankful Howard had come along when he did and saved their lives. He was also glad for the good night's rest and food. But he didn't have any intention of *staying* for very long. Not if they wanted to find answers.

Sure, Howard had built up a nice little compound. He seemed to know how to keep himself safe. But Mitch didn't want to simply stay safe. He wanted to fight.

If Howard's theory was true and Earth had been invaded, they needed to fight back. Find the aliens' weakness and exploit it. Their original plan was to head east. To Washington. There was no reason they shouldn't stick with it.

Howard poured the last of the gasoline and climbed down. Wiping his forehead with a handkerchief, he frowned and nodded up the street.

"Looks like there's one more house up there. Let's go see if they want to donate."

Mitch groaned and rolled his eyes.

Howard shrugged. "Just one more house."

Mitch grabbed the pump and gas can and headed up the street. It was a small house. A shack really. Dingy and unkempt. Paint peeled from the weathered clapboards, and the roof had a slight bow to it.

Mitch trudged around to the garage in the back. It was in even worse shape than the house. The side door was locked, so Mitch plowed his shoulder into it. The rotted jamb gave way and Mitch tumbled inside.

A Dodge van nearly filled the entire space. There was little more than a few feet on either side, so Mitch squeezed around the back in search of the latch for the overhead door. He turned it but couldn't get the main door to open. It was jammed somehow, and it was too dark for Mitch to see what was causing the problem. Muttering to himself, he opened the gas cap and fed the hose down into the tank.

A gust of wind rattled the rafters and blew the side door shut, cutting off his light. Darkness fell around him like a cloak. And in the darkness, Mitch heard something. A soft rustle. Not wind, but movement. A chill crawled down his spine. He wasn't alone. A dark figure stood at the back of the van.

Mitch fumbled for his flashlight and flicked it on.

The beam fell on a woman's face. Thin and pale. Wide brown eyes stared at him. Straight dark hair fell down past sharp cheekbones to her shoulders.

Mitch's eyes widened, and his breath caught in his throat. *"Linda?"*

Linda stared at him. "Mitch? Are you all right?"

Mitch backed away. The light trembled in his hand.

Linda tilted her head, her eyes showing concern. “I was worried about you.”

“Who are you?”

Linda blinked. “Don’t you recognize me now?”

Mitch shook his head. “You’re not real. You’re one of them.”

“No, I’m not. Mitch, it’s me.”

She took a step toward him. Mitch fell back, against the wall. His hand fumbled for his gun and drew it out. “Just stay away from me.”

Linda glanced at the gun then back at Mitch. “You’d *shoot* me?”

“Just stay away!”

“Mitch, you don’t have to be afraid. You don’t have to fear them.”

Mitch brought the gun up. His teeth clenched. “What are you? Why are you doing this to me?”

Linda held out her hand. “Please don’t be afraid of me. I love you, Mitch.”

Mitch’s hand trembled. “I love you, too, baby. More than anything.”

“Then come with me.”

“No. Not until I get some answers!”

“You’ll find the answers, Mitch. They don’t want to hurt you. You’ll find the answers to everything."

Mitch shook his head. "What's happening? Why are they here?"

"They want to live in peace. They just want to coexist."

"*Coexist?* They don't want to coexist. They invaded our planet. They're trying to destroy us!"

"They didn't invade our world, Mitch. *We* invaded *theirs.* They were around long before we got here. They're just trying to survive. Don't you get it?"

Mitch stared at her. His head spun. "How . . . ?"

"They're old, Mitch. They have so much knowledge."

Mitch blinked. Old? How long had these creatures been on the planet? Millions of years? Had they evolved even before humans? "Why haven't they contacted us before? Why haven't we seen them before now?"

"There wasn't a need before now. We weren't a danger to them before. Now our technology has made us a threat. We're destroying their world. Destroying *our* world. Polluting it. Using up its resources. Creating weapons that could destroy all life on the planet. They didn't want to intervene, but they *had* to. To save us all."

Mitch's gaze fell. Is that what this was all about? Sending a message to mankind? He slowly lowered the gun. "Where is everyone?"

Linda reached out. Her fingers beckoned him. "Just come with me. I'll show you everything. But you have to trust me."

Mitch hesitated. His mind reeled with a thousand questions. More than anything, he wanted to find answers. More than anything, he wanted to be with Linda again.

More than anything . . .

A loud thump drew Mitch from his haze. Linda turned around as daylight poured into the garage. The overhead door rolled up.

Howard stood there, smiling. "What's taking so long?"

Mitch blinked. His eyes adjusted to the light.

Howard peered at him and frowned. "What's wrong? Did you see something?"

Mitch looked up. He stood against the back wall of the garage with his gun drawn. But Linda had disappeared.

42

Helen ran back to the house, stumbling over the uneven ground. Afraid to stop. Afraid to look back. What had she just seen? Was it Devon turning into one of those creatures? Or was it one of them posing as Devon? She shuddered as she climbed onto the porch and collapsed into one of the lawn chairs. Her heart raced. There was no sign of him in the field.

Whatever that thing was, it had tried to lure her into the woods. Was there something waiting there to abduct her? Was it some kind of trap? She rubbed her temples and struggled to catch her breath. Slowly her terror subsided. She cursed the others for leaving her here all alone.

She'd be safe, they had said. The creatures didn't come out during the day. But she had seen them in Chicago. They had taken Devon's friend in broad daylight. They couldn't be sure of anything. They didn't know anything about these creatures.

Her arm tingled where Devon had grabbed her. She rolled up her sleeve. A large, purple bruise encircled her forearm.

She touched it and pulled her hand away. It was cold. It stung almost like a burn but was cold to the touch. Like Devon and Conner. Like Terrell and Ray. Now she was infected too. She shook her head. No, not her, too!

Suddenly the back door opened and Devon stepped out onto the porch.

Helen screamed and jumped out of her chair.

"Whoa!" Devon lurched backward. "What? What's wrong?"

Helen picked up the chair and held it in front of her. "Stay away from me!"

Devon peered at her and scowled. "You crazy? What's the matter?"

Helen glared back. "Just stay away!"

"I didn't do anything!"

"What do you want with me?"

Devon shook his head. "What are you talking about? It's me. Are you seeing things again?"

Helen wasn't about to let her guard down. "I just saw *you*. A few minutes ago. You tried to get me to follow you into the woods."

"The woods?" Devon wrinkled his nose.

"You think I'm crazy? I ain't going in those woods. I've been in my room for the last half hour."

Helen tried to control her breathing. She had to keep control. "You . . . you said you had seen your friend. You said he had gone into the woods and you were going to follow him."

Devon suddenly looked nauseous.

Helen frowned. "What's wrong?"

Devon sat down and stared at the ground. "I . . . I *did* see Terrell this morning. I woke up to go to the bathroom and . . . it was early and I saw him outside by the barn. He was waving for me to follow him."

"What did you do?"

Devon looked up at her. "Nothing. I wasn't going out there. I thought maybe I was seeing things. I thought I was going crazy or something, so I didn't tell anyone."

Helen slowly straightened. She set the chair down. "They're trying to trick us. They can't get to us so they're trying to bring us to them."

"Why?" Devon shook his head. "Why are they doing this?"

Helen stared across the field. The trees rose up thick and black against the overcast sky. "There's something in those woods."

"You think that's where everyone is? You

think that's where they're keeping them?"

Helen shrugged. "I don't know."

Devon stood. "Man, I wish those guys would hurry up and get back." He stopped and tilted his head. "You hear that?"

"What?" Helen listened. "I don't hear anything."

Devon scratched his head. "It's like a h—" Suddenly his jaw clenched and his back arched. He fell to the ground, his hands and legs trembling.

Helen hesitated a moment. "Devon?" Then she knelt beside him. His hand was cold. His whole body trembled. He grimaced and tried to cry out but seemed unable to move.

Then his mouth opened. His eyes grew wide. He stared at her, through her. Past her.

Helen gasped. "Devon?"

There was a bright flash of light. It knocked her backward, blinding her momentarily. Her vision returned and she scrambled to her feet.

But the porch was empty. Devon was gone.

43

Conner rode back to the truck. His heart was racing, more from his encounter in the library than from his ride. His arm still tingled as well. The discoloration had spread even farther up his forearm. He had gone there for answers. He had come away with only more questions.

Howard and Mitch were walking up from the garage as Conner pulled up. Mitch looked white as a sheet. Conner frowned. "What happened?"

Mitch didn't reply. Howard only shrugged. "I think he saw something inside the garage. I think he's in shock."

"I saw one of the creatures inside the library," Conner said, catching his breath. "There's probably more of them around. We better get back to the farm."

"In the library?" Howard shook his head. "I don't understand. They're never this active during the day. What's going on?"

"I think they may be up to something," Conner said. "Planning something. I don't know." He described his encounter and how the creature had communicated to him.

"Soon?" Howard said. "What d'you suppose it meant?"

"I have no idea, but I don't think it's good." Conner grabbed Mitch by the shoulders and gave him a shake. "Mitch!"

Mitch blinked. Color returned to his face, and his eyes rolled down and finally focused on Conner.

"Mitch, what did you see? Was it one of them?"

Mitch stared at him for a moment, then shook his head slowly.

"What? What did you see?"

Mitch pulled away. "I'm all right. I just . . . I thought I saw my girlfriend. Linda."

"Your girlfriend?"

"It was nothing. Just another hallucination."

"Did she say anything? Did she talk to you?"

Mitch leaned against the truck and rubbed his eyes. "Yeah, she said . . . She told me about them. The aliens."

"What did she say?"

Mitch looked down. "She said they weren't really aliens. They were here before us. This was *their* planet too. She said they were only trying to keep us from destroying it. Y'know, with pollution and bombs. She said they just wanted to coexist with us. She wanted me to go with her and she'd show me the answers."

Conner stepped back. "*Their* planet?"

He tried to process this new information. Was it possible these things weren't aliens at all but another terrestrial life-form? one that hadn't been discovered yet? Could there be a totally separate species of intelligent life that had evolved simultaneously with human beings? Or one that was far older and far more advanced? Developing telepathic abilities. Staying hidden. Avoiding contact.

Mitch was shaking his head. "But she just disappeared. She was just an illusion."

Conner nodded to himself. "Maybe they were just using her image to communicate to you."

Howard climbed into the truck. "It's about noon," he said. "We should be getting back. Your friends will be getting worried."

Twenty minutes later they pulled up the long gravel drive to Howard's farm. As they parked in the back, they found Helen sitting on the porch steps. Her face was stern and her eyes were red.

She stood up and glared at Conner as he got out of the truck. "Don't you ever leave me alone again!"

"Alone?" Conner blinked. "What happened? Where's Devon?"

The fierceness in Helen's eyes wavered, then gave way to tears. "He's gone."

Mitch swore. Conner shook his head. "Gone? What do you mean? Where'd he go?"

"He just . . ." Helen waved her arms. "Just disappeared. Vanished into thin air!"

Conner and Mitch looked at each other for a moment, then back at Helen. Mitch ran inside calling for Devon.

Helen shook her head. "Didn't you hear me? I said he *disappeared!* He didn't just *run away.* He's not hiding. He just disappeared right in front of me! One second he's talking to me, then he starts going into this convulsion. Like you had on the boat. Then there was a flash, and when I looked up, he was gone."

Howard scratched his head. "Where did this happen?"

Helen nodded toward the house. "Right there, on the porch."

Conner narrowed his eyes. "You said he had a convulsion. A seizure like mine?"

Helen nodded and choked back tears. "I

didn't know what to do. . . . I tried to help him, but then this light came from nowhere."

Conner drew close and placed an arm around Helen's shoulder. "Sit down. Tell me exactly what happened."

Helen recounted her experience that morning. How Devon, or something that *looked* like Devon, had tried to get her to go into the woods. Then how she had fled back to the house and discovered the bruise on her arm. And then how she had met the real Devon again.

Conner examined the rash on her arm. It was even larger than his, nearly covering her entire forearm. "Does it hurt?"

"It stings a little," she said and then looked up. "Conner, what's happening to us? Did you find anything in the medical books?"

He shook his head. "I couldn't find anything like this. Nothing with all the symptoms we have. I'll keep at it, though. I'm not giving up."

Helen went on to describe Devon's seizure. The light. Conner frowned. He wondered if that had anything to do with the bright light he had seen during his own convulsions. He hadn't had an episode since two nights ago on the boat. Either they had stopped altogether or he was due for another one soon.

Was that what had happened to everyone else? Did these creatures have some means to make people disappear? Had Devon been transported somewhere, or had he just been disintegrated? Was that what was going to happen to him as well?

What about the creatures, then? If they were, in fact, terrestrial, were they responsible for Devon's disappearance? The others had been physically dragged away. Why had he simply vanished? Was this something new, or did the creatures have abilities they weren't aware of yet?

Conner rubbed his eyes. Something was missing. A huge piece of the puzzle. Helen, Devon, and Mitch had all had hallucinations where someone they knew had tried to get them to follow. To go back to the forest.

The forest. Was that where the answers were? Conner shuddered. That was the last place he would go to find them. It was all too convenient. It reeked of a trap.

Conner's own experience in the library had been different. The creature there could have dragged him off, yet it didn't. It acted almost as if it had come simply to deliver its message.

Soon.

What though? What was going to happen soon? Was it a threat or merely a warning? And precisely *how* soon was *soon* intended to be? Soon, as in a few days? Or a few hours?

They would have to wait. Conner's jaw tightened. They would just have to wait.

44

The four of them sat around the kitchen table. Conner stared at the half-eaten granola bar in front of him. He was no longer hungry. Thirsty, yes. But he had long since lost his appetite.

He downed his third glass of water before speaking. "I think we should assume these things have some type of hostile intent. Their pattern of behavior has been one of deceit and guile. They haven't given us any reason to trust them."

Mitch leaned back in his chair, arms folded. "You think they're responsible for Devon's disappearance too?"

Conner shrugged. "At this point, I don't see any other explanation."

Helen rubbed her bandaged forearm. "So what then? What are we supposed to do? Just wait around until they pick us off one at a time?"

"No," Conner said. "No, as I see it, we

have two options. Fight or run."

Howard frowned. "What about holding our ground? We know they're afraid of the lights. I've been living here for years with these things right in my backyard. Why is it they've never dragged me off? And I'm just one man."

Conner drummed his fingers on the table. Howard had a point. However, the creatures' hostility had apparently increased when they arrived. The same thing had occurred at Ray Cahill's house the day before. Ray had been living for weeks without incident until they showed up. Then a few hours later, the creatures dragged him off.

"I think it's us," he said, gesturing to Helen, Mitch, and himself. "I think their focus has been on us. They left you alone this long, but as soon as we showed up, they became more hostile. They're disguising themselves as people we trust. They're trying to get us to follow them into the forest."

"But what did we do?" Helen said. "Why are they after *us?*"

Conner sighed. "I don't know. Maybe we've done something they view as a threat. Maybe we're not supposed to be here. I don't know."

"I couldn't care less," Mitch said. "I just want to figure out how to kill them."

Howard snorted. "Son, how're you gonna kill them? They can make you see things that aren't there. You could be fighting phantoms and not even know it."

"But we do know their weakness," Conner said. "I think it may be time to exploit that."

Howard raised his eyebrows. "How?"

"Your harvester. They hate the lights and the noise. What if we rig up more of those? If we can get our hands on a few more tractors . . ."

"Or bulldozers." Mitch perked up. "Some of those big earthmovers. We could level that whole forest and torch it. That'd brighten things up a bit."

Howard shook his head. "Son, you'd be stirring up one heck of a hornets' nest."

"Maybe." Mitch shrugged. "But I don't care anymore. I'm tired of playing defense. I say it's time to take the fight to *them.*"

"How big an area are we looking at?" Conner said.

Howard stood up and looked out the window. "That's a couple hundred acres of forest."

Mitch grunted. "Then we got our work cut out for us, don't we?"

Howard looked at his watch. "I need to get the generators ready. It'll be getting dark in a couple hours, and I need to fill the tanks."

They followed Howard out to the yard, where he filled six gas cans from the large central tank next to the barn. He had transferred the load of gas from the milk truck earlier.

He sent Mitch and Helen off to fill up the three generators inside the maintenance shed, while he and Conner set out to fill the three in the larger barn. An old tractor was parked near the entrance, and they had to squeeze around it and several other farm implements to get to the generators at the back.

Conner began filling the tank of the first generator as Howard knelt down to check the oil levels and AC connections.

"It's not that I don't think you should do something," Howard said. "I'm just wondering how smart it is to plan an attack when you don't know enough about them. You don't really know what you're getting yourselves into."

Conner knew they had made the same mistake when they had gone out onto the lake. They had chosen to act despite their lack of information. They assumed they would be safe, not knowing the creatures had adapted to water as well as land. He recalled being uncomfortable with acting before knowing more facts. It had nearly killed them. Now they were planning to do the same thing. But he didn't care anymore. He was tired of trying to think his way through this mess. It was time to act. They had a sound, working theory on the creatures' weaknesses. They weren't going to get much more information than what they already had.

"Well, you may be right," he said finally. "But we have to do something."

Howard peered at Conner. His expression grew cold. "So your mind's made up then, is it?"

Conner nodded. "I'm tired of running away. It's time to stand and fight."

"Fight. Puh!" Howard stood up and turned away.

Conner frowned. Had he said something to upset him? "Howard?"

"You have no idea what you're fighting," Howard grunted. "But you're always so quick to do it."

"What are you talking about?"

Howard just rubbed his jaw. "That's been your problem since the dawn of time. Always acting before knowing the consequences." He chuckled softly. "Some things never do change."

Conner felt the air go suddenly cold. A gust of wind moaned through the rafters. His arm jerked as a sudden bolt of freezing pain stung him. He dropped the can and clutched his wrist. His heart raced. "Howard?"

Howard turned around to face him. A shadow crossed over his face. His eyes were white. Cold. Empty. Expressionless.

Conner backed away. "What . . . what are you?"

Howard shook his head. "You have no idea what you're up against."

Conner's mind reeled. What was going on? This was the old man who had saved them. He had built a sanctuary out of his farm. A haven. He had given them rest and nourishment. He . . .

He was one of them!

Conner had to warn the others. "Mitch!"

He heard a low whisper and spun around, peering into the shadows. Something moved. A tall, thin shape emerged from behind the tractor.

Conner's eyes widened. He backed against the wall. *"Mitch!"*

Another voice whispered in the darkness to his right. A second creature stepped out from the shadows, as if it had materialized out of nowhere. Conner slid to his left, pressing back into the corner, away from both creatures. They approached slowly with shoulders back and heads forward, tilting and sniffing the air.

Howard watched the creatures advance on Conner like a man watching his hunting dogs corner their quarry. His face was still obscured by shadows. His pale eyes glowed. "You think you can fight them? You think you can actually win?"

"Why?" Conner's head was spinning. "Why are you doing this?"

"You wanted answers. And now it's time."

The creatures moved closer. In the darkness, Conner could see soulless white eyes appear against their gray flesh. He could see black jaws opening. He could smell their stench. They reached out spidery hands. . . .

But before they touched him, Conner's muscles stiffened as another seizure raked his body. His back arched; his teeth clenched. Searing white light pressed in upon him. Blinding him. A frigid blast of air tore through him. He fell back against the wall. Wind roared in his ears, a thunderous, pulsing torrent that tugged at him with its force.

But beneath the light, the cold, and the fury was something else. . . .

45

Mitch and Helen lugged three gas cans into the maintenance shed and started filling the generator tanks. A bundle of power cords snaked out the main doorway and stretched across the yard.

Helen stood back for a moment. She had been having doubts about their plan to burn the forest. "Do you really think it's a good idea to attack them?"

Mitch looked up. "Do you see any other options? I mean, the way I see it, Conner's right: we either fight or keep running." He gestured around him and grunted. "Or get comfortable here on the farm."

"We'd be safe as long as we can keep the lights going."

"Safe?" Mitch frowned. "For how long? They haven't stopped trying to lure us into the woods. They used Devon, even my girlfriend to trick us." He shook his head. "We shouldn't trust them. They're not going to stop. They won't give up until . . ."

Helen looked down. "I just wish I knew what they wanted."

"Linda said — or my *hallucination* of Linda said — they were trying to keep us from destroying the planet. That they just wanted to coexist." He grunted. "I don't believe it. She was just trying to get me to trust her. To go with her."

"What do you suppose is in there?"

Mitch raised his eyebrows. "The forest?" He shrugged. "I don't know. Their spaceship. Their colony. I'm not the curious type. Whatever it is, I say we burn it down."

They filled the last of the generators with gas and headed back toward the house. The sky was showing the first signs of dusk, and a cool breeze had picked up. Inside, Helen started to wash up.

It was several minutes later when Howard burst into the kitchen, out of breath.

"Trouble," he gasped. "We got big trouble!"

Mitch stood up. "What do you mean? Where's Conner?"

"He . . . he *disappeared!*"

"What?" Helen heard the words but couldn't move. For a moment, she felt paralyzed.

"Just like the other kid. Devon," Howard

said. "There was a flash of light and then he was gone. Just into thin air!"

Mitch blinked. "Where?"

"In the barn." Howard stuck a thumb over his shoulder. "We were filling the generators when he had this . . . like a convulsion. Then, poof! he just vanished!"

"Just like Devon!" Helen's eyes widened. "What's going on? What are they doing?"

Mitch stared at them for a moment. Then he shook his head. "We better get those generators running. Get the lights on."

"That's the other trouble," Howard said. "It looks like they've been here, too. The creatures. They sabotaged us. All the cables have been cut."

"Cut?"

"Sliced right through."

Mitch looked like he was going to punch the old farmer. "I thought you said they don't come out during the day!"

"They must have burrowed through the ground into the shed and the barn."

"What about Conner?" Helen said. Everything was happening too fast. What if he was hurt? What if he needed help?

Mitch gave her a stern look. "We need to get those lights on first. We can figure out what to do about Conner after that."

He rushed out the door with Howard on his heels.

46

Freezing. It was freezing.

Conner felt his body floating limp and numb. Brilliant white light flooded over him, permeating him, though he couldn't tell whether his eyes were open or closed. Either way, they ached with the brightness. His whole head ached.

He could still hear the wind pulsing, much louder now.

Woosh. Woosh. Woosh.

His body felt thick and disjointed. And heavy.

And freezing cold.

He tried to remember where he had been. Images circled in his head. A farm. A barn. Swirling shadows. Faces, dark and hideous. And eyes. Cold, white, and empty.

He felt himself being pulled upward, as though through bone-chilling water, and his body seemed to grow heavier with every inch. He tried to move his limbs, but they were far too heavy.

Woosh. Woosh. Woosh.

Beneath the pulsing, sloshing torrent, Conner heard . . .

Voices!

Human voices! People!

They were speaking to each other. He couldn't quite make out the words. It was English, he thought. There were several people, all talking at once. All talking over each other. Worried. Excited. They grew louder and more distinct as the pulsing wind faded into the background.

The light seemed to take form. His eyes were open. Wide open. Five enormous, circular lights floated in front of him.

Other sounds fought through the voices. Clattering, shuffling. The sound of people moving around. He could make out a few disjointed words now. Echoing off in a cavern.

". . . one hundred milligrams . . . lidocaine . . ."

". . . sinus rhythm . . ."

". . . looks . . . regaining consciousness . . ."

". . . Hayden . . . Mr. Hayden?"

Someone was calling his name. Someone was talking to him!

A dark image swept in front of the lights.

Conner tried to focus. He tried to squint, but he couldn't move his eyes.

"Mr. Hayden . . . can you hear me?" The dark image came into focus. A face. A woman's face, with worried eyes and something covering her mouth.

Conner blinked. The face leaned close. A smaller light shone in his eye, then flicked away. Conner blinked again.

He tried to lift his head. Move his arm. But they were too heavy. Or he was too weak.

More faces moved in. Then moved away. Hands and arms passed things back and forth. His head rolled to the side. A man was holding a pair of shoes. One in each hand. No. No, not shoes. Something else. Something plastic and . . .

Someone moved his head back again. Back to the lights.

The wind was still pulsing in the background, though it wasn't actually wind any longer. Conner recognized it now.

Woosh. Woosh. Woosh.

It was his heart. Beating.

The face drew close again.

"Mr. Hayden? Can you understand me?"

He tried to answer. *Yes.* His tongue felt thick and dry, like a piece of wood in his mouth. "Ehhthh . . ."

He blinked again. He was so cold.

"Mr. Hayden," the voice said, "you're in the Lake Forest Hospital ER. You're having a heart attack."

Where? Conner blinked. *What?*

"Mr. Hayden, do you understand what I'm saying?"

Conner tried to nod. His head felt like it was made of lead. He was having a . . .

A heart attack.

Heart.

Attack.

He was having a heart attack?

His head fell to the side again. The man holding the shoes that weren't shoes had put them back on a machine. And he recognized them now. Paddles. What did they call them? De- . . . defibrillators? Or something like that.

His eyes rolled to examine his surroundings. He was in a white, tiled room. Brightly lit. And cold. Fleeting images passed by his face: stethoscopes, syringes, monitors. Where did she say he was? Lake Forest Hospital ER?

Lake Forest? Not Indiana?

Lake Forest! His home. His head flopped to the other side. There were people all around him. Dozens of them. Nurses! Doctors! His eyes caught a glimpse of a face he recognized. A face beyond the ER staff. Beyond the room. Through the double doors. Peeking in . . .

Rachel!

Her eyes were red. Her face was pale. She looked concerned. Scared. But it was Rachel. He was sure it was Rachel. Conner's breathing quickened. He tried to talk. To call out to her. He wanted to jump up and hug her. Just to touch her. Just to make sure she was real.

And with Rachel he saw . . . Marta! They were standing in the hall. Hugging. Marta's hand was over her mouth. She was crying. He could see the tears streaming down her cheeks.

What had the nurse said? He was having a heart attack. Rachel was there. Conner tried to recall what had happened. He was in his study. He saw the storm. His neck . . .

His pain. All day he'd been having pain. His chest and shoulders had been tight all day. A heart attack? He was in the ER. He was . . .

His eyes widened. *He was dying!*

The ER staff bustled about. The nurse was trying to speak to him. But he couldn't understand what she was saying. He couldn't respond. His mind was spinning. He was dying!

But he could remember. He could remember everything! Mitch. Helen. The dark-haired kid. Devon and Ray Cahill. And Howard . . . Howard who wasn't what he seemed. Who wasn't what he claimed to be. Howard who sent Conner into the hands of . . .

Conner had to get up. He had to help them. He had to warn them. An image flashed into his head: Ray Cahill, gray spider claws digging into his chest, pulling him outside. Out into the darkness. Out into . . .

Conner could feel his chest pounding. His heart raced. He had to tell them! He couldn't go back. *Don't let me go back!* He lifted his head and tried to speak. There was an oxygen mask over his nose and mouth. He had to tell them. . . .

Help me!

". . . ellff m-me . . ."

His voice was weak and pathetic. His tongue wouldn't move correctly.

He tried again. He focused his mind. Focused all his strength.

"He-elp m-me!"

The nurse glanced down. And looked away.

"P-pleeease!"

She looked at him again. Conner tried to touch her. His arm flopped awkwardly. His hand clutched her shirt. He couldn't go back. He couldn't go back! They were going to take *him!*

She peered at him. She frowned.

"Pleease!" He struggled with each word. "Don't . . . let . . . th-them . . . t-take . . . me. . . ."

She looked into his eyes. Her frown deepened. But did she understand?

". . . pressure's falling . . . ," a voice said.

The nurse looked away.

No!

". . . v-tach . . ."

The voices grew urgent but began to fade. The lights were growing dim.

Conner could barely see the nurse now. Was she looking at him? He struggled again to tell her. His voice was fading.

"Don't . . . let . . . them . . ."

The lights were swallowed in shadow. Somewhere far off a voice said faintly, ". . . losing him . . ."

Darkness folded around him again.

47

37 Minutes Earlier

Rachel Hayden went to her room and flopped onto the bed. She frowned at the ceiling, biting her lip until it hurt. Supper with her father had gone less than swimmingly. She hated when he was like this. He thought, for all the world, he was this progressive, open-minded man, so thoughtful, so devoted to reason. But he couldn't even see how bigoted he had become.

Life had been miserable for the last two years, since her parents divorced. Really for the last five, since Matthew died. Her father had turned into a dark, brooding man after that day. He spent most of his time at the office, and when he was home, the tension had been unbearable. He rarely said more than a few words to her mother, and the slightest mishap would send him into a fit of rage. It was as if he was blaming *them* for Matthew's death.

When her mom started going to a friend's house for a Bible study, she told Rachel not to mention it to her father. Rachel felt trapped between them, like having to choose allegiances. Since her father remained locked in his own world, Rachel had no choice but to side with her mother.

But when her mom came home one day talking about Jesus and about joining a church, Rachel wondered if she hadn't gone off the deep end as well. It was as if her parents had gotten on separate trains headed in opposite directions and she had to make a choice or be left at the station. She resented it at first. Why couldn't things be like they had been before Matthew died? Things weren't perfect, but at least they were happy.

And she resented the people at her mother's church. Part of her blamed them for the change in her mother. They all seemed so happy. What right did they have being joyful when she was suffering so much?

Yet during that time her mother had become a different person altogether. Rachel caught her actually *reading* her Bible, and she said she'd even taken up praying in the mornings. Rachel couldn't believe it. What if her father found out? He seemed to tolerate her mother going to church once in a while, as long as she didn't take it too seriously. But when she tried to get him to go with her . . . it was like a match in a powder keg.

Her parents had drifted so far apart that it was like they were living in separate houses. Rachel couldn't figure how they could just stop loving each other. They had gone through so much together. They had seemed so much in love. . . .

After the divorce, Rachel had been devastated. She wanted to get back at them for ruining her life. She thought of dabbling in drugs but decided it wasn't worth the risks. She was pragmatic if nothing else. What good would it do to get their attention and then have to deal with the other effects of drug addiction? She even flirted briefly with the Goth look: black clothes and dark lipstick. Frankly, she didn't like the way she looked, but she thought it would bug her parents more than her. She also hoped it would make the people at church feel uncomfortable. She blamed them in part for her parents' divorce. But hardly anyone there seemed to notice — or *care* — how she looked. They seemed to accept her as she was. And while part of her still harbored resentment, another part was starting to soften.

So it was over the next few months that Rachel began to research what her mother had gotten into. The beliefs her father despised. She talked to the leaders at the church. She searched through various Web sites and read more than a dozen books. There were days she felt confused and didn't know what to believe. Ultimately, it was a question of evidence. One thing she had learned from her father was a fierce devotion to logic and to following the evidence wherever it led. Did the structure and complexity in nature point to a Creator? She had to acknowledge it did. But if there *was* a Creator, was it possible to know what He was like? Jesus, Buddha, Muhammad, Krishna . . . there were so many paths. They all had similarities but also some big differences. In the end, it came down to only one issue: an empty tomb. She had no choice but to follow the evidence, despite how her father felt. And that led her to a humble carpenter who claimed to be God.

And her father hated it.

"Rachel . . ."

From downstairs, her father's muffled voice brought Rachel up from her thoughts. She went into the hall. "What?"

He didn't answer.

Rachel sighed and rolled her eyes. "Dad, what?"

There was a loud thump.

"Dad?"

Rachel bounded downstairs to her father's study. She entered the room and time seemed to slow down. Her father lay on the floor by the patio doors.

He was limp. His face was drained of color and his eyes were wide open.

"Dad?" she heard herself say. "Daddy?"

She fumbled for the phone on the desk and threw herself down next to her father's limp body.

"Oh, God." Her voice quivered. It didn't even sound like her own voice. "Please don't let him die! Daddy, can you hear me?"

Her mind raced as she dialed 911. The operator answered, calm and emotionless.

"My — my father is unconscious on the floor! He's — I don't think he's breathing!"

The operator calmly verified her name and address. She asked for details of her father's condition, assured her that a rescue squad was on its way, and walked her through how to check his vital signs.

Check for breathing. Check for pulse. Rachel laid her ear to his mouth. She looked for anything that might be obstructing his airway. She put her head to his chest. No breathing. No heartbeat. Nothing.

Next the operator asked Rachel if she knew CPR. Rachel tried to recall her babysitting classes. They had gone over CPR, but now she struggled to remember the steps they had taught her. She tilted his head back. That was important, though she couldn't recall exactly why. His lips were still warm as she pressed her mouth to his and breathed in two quick puffs. Was it supposed to be two? Or was it three?

Her mind raced through the next steps of CPR. Hands on his chest . . . his sternum — not too low — what was that thing called again? She had to be careful to push in the right spot. What else, what else? She was forgetting something. She rose up on her knees, locked her elbows, and got ready to push down on her father's chest. *Fingers up, off the ribs. Push with the ball of your hand.*

She pushed down. The feeling was strange — not at all like the CPR dummy she had practiced on six months ago. This was her father. This was her dad. She had sat on his shoulders. He had pushed her on swings. . . .

Was she doing this right? Was she pushing hard enough? *Oh, God, please help me!* How many times was she supposed to push before breathing again? Twenty? Thirty?

How long would it take the rescue squad

to get here? At least ten minutes, maybe more.

. . . twenty-eight, twenty-nine, thirty. Now how many breaths? Two. Two breaths. Thirty to two. She thought that was the ratio. She pushed again on her father's sternum. His face was white.

"Daddy," she said, losing count. "Can you hear me? Please don't die!"

His eyes were still wide open. . . .

In the distance she heard a siren.

She pressed her lips to his and breathed in four more breaths. She could taste liquor on his mouth. And the salt of her tears. Where were they? Where were they?

Rachel worked her way through two more sets of CPR, fighting back her tears. Trying not to sob.

The doorbell rang, and she sprinted down the hall to the foyer, flinging the door open. Two men in blue uniforms and a female police officer stood outside. Rachel ran back to the study, waving them in. "This way. He's in here. . . ."

They rolled a stretcher into the room. A third paramedic brought a medical kit. They worked calmly. Quickly.

"I — he's not breathing. I couldn't get a pulse." Rachel's voice was quivering again.

They seemed to ignore her. Finally the

police officer took her name. One of the medics asked her a myriad of questions about her father. How old was he? Was he taking any medication? Had he been acting odd lately? Had he complained of chest pains? Had he had any history of heart problems?

They tore open his shirt. They opened his mouth, flashing a penlight into his throat, then in both his eyes. They covered his mouth with an oxygen mask.

One of them unpacked the defibrillator and grabbed the paddles.

"Charging!"

Rachel's eyes widened.

"Clear!"

The paramedic pressed the paddles to her father's chest. His torso lurched up, back arching as the current coursed through him. His head rolled back and his eyes met hers. . . .

But they were empty. A vacant, mannequin expression spread across his face. Then he sank back onto the hard, wood floor. They squeezed air into his lungs, pressed a stethoscope to his chest.

The police officer was trying to keep Rachel's attention off the paramedics. "I'll give you a ride to the hospital. Is there someone else we should call?"

But Rachel was staring at her father's limp body. He had been moving. Talking, eating just a half hour ago. Not more than thirty minutes.

"Miss?"

She looked back at the woman officer and nodded.

"My . . . my mother."

"Do you know where she can be reached?"

Rachel's mind was spinning. Reached? Yes. She nodded. Yes. She gave the officer the phone number.

"Clear!"

A second charge coursed through her father. Rachel winced. She had seen this in countless movies, but never live. Never this close. Never on her own father.

They transferred him to the gurney. One of the men was performing CPR even as they rolled him outside. They slid him into the ambulance, closed the door, and drove away.

Rachel sat in the back of the squad car as it snaked through traffic, following the ambulance. Sirens blared outside, yet the officer drove with one hand on the wheel. She seemed so calm, like they were just going for a drive in the country. "Your mother will be meeting you at the hospital," she said. "I believe she's on her way."

The officer didn't bother with small talk after that, and Rachel didn't mind. She didn't feel like talking. She didn't feel like feeling either.

Please, God . . . don't let him die. He's not ready to die.

48

Mitch ran to the maintenance shed. The doors were opened slightly and an orange glow poured out onto the gravel. The bundle of cables that snaked out from the shed had been sliced neatly through. He found himself staring at the light. There was something familiar about it. It seemed to draw him closer.

Howard walked up behind him. "See? Cut clean through."

"Where's that light coming from?" Mitch started to feel dizzy. The ground seemed to shift beneath him. Something drew him toward the shed. Beckoning him.

Howard leaned close. "You'll have to see for yourself."

Mitch hesitated. A warning sounded inside him, telling him to go no further. But still another silent voice — a gentle prodding — beckoned him closer. He pushed the doors open and peered inside.

This wasn't the maintenance shed.

Mitch found himself standing once again in his mother's bedroom. In the old house back in Illinois. It had the same dismal wallpaper, the same stale warmth and oppressive odor. The dull glow fell from a lamp on the nightstand next to the bed. But this time, there was someone else in the room. A skinny blond teenage boy sat on a wooden chair at the foot of the bed.

The boy was *him.*

A fetid stench hung in the room. Mitch could smell it still.

A body moved beneath the sheets. His mother. Mitch could hear her raspy breathing between soft moans. She was restless again. She was in pain.

"Look familiar?" Howard's voice startled Mitch.

Mitch shook his head. "What . . . what's happening?"

Howard shrugged. "Looks like a scene from your childhood."

"You can . . . you can see this too?"

Howard gave a slight chuckle and nodded to the boy. "What are you, thirteen? Fourteen?"

Mitch turned and fixed his eyes on the old man. "Are *you* doing this?"

"Actually —" Howard rubbed his jaw —

"you are."

Mitch glanced around the room. His mind reeled. He steadied himself against the wall. What was happening to him? He turned back to Howard. "Do you know what's going on?"

Howard nodded. "This is your mother. She's dying."

"Who *are* you?"

"How could God do this to her? you wondered." Howard went on. "She was a saint, after all. Selfless and loving. And this was her reward."

Mitch stared at the image.

The boy's eyes seemed to hold an icy gaze. He spoke softly, but his voice was unwavering. "Nobody else cares that you're suffering, Mom. No one but me."

His mother writhed in pain, barely noticing him. She could not speak.

"She was in such pain," Howard said.

Memories stirred inside Mitch. Dark memories, long since buried. They unfolded like black wings. He shook his head. "No! I . . . I don't want to see any more."

"You prayed for her, didn't you?"

Tears stung Mitch's eyes. "Stop it!"

"I can't stop this, Mitch. This is your doing. Remember?"

"No." Mitch shut his eyes tight. "I can't

watch her anymore."

"You *must.* Or it will never go away."

Mitch's shoulders slumped. He couldn't ignore the memories any longer. He couldn't fight it. He had only ever asked God for one thing. And that was not for himself. . . .

After a moment he opened his eyes again. "I prayed for months when she got sick."

"He didn't answer you, did He?"

Mitch's jaw clenched. He'd persisted. He'd begged. He'd even bartered, but still it was denied him. It was that silence, that . . . *rejection* more than anything that turned him away from the God of his father. "He never even heard me."

"The doctors couldn't do anything. Not even the morphine helped."

"She was in so much pain. . . ."

"So what could you do? What could you do in the face of such pain?"

Mitch breathed through his teeth. His heart pounded. Tears dripped like salty rivers onto his open lips. "I was . . . I was just a kid."

"You were only a boy. What could you do?"

Mitch watched as the boy got up, went to the bedroom door, and locked it. Then he drew close to the bedside and slid one of the pillows out from under his mother's head. He clutched it tight to his chest, now weeping. Sobbing.

"So you took matters into your own hands."

Eyes filled with tears, the boy placed the pillow gently on his mother's face . . .

And pressed.

Mitch watched. Helpless. Unable to move. Through his tears he watched his mother struggle. Her thin arms flailed. Her chest heaved as she fought for breath. As weak as she was, as sick as she was, still she struggled to live. A hand, pallid and shriveled, reached up to the boy's face. It slid up, up, and clutched his blond hair.

Tightly . . .

Tightly . . .

And then released.

It slid back down to touch his cheek, paused for a moment. Then it fell limp.

Mitch's body shook as he fell to his knees. "Mom . . . ," he whispered through choked sobs. "Please forgive me. . . ."

"Mom?" Howard spoke with mock surprise. "What good would *her* forgiveness do you?"

Mitch looked up. He couldn't stand.

Howard bent down. "It was your father who couldn't forgive you."

Someone pounded on the bedroom door. A moment later it burst open, and Mitch's father stood, beholding the scene in front of him. He blinked as if in disbelief. Mitch watched his expression turn from anger to horror to sorrow and then to uncontrollable rage. He cried out in such guttural, visceral agony. He picked the boy up by his neck and threw him across the room, out into the hall. Then he turned back to his dead wife, his arms held out, tears falling, and collapsed upon the bed and wept.

Howard just shook his head. "He didn't speak to you for months."

Mitch stared at the sight of his father's grief. He hadn't realized then how deep it was. How intense the pain had been. He nodded. "Things were never the same again. He never smiled. He never . . ."

"He never again told you he loved you."

Mitch watched as the light faded, the room fell into shadows. The walls of the shed emerged, the tools, the generators. Mitch felt the cold cement floor beneath him. His breathing grew labored. Slowly, he shook his head. "I killed her."

Howard drew in a breath. "Yet he never called the police. Never turned you in."

"No."

"And how could he? How would it look?

A congressman's son." Howard sniffed. "The *scandal.*"

Mitch picked himself up, stumbling to his feet. He looked at Howard. "Why? Why am I seeing this?"

Howard shrugged. "We all have our demons, Mitch. The deeds that haunt us through our lives. We may try to hide them away in dark closets, far from prying eyes. Where we think no one else will ever find them. No one will ever see. We sometimes even forget they're there. But they never stay hidden, do they? Those demons. They never go away." He pointed to the darkened shed. "This was a significant episode in your childhood. You might call it a watershed moment. This single event shaped the rest of your life. It altered your journey. And ultimately led you here."

Mitch narrowed his eyes. "Who are you?"

Howard chuckled. "I'm just a farmer. I just harvest the crops."

"Where are we? What is this place?"

Howard only smiled. Then he looked up. "The sun's going down. I'm afraid there won't be any lights tonight."

Mitch blinked. His eyes widened. Behind Howard, across the field, a mist was rolling in from the forest.

49

Helen sat alone in the kitchen, staring at the door. Just staring. Her mind felt like it was shutting down. Closing her off to reality. She felt oddly detached . . . and completely alone.

Devon and Conner were gone. Just disappeared. Mitch had gone as well, with Howard. She had watched them enter the darkened maintenance shed, leaving her alone again. And it was getting dark.

She glanced down at the rash on her arm. It had spread to her shoulder and now covered her hand. She could see it spreading, moving over her. Tingling. Burning. Chilling her skin.

A gust of wind moaned past the house.

A voice behind her jerked her up from her thoughts.

"They left you all alone again, didn't they?"

Helen shuddered internally, but her body

was too numb to respond. Her heart raced. She knew the voice. She turned slowly to see Kyle across the table from her.

He was practically unrecognizable. His face and head were completely covered by charred and peeling skin, his eye sockets swollen shut by red blisters. His ears and nose were blackened lumps. His mouth was merely an opening in the charred flesh.

"You're all alone."

Helen blinked. Tears rolled down her cheeks, but she only stared at him.

"Go away. You're not my son."

Kyle laughed. Or at least that was the impression she got. His face had no way to show emotion, but his breath came in choppy beats and he tilted his head back slightly. "You pushed them all away. Everyone in your life. And now, here you are. Alone."

Helen's breathing quickened. She was growing tired of the accusations. "You know, whatever you have to say, I'm not interested. You don't know me. I refuse to give you the reaction you're looking for."

"Oh, I know you better than you think. I know all about you."

"You're even not real. You're just an illusion."

"I'm as real as you are, Mother."

Helen glared at him. *"Leave me alone!"* she hissed and turned away.

Kyle sat still, tilting his head as if examining her. As if his burned-out eye sockets could still see. After a moment, he spoke again. "Why did you make him leave?"

"What are you talking about?"

"My father." Kyle leaned forward. "Why did you make him leave?"

"Your father?" Helen's jaw tightened. She turned back to him. "I didn't make him leave. He left me. He left *us!*"

Kyle shook his head. "You had a good thing. Such a good thing. Most people live their whole lives never having a relationship like that. And you threw it away."

"I wasn't ready for what he wanted! I didn't ruin anything. I wasn't ready and he wouldn't wait!"

"And after he left, you pranced through a string of boyfriends who didn't care a thing about you."

"Stop it!"

"You used your body like a . . . like a credit card. You bought whatever you wanted with it."

Helen's eyes slowly lost their fury. "Please stop. . . ."

"You were nothing but a cheap . . . *whore!*" He spat the word through his teeth.

"You're not Kyle," Helen hissed. "You're not my son!"

"And your parents?" Kyle sat back again. "Why didn't you ever let me meet them? Did you ever even tell them about me?"

Helen closed her eyes. She couldn't look at this apparition any longer. Yet she found she couldn't run. Like in a dream — a nightmare — she felt paralyzed.

"You drove away anyone who ever loved you. And now here you are. Completely alone."

Helen clenched her jaw against his words. She wouldn't give in. She wouldn't. . . . But slowly, her resolve abandoned her. She started to weep and buried her face in her hands.

Kyle stood and moved toward the doorway. He leaned down and whispered in her ear. "You're going to die alone."

Helen looked up. Kyle had disappeared. Her body went cold. The rash had spread, enveloping both arms and her torso. She could feel the sensation creeping down her legs and across her face. She stared at the open doorway, eyes wide. Her whole body trembled now.

From the darkness outside, two gray figures entered the house. Heads forward. Eyes white. Jaws open. Hands reaching toward her.

What horrible darkness! What complete and terrible darkness!

She shook her head and tried to scream. . . .

50

The ambulance arrived at the ER entrance, followed by the squad car with Rachel inside. The paramedics rolled her father through the wide double doors. The officer led Rachel in through a secondary entrance and up to the registration desk.

Rachel searched for her mother's face among the people in the waiting room. It looked like a fairly slow night. Only a half dozen or so people were there.

The middle-aged, heavyset woman behind the glass asked Rachel for some information on her father. Name, age, address. Insurance? Rachel had found his wallet before she left. The officer had reminded her. She thumbed through her father's credit cards until she came across what she thought was his insurance card.

Was this it? She slid it across the counter. The lady nodded — yes, it was.

Social Security number? Rachel shrugged.

She barely knew her own. Fine, the lady said; they could get it later. Then she rattled off a list of other questions, health related. Rachel knew the answers to less than half of them.

"I think my mother would know that. . . ." Rachel craned her neck to search for her mother again.

There she was.

Her mom rushed through the entrance. Her eyes fixed immediately onto Rachel. She slid into the seat next to her daughter, answering all the questions Rachel had missed. As if she knew them by heart. Her hand stayed on Rachel's leg the entire time.

They finished with the questions and went to a smaller waiting room down a side corridor. Rachel could see a flurry of activity through the windows of a double door at the end of the hall. Her mother drew her close and, finally, Rachel wept. Full and hard.

She relayed the events through tears and choked sobs. "His eyes were still open," she said. "He was just laying there. Even when they shocked him . . . nothing happened."

Her mother held her tightly and whispered a soft prayer in her ear.

The activity continued for several minutes. Someone bustled a cart into the room, propping the doors open. Rachel moved closer.

"Rachel . . ." Her mom urged her back but followed her down the hall.

Her father lay on the table in the center of the room. Shirt open. Chest exposed. An IV was hooked into his arm. Wires ran from white pads on his chest and hands. Someone was still squeezing air into his mouth and nose. They had another defibrillator next to the gurney, and one of the ER doctors picked up the pads.

He looked over his shoulder at a monitor. "Clear!"

Everyone backed away as he placed the pads on her father's chest. His body arched up, held there for a moment, then sank back down. The lines on the monitor jumped. Flattened. Then pulsed. Slowly at first. The activity increased. Rachel only caught snatches of the conversation. Someone called for lidocaine.

"We have sinus rhythm," one of the nurses said.

"It looks like he's regaining consciousness."

The nurse bent to look in his face. "Mr. Hayden? Mr. Hayden?" She checked the monitors, then bent close again. "Mr. Hayden, can you hear me?"

A doctor checked his pupils with a penlight.

Rachel turned to her mother. "They're talking to him! Is he awake?"

"Mr. Hayden, can you understand me?"

Through the bodies crowded around him, Rachel could see her father move. She thought she saw his mouth open slightly.

He moved! He was answering the nurse!

A wave of relief swept over Rachel. She turned and hugged her mother.

"Oh, thank God," Marta whispered. "Thank You, God."

"Mr. Hayden, you're in the Lake Forest Hospital ER. You're having a heart attack. Mr. Hayden, do you understand what I'm saying?"

Rachel could see him turn his head. His eyes caught hers. He saw her. She could see that he saw her! She could see recognition in his eyes. If only for a brief moment.

His head rolled back. He looked like he was trying to move his hand. He was trying to talk again. He was saying something to the nurse. She looked down, into his face. She bent close, as if to hear. A moment later, she straightened up. She looked around the room, then back at Rachel and her mother in the hall. For a moment, her eyes held a look of surprise and concern.

Then she turned away.

The steady beat of the monitor began to increase.

"His blood pressure's falling," someone said.

"We have v-tach," another voice echoed.

The monitor chimed a steady tone now.

Rachel's eyes widened. No, he was awake. He had looked at her. *No!*

"We're losing him. . . ."

51

Conner sat up with a start, staring wide-eyed into the darkness. His chest heaved as he gasped for air. Shadows surrounded him, but after a moment, his eyes adjusted to the dim light. He could make out the shapes of shovels and rakes hanging on the wall and large farming implements. And beyond them, the old tractor. He was inside the barn again. The barn where he had been attacked. Where Howard had betrayed him. The memories of his encounter flooded back along with memories of something else. The seizure and the light and . . .

Rachel? Had he just seen Rachel? And Marta as well?

What had just happened?

Where had he just been?

His head was spinning as he tried to make sense of the images he had seen. No, they weren't images. They were real. He had felt like a stranger in his own body. It was thick, awkward, and cold. Yet it had an odd familiarity, like the sensation he would have after driving for a long time in a different car, only to return to his old vehicle. It was familiar though still a little awkward.

The memories swirled in his mind. They seemed so real and yet so distant. He had been lying on a table. A nurse was looking down at him. And doctors. He was in an ER. The ER at Lake Forest Hospital. He was back in Lake Forest!

What had she said to him? He was having a . . .

Conner's eyes widened. A heart attack!

He struggled to his feet, shaky and disoriented. He felt as if he were trying to put together a large puzzle and all the pieces were lying on the floor. Just close enough together for him to see what kind of picture it might be but not close enough to make complete sense.

Was it real or just another illusion these creatures were giving him? This hallucination wasn't like the others he'd had. This was louder, colder, and more intense. Either way, he had to find Mitch and Helen. He had to warn them about Howard. The man was not what he appeared to be.

Conner made his way back to the entrance of the barn and peered outside. Darkness had settled over the farm along with a thick mist. Yet there were no lights on. The generators weren't running. There was no power. His stomach tightened. Something terrible had happened.

Nothing moved in the mist. No sign of the creatures. No sign of Howard.

A dim, orange glow spilled out from the windows of the farmhouse. Conner moved across the yard to the back porch and slipped inside.

Candles flickered on the kitchen table, the counter, and the windowsills. In the living room beyond, more candles had been set on the coffee table and upright piano. Mitch sat on the sofa, staring at the candlelight with an empty expression on his face.

"Mitch?" Conner whispered.

Mitch didn't move.

Conner waved his hand in front of Mitch's face. "Mitch, can you hear me?"

Mitch blinked. His eyes drifted up to Conner. After a moment, a slight glow of recognition appeared. "Hey, Conner. Where'd you go?"

Conner narrowed his eyes. What was wrong with him? Why was he acting so strange? "It . . . it's a long story. Where's Helen?"

"Helen?" Mitch wrinkled his forehead,

almost as if he was trying to remember who she was. "She, uh . . . I don't know. I think she left."

"Left?" Conner frowned. "Mitch, what's wrong? Where did she go? Did she go with Howard?"

Mitch's gaze fluttered back to the candle. "Yeah . . . I'm not really sure."

Conner glanced around the room. "Mitch, I think we should get out of here. We need to find Helen. I think she's in serious trouble. I think we're *all* in danger."

Mitch shook his head. "Yeah . . . I think we should wait for Howard to get back."

"No." Conner took Mitch by the shoulders. "Howard *is* the danger. We've got to get out of here! Before he gets back!"

A sudden shriek echoed in the darkness outside. Conner froze. He recognized it. "Helen?"

He went to the back porch and peered out into the darkness. The chilling sound echoed again. High-pitched. A scream of complete terror. It came from the forest.

Conner turned back to Mitch. "Did they take her?" He ran back inside and shook Mitch by his shoulders, dragging him off the couch. "Wake up! Did those things take her?"

Mitch scowled, drunkenly. "How should I

know? I wasn't around. I just went out to fix the generators, and when I came back, she was gone."

"She's in the woods! I can hear her. Don't you hear that?"

Mitch shook free from Conner's grasp and plopped back onto the sofa. "Just go away and leave me alone!"

Conner swore at him. *"We've got to save her!"*

"*You* can go," Mitch grunted. "*I'm* not going anywhere."

Conner peered at him. "What's happened to you?"

"Just leave me alone."

Conner rummaged through the house, explaining his experience to Mitch, hoping some of it was getting through. Could they be dying? Could they all be dead? Was all this some kind of hell? Mitch didn't seem to care.

Conner found a large flashlight and headed outside. He made his way back to the barn. His mind was churning. He needed a plan. But what? He wasn't even sure what was happening to them. Had his experience in the hospital been just another illusion?

Helen's voice echoed again. Pleading for help. Conner shuddered. He had never heard anyone sound so deeply frightened. He found Howard's harvester behind the barn. Maybe he could figure out how to use it. He climbed into the cab and searched for the keys. Or an ignition switch. He had no idea how to even operate the thing. He slammed his fist onto the steering wheel and cursed. He struggled against his own panic. Part of him knew he had to rescue Helen — or at least try. But part of him was paralyzed with fear.

He climbed back out of the tractor and swept the flashlight across the field. Tendrils of mist coiled and swirled in the light. Darkness seemed to swallow it completely.

"Help me! Help! Someone, please help me!"

Helen's voice sent chills down his spine. The sheer terror he heard in it. He swore again, cursing Howard and Mitch and even God Himself.

Then slowly, as if fighting against a strong current, he made his way forward across the open field. Everything inside him screamed not to go forward. He turned and peered behind him. Darkness and mist enveloped him completely. He couldn't see the house or the barn. Ahead lay even thicker darkness and fog, beckoning him — daring him almost — to continue. He stood alone in the dark, holding the flashlight, trembling.

At length, he willed his legs to move forward again. After several minutes, the light caught the branches of trees, rising out of the mist. Black, twisted, and bare. He stood at the edge of the forest. He could feel the air, cold inside. His breath puffed out in steamy billows.

Whispers echoed from the darkness. Rasping, inhuman voices surrounded him. Then his eyes caught something. . . .

Far off among the trees, a single light glowed. It flickered, dimmed, and then glowed again.

Conner's heart pounded, shaking his ribs. He took several long, deep breaths, clenched his teeth tightly, and plunged into the woods.

52

Branches snagged on Conner's clothes and scraped against his skin. He lowered his head and pushed through the undergrowth, pressing forward toward the tiny glow. The wood seemed dry, snapping as if every bit of moisture had been sucked from the trees, leaving charred, skeletal remains.

The voices closed in on all sides of him. Rasping whispers buffeted him with words he could not understand. Taunting, jeering. Warning. Threatening. He clenched his teeth against his fear until his jaw ached. Still he pressed onward.

After several minutes, he broke into a clearing and found himself staring wide-eyed at a small cabin. It was a simple timber structure with a single door and window along the front. A rusted stovepipe emerged through one side of the sagging roof. It looked completely abandoned and forsaken except for the orange glow pouring out through the window.

Conner swallowed. His throat was still dry. Why hadn't he thought to drink anything before he left? Why hadn't he come more prepared? He switched off the light, stole quietly to the front window, and peered inside.

Through the weather-stained glass, he could see a single table and three chairs. A potbellied stove sat off to one side. An assortment of hunting gear and other items cluttered the walls and remaining floor space. Several fat candles glowed on the table, and a small fire had been lit inside the stove.

Conner's heart raced as he tried to determine whether anyone was hiding amid the junk, but the place looked empty. He creaked open the door and slipped inside.

It smelled like a musty attic. Conner looked around. He held his hand to the open door-plate of the stove and frowned. It glowed, but he could feel no warmth. He examined his arm again. It was entirely enveloped by the purple rash. He could feel the prickling, cold sensation on his shoulder.

"I see you decided to join us again." Howard's voice jolted Conner. He spun around to see the old farmer behind him, in the doorway.

Conner backed away. His heart pounded. "Stay away from me!"

Howard drew a deep breath and sighed. "I suppose I can't blame you for being upset."

Conner narrowed his eyes. "What's happening? What is this place?"

Howard lifted his eyebrows. "It's Indiana."

"This is *not* Indiana."

"Well . . ." Howard shrugged. "It's more like what you remember you always thought Indiana *might* be like."

"That doesn't make any sense."

Howard stepped inside. "It's everything your mind is still clinging to of your life. Like an afterimage of your world."

"My *life?*" Conner swallowed. His throat felt like sandpaper. He didn't want to believe it. He didn't want to give voice to his fears. But still, he needed to know. "Are we . . . are we dead?"

"No, you're not dead," Howard chuckled. "Not yet."

"I don't get it."

"This place is not your final destination, only the road that leads to it." Howard nodded out the window. "This . . . Interworld . . . is that gossamer veil between life and death. A curtain, if you will, between Time and Eternity. And everyone, sooner or later, passes through it."

Conner shook his head. "Then who are you?"

"Me?" Howard raised his eyebrows and scratched the back of his neck. "Well, I'm just a gatekeeper of sorts. Just the doorman, really."

"So that storm we all saw, with the lights . . ."

Howard nodded. "That was the portal — for lack of a better term. The threshold of perception. It's only truly visible when death is imminent."

"My heart attack," Conner said. "And Mitch, and Helen?"

"Yes. Each of you is dying. And your spirits are passing through this dimension." Howard rubbed his jaw. "It *is* somewhat of an anomaly that you happened upon each other as you did. Spirits rarely cross paths here. And even when they do, it's rare for them to have any interaction."

"Spirits?" Conner's gaze beat a trail across the cabin. He looked down at his hands. "But I'm no . . . I'm no spirit. See? I have a physical body." He rubbed his arms. His own flesh was solid to his touch. "This is just some kind of illusion."

Howard shook his head. "You still cling to life. You only appear to have a body because your mind still believes it. It hasn't yet accepted the truth."

"What do you mean?"

Howard circled the room. "Life is like a flame, Mr. Hayden. Some people die so suddenly that their flames are just snuffed out." He brought his hand down on one of the candles on the table. Smoke curled up from the bent wick. "They pass through this place so quickly, they're scarcely even aware of it. But for others . . . for others, death comes more slowly. An illness or a coma. Or in your case, a heart attack." He bent down and blew gently on a second candle. The flame flickered, bowed, and went out, leaving the tip of the wick glowing. "For them, the flame goes out but the ember still glows for a time. And they linger here until the last vestige of their life fades completely." He straightened up again. "But this body you touch — what you *think* you *feel* — is only your perceived physicality. Only what your spirit remembers of its shell. And as your life fades, so will your perception."

"What about those creatures?" Conner's frown deepened. "What are they? Why are they after us?"

Howard's lips tightened. "Mankind is not alone in the universe, Mr. Hayden. There are creatures here that you cannot even begin to fathom. Creatures far older and wiser than you, who existed long before mankind ever drew his first breath. Some whose beauty defies description. And others more hideous than you could possibly imagine."

Conner recalled the chilling hallucinations he'd been having earlier. Even before the storm. "I thought I was just seeing things. People staring at me. And the guy on the roof with no face . . ."

Howard nodded. "Sometimes, when a person is near death, they may get a glimpse behind the veil."

Conner shook his head. "But I was fine. I felt . . ."

"No, Mr. Hayden." Howard leaned his gaunt face toward Conner. "You were dying since breakfast. You just didn't know it."

Conner's mind reeled. What was he talking about? Angels and demons? He had never believed in such nonsense. He still wasn't sure he did. He started to feel dizzy.

"Then which kind are you? You saved us from them, but then you led me right to them. Back in the barn."

Howard smiled and looked down. "Well, I must confess, I do have a flair for the dramatic. I love to play the savior on occasion."

"Savior?"

Howard frowned. "But you weren't supposed to go back. You were too far gone. I thought for sure you were ours."

"But they *did* bring me back," Conner said. "In the hospital, they . . . they revived me."

Howard nodded. "Most unexpectedly, I might add."

"So . . . so I'm not dead yet." Conner fought back his fear. "You said I'm still clinging to life, right?"

Howard shrugged. "A technicality."

Conner caught a glimmer of hope. "Then there's still a chance. If they revived me once . . ."

"Oh . . ." Howard's expression turned to what Conner could only interpret as pity. "Oh, Mr. Hayden, I'm afraid you may be setting yourself up for a big disappointment. It's very rare."

"But not unheard of," Conner persisted. "It does happen."

Howard shrugged again. He seemed to concede the point, if only as a technicality. But Conner was shifting reflexively into lawyer mode, as if he might barter his way out of this situation. An entire case could swing on a single technicality or loophole. He had done this countless times before. It was just a question of bringing it to light. Exploiting it.

"Yes," Howard said. "But your life is fading. Your heart has stopped. And your breathing. Even now, your cells are going without oxygen. Soon they will begin to die and your brain synapses will cease. In minutes you will be beyond anyone's ability to revive. It is inevitable." He pointed to the discoloration that now enveloped Conner's arm. "Once it covers you completely, there will be no going back."

"But if I can just hold on until —"

"Hold on?" Howard raised his eyebrows. "Do you think any of this depends on your efforts? Do you think you can add a single second to your allotted time? Or affect your fate by sheer force of will?"

"Fate?" Conner's face darkened. "I don't believe in fate."

"I know," Howard chuckled. "And that is precisely how you got to this point. Your arrogance. Your unbelief."

"You mean in God?" Conner shook his head. "You're wrong. I do believe. I just believe in a God who doesn't take the least bit of interest in what He created. Just look at His world: famines, floods, earthquakes, diseases. There's no real justice. No rhyme or reason. It's all suffering and chaos. My fate is my own. It's what I make it. And yes, I do think I can lengthen my time by sheer force of will."

Howard sighed. "Why do you persist in trying to be the master of your destiny?"

"Because I am!"

Suddenly the entire cabin shuddered. Dust seeped from every crack within its framework. The ground trembled and a deep groan echoed through the forest. Conner stumbled to his knees. After several seconds, all was quiet again.

"What was that?"

Howard steadied himself against the doorway and brushed off his shirt. His lips tightened. "You spoke the Name, Mr. Hayden. Those words are dangerous here."

"What name?"

"*The* Name, Mr. Hayden. *His* Name."

Conner furrowed his brow. "What're you talking about?"

Howard leaned close. His thin lips peeled back. *"Ego Sum."* His voice was barely above a whisper. "*I Am.* You appropriated it for yourself. A thing you do at your own peril."

Conner frowned. A memory flitted back to him from his childhood. When his parents brought him to Sunday school. An old man and a burning bush. He shook his head and fought to stay on the offense.

"I don't care." Conner examined his arm again. "I intend to hold on. I'm going to fight this. I'm going to fight *you!*"

Howard only smiled. "I knew you would. But it won't do you any good. You cannot fight that which is inevitable."

"I can try."

Howard looked at him for a moment. His gray eyes seemed placid and thoughtful. "Mr. Hayden, you don't have a clue what lies beyond this place, do you?"

Conner stepped back. It was the question he had been trying to thrust from his mind. If this place was merely the path . . . what was the ultimate destination?

At that moment, Helen's shrill cry echoed again from deeper inside the forest. Conner stepped outside and peered into the woods.

Howard folded his arms. "You want to save her, don't you? Your chivalry is noble and quite noteworthy considering your present circumstances. But really, Mr. Hayden, do you honestly think you can do anything for her?"

She screamed again. Conner's heart pounded. He was being drawn farther into the forest. Every sense inside him shouted a warning. It was a trap. Yet he could not listen to those cries for help and do nothing. He had to at least try. . . .

"I have to try," he said, drawing a breath. He gritted his teeth and pushed himself forward, into the woods.

53

Conner forced himself onward. Helen's cries sounded close, just a little ways ahead. He shuddered again; his knees trembled. What were they doing to her? What would they do to him? How could he possibly hope to save her? And why would he even try? They were strangers, after all. They hardly knew each other. Would she be doing this for him if their places were reversed?

Howard's words echoed in his mind: *You cannot fight that which is inevitable.*

The flashlight cast contorted shadows amid the gnarled trunks and branches. The mist lit up like a thick, glowing wall before him, not allowing him to see more than ten or fifteen feet in front or behind. He could very likely wander through the woods all night and miss Helen completely.

His progress was limited by the frequency of Helen's cries. He traveled in the direction her last scream had come from, but just as he would be ready to give up completely, he would hear her voice again, somewhere up ahead.

Before long, the ground began to rise steadily. Rocks peppered the forest floor, slowing his progress. The trees quickly thinned out, and soon he found himself scrambling up a steep incline. Helen's cries were close now. Just beyond the crest . . .

He emerged onto a wide, level clearing and stopped. Ahead of him, Conner could see, far off, a pale sky on the horizon. Whether it was from the onset of dawn or for some other reason, he could not tell. He had long since lost track of time. But he could not see anything between himself and the far horizon. He swept the light across the ground in front of him and gasped. The rocky embankment ended abruptly. He was standing on the edge of a massive cliff. The horizon continued to grow brighter, and before long, Conner was able to make out more of his surroundings.

He was indeed standing on the edge of a cliff. A vast abyss opened before him, stretching into the distance. Yet to the east was a distant plateau, like the far shore of a wide lake, now lit more brightly. The clouds were breaking there, and Conner could see distant shafts of sunlight pouring down upon that place. He peered into the distance and rubbed his eyes. Green? Was it green grass he saw? Rolling hills and lush foliage?

Yet immediately overhead, he could see only thick, gray clouds. Behind him and to each side stretched the dry, black forest. To the north and south, the jagged ledge extended as far as he could see.

The wind swept around him now, gusting and swirling, tugging him to the edge. And he could still hear the haunting, disembodied whispers coming from both the woods behind him and the chasm ahead.

Conner swallowed and inched his way forward. The rocky ledge dropped off sharply and disappeared into blackness. The sheer face of the cliff dissolved into an inky void. A gust of wind shot up from the depths, carrying a choking, fetid stench and something else. . . .

Agony.

For an instant, Conner caught the full brunt. A wave of voices, crying out. Human voices. Thousands. Millions. Each one distinct and yet all blended together into a seemingly solid force: sorrow, hatred, anger, and unfettered, unbridled rage. And terror. As deep and bottomless as the chasm itself seemed. Conner heard them all at once.

The sound of it, the depth and vastness of

it, physically knocked him backward. His chest seized with icy talons as he fell onto the rocks and scrambled away from the edge. The horror of it stole his breath away. He shook his head, gasping for air.

He felt a presence behind him, looming over him, and turned to see a gaunt silhouette against the gray sky.

Howard curled an eyebrow. "You never believed in the afterlife, did you?"

"What . . . what is this place?"

"It is the abyss, Mr. Hayden. Endless darkness. The threshold of eternity."

Conner closed his eyes. He tried to control his fear. To let it pass over him and through him. "Is that . . . ?" His voice sounded weak and pathetic. "Is that where Helen's gone?"

Howard's pale face grew solemn. "I'm afraid so."

Conner struggled to his feet and stared at Howard. The old farmer seemed completely absurd, standing in his plaid shirt and overalls. Conner's expression faded from fear into a scowl. "Why? Why is *she* there? She was a good person."

Howard's eyes flared. "Do you even know the meaning of the word?" He closed his eyes and drew a long, slow breath, as if Conner had irritated him somehow and he was trying to control his outrage. "Nice, perhaps. She may very well have been a *nice* person. But she was hardly good."

Conner shook his head. This was like some twisted, macabre fairy tale. A cartoon version of Dante's Inferno. It had to be some kind of illusion. This couldn't be all there was. He glared at Howard. Here at the brink of eternity, this was all there was? This was the best they could do?

"Why?" he spat again. "What did she do that was so terrible?"

"Do?" Howard narrowed his eyes. His lips peeled back in a twisted smirk. "It's not what she did so much as what she *didn't* do, Mr. Hayden. It's what you didn't do. Or Mitch. It's what all those who stand here neglected to do."

"What's that?"

Howard leaned close and whispered through his yellow teeth, "Believe."

Conner felt his anger roiling. "Believe? Believe in what? You know what our world is like. You tell me what there is to believe in. You tell me what religion was worth my attention."

"Not religion, Mr. Hayden. Religion is too often mere rote and regimen. And at worst, a license to slaughter the unfaithful. No, He hates that kind of religion as much as you do." Howard shook his head and grunted.

"But your species is unparalleled in its hypocrisy. How you could turn such a remarkable thing, and sublime, into something so mundane. He beckons you into His very presence — where angels fear to tread — and you contrive a myriad of obstacles to put in the way. Too often you've constructed traditions and formalities that serve more to keep others out than to usher you in. Then, when you've squeezed every drop of life and vitality from your worship, you sniff at the ritual you've created and blame it on Him." Howard stepped to the edge of the abyss and cast a glance downward. "Do you know how many religious souls are down there? How many people who thought they were good enough? who went through all the motions just to feel comfortable with themselves but ignored the one thing required of them."

"Perfection?" Conner scoffed.

"Humility," Howard intoned. "A penitent heart."

"There's no way to please Him. He's as cruel and uncaring as I always thought Him to be."

"Uncaring?" Howard chuckled. "For all your education and intellect, you're a great fool, aren't you? Like a man who goes to a ball game with no tickets and no wallet, no ability to pay for his admission. And yet when you arrive, you think you should just be let inside the park."

Conner peered again at the far side of the gulf and shook his head. "If He is good and loving, why is there a price to get into heaven?"

"Everything has a cost, Mr. Hayden. You of all people should understand that. And you don't have the slightest clue how great that cost was."

"What cost?"

"Redemption," Howard said and narrowed his eyes. "But then again . . . you don't believe in that, do you, Mr. Hayden. You don't believe you need it."

Conner turned away from the edge. He'd had his fill of this conversation and this old fool. The whole scene had gone beyond being absurd. "I've had enough of this."

He had started back into the woods when his body jerked suddenly. Pain coursed down his spine and ribs. White light flashed momentarily in his eyes. Then, just as quickly as it had come, it was gone.

Conner stood there, clutching his heart. What was that? It felt like one of his seizures, though not as strong as the others. Not nearly as strong.

Howard peered at him. "It seems they're

not giving up on you yet, Mr. Hayden."

Conner furrowed his brow. That seizure had been far less intense than the previous ones. He recalled the defibrillator he had seen — or thought he had seen. Were they trying to shock him back to consciousness? Were they trying to revive him again? Conner's face clouded with a puzzled look.

Howard chuckled again. "Not as strong as the others, was it? They're losing you. The longer you remain here, the less you will feel. And the less likely it is that you will be brought back."

Conner looked up. *Losing him.* He remembered one of the voices in the ER. He had caught only a few words before he faded out, but he could have sworn that's what they had said. His heart started racing. They couldn't give up on him. He couldn't let them give up!

"Try it again!" he screamed with all his strength. His dry throat was raspy. He waved his arms at the sky. "Don't give up!" He broke into a fit of coughing.

Howard was laughing. Not his usual insincere chuckle. This was hearty laughter. "Yes, keep it up, Mr. Hayden. I'm sure they can hear you. Keep screaming."

Conner could feel the icy chill of the rash spreading across his chest now. "Don't give up!" he screamed again into the sky. "Please!"

"Was that your strategy?" Howard taunted. "Was that your plan?"

Conner turned around. Anger flowed through his veins now. But only for a moment. His nerve drained from him as two contorted, gray figures climbed up over the edge of the chasm. They straightened up, standing on either side of Howard. Heads forward, pale eyes glowing, black jaws opened wide. They lunged toward him.

Conner's eyes widened and he turned to run, but his legs felt thick and sluggish. His foot caught on a rock and he tumbled down the slope. Scraped and bloody, Conner picked himself up and dashed into the woods. He threw a glance over his shoulder to see the two creatures descending after him.

He burst through the dry undergrowth. Branches whipped past him, tearing at his skin as he stumbled on through the forest. He could hear Howard's laughter echoing from all directions. His mind reeled. This had to be a dream. This couldn't be happening.

He hurried on, not daring to look back but feeling the presence of the two creatures closing in on him through the trees. Black trunks loomed around him. Gnarled branches like giant arms seemed to reach down and block his path. It was as if the forest itself was alive and trying to trap him.

He gasped for breath; freezing cold crushed in on his chest and arms. He caught a glimpse of the discoloration creeping across his other arm now. He closed his eyes. *Please, not now.* His legs chugged, as if in slow motion. He felt like he was in one of his childhood nightmares, struggling to run, unable to move. Unable to put any distance between himself and his attackers.

Suddenly he felt the branches pull away. He fell forward. His eyes snapped open as he tumbled to the ground. Squinting. Sunlight blazed around him, poured over him. He covered his eyes and scrambled back to his feet. Where was he?

The brightness overwhelmed him, blinded him. He felt a warm breeze on his face. He smelled the scent of freshly mowed grass. It was a sensation that normally would have filled him with cheer but now only filled him with dread.

54

Conner looked around, shielding his eyes. Sunlight poured down from a cloudless blue sky. After a moment, he recognized his surroundings. He stood at the edge of a large, well-manicured yard. A wooden play set and a trampoline were set off to one side. The carpet of grass butted up to a gated cement patio around an inground pool.

This was — used to be — *his* backyard. In Lake Forest.

He closed his eyes and breathed in the scents: freshly cut grass, chlorine, and charcoal burning somewhere in the neighborhood. Someone was running a lawnmower. And birds! He heard birds chirping in the lush, green trees at the edge of their property.

Conner walked toward the house. His arms were scraped and bruised. His ankles were sore where he had bashed them against rocks earlier. But now the sunlight warmed him.

A voice came from behind him. "A beautiful day, isn't it?"

Howard stepped through the trees at the edge of the property and crossed the yard, squinting in the sunlight.

Conner tensed and peered into the foliage for any sign of the creatures that had been pursuing him. He knew he should be fleeing in panic, but he felt dazed somehow. Detached and dizzy. "What is this?" he said. "What's going on?"

Howard moved closer and shrugged. "It looks like your home."

Conner said, "Why are you doing this?"

"Well, it's mostly your doing. As you die, your brain recalls images from your life. Different events. Sometimes pleasant. Sometimes not so pleasant. And sometimes things we try to forget."

A sick feeling grew in Conner's stomach. "I don't want to see this."

"Really, Mr. Hayden," Howard said coolly, "do you honestly think this is about what *you* want?"

Then Conner heard a voice. It was *his* voice. Muffled. Coming from inside the house. Conner walked up to the window. He could see papers strewn across the table in the breakfast nook. His work had spilled over from the office into the kitchen. Then he saw himself, dressed in jeans and a green golf shirt, moving around inside. He was on the phone.

Conner frowned. He was watching himself.

Then a second image darted down the hallway.

Matthew.

Conner gasped.

Matthew was chasing his soccer ball. It rolled into the kitchen and Matthew bounded in after it, blond mop bouncing, catching the sunlight. The ball rolled under the table and the boy crawled under as well. He scrambled out the other side and stopped to peer out the window. For a moment Matthew seemed to look directly at Conner.

Conner caught his breath. What a beautiful boy. He had forgotten how handsome he was. Wide blue eyes. Mischievous grin. Front tooth missing.

"Matty," he whispered. He laid his fingers to the glass, but then Matthew's face turned away. Inside, Conner could see his own image enter the kitchen, still on the phone. He snapped his fingers and shooed the boy out of the breakfast nook. Matthew disappeared again down the hall.

Conner watched himself riffle through the stacks of papers, engrossed in the conversation. He had been talking to Gus Brady at the time.

Howard peered over his shoulder. "You remember this day, hmmm?"

Conner stared. Yes, he remembered. But he didn't answer.

"It wasn't so long ago, was it?"

Conner shook his head. Five years, one month . . . *twelve* days.

Howard nodded to Conner's image inside. "You look like you're working on something important. A big case, was it?"

Conner was slow to answer. "Pretty big, yeah."

"Important stuff?"

Conner blinked. "I . . . I don't want to see any more."

Howard chuckled. "Well, I don't think you have much of a choice."

Conner turned away. He stared out at the yard. So full of things: play sets and bikes and inflatable rafts and balls.

So full of . . . life.

"Ah, here it is." Howard nodded toward the window. "The fateful moment."

Conner turned and peered inside. He didn't want to watch it, but he couldn't bear to look away. The soccer ball bounced across the hall into Conner's front office. Matthew darted after it.

At the same time, Conner's double turned from the kitchen table and headed back down the hall.

"You were forever shooing him out of your office," Howard said.

Conner shook his head. "He was always kicking that ball in the house. . . ."

They heard a muffled crash and Conner's voice from inside, yelling.

"How many times do I have to tell you? Play with that ball outside!"

A moment later, Conner emerged from his office, herding Matthew by the scruff of his neck. Matthew ran on his tiptoes, clinging to the ball with both hands.

Conner slid the patio door open and pushed him outside. "And if I see you with that ball in the house again, I'm going to throw it away! You understand?"

Matthew rubbed the back of his neck and nodded sheepishly. Conner slammed the door shut and returned to his cell phone. "Sorry, Gus, my kid just knocked over my lamp. . . ."

Outside, Conner watched Matthew dribble the ball on the patio. Inside, he saw himself engrossed in paperwork.

Howard drew close behind him. "Not exactly father-of-the-year material, were you?"

Conner's breathing grew more rapid. "Please . . . I don't want to watch any more."

"No?" Howard said. "But this is where it starts to get good."

Matthew kicked the ball. He went onto the grass and kicked it across the yard.

Howard grunted. "The kid's got a pretty good leg."

Matthew ran to the far side of the yard, backed up, and kicked the ball toward the house. It lofted up, bouncing off the top of the chain-link fence, onto the cement. Then bounced once, twice . . . and into the pool.

Conner tensed. He could see Matthew's face. He looked to the house first. Was Dad watching? Conner followed his gaze. Through the window, he saw himself get up from the table and head back to his office.

No!

Howard shook his head. "Your wife was where? At the mall with your daughter?"

Conner nodded. He couldn't speak. He spun back to Matthew. The boy ran to the gate and opened the latch.

"So many tiny, fateful decisions," Howard said. "Change just one of them and the course of your entire life would have been altered." He chuckled. "Not to mention your son's."

Conner ran to the fence. "Don't go in there! Please, don't go in there." He tried to pull Matthew away from the gate. But Matthew's body did not feel like flesh and bone. Rather it was cold and solid, like a marble statue. Conner tried to block his path, but Matthew was moving by some other force — too strong for Conner to stop. Like trying to stop a rolling locomotive. Conner tugged at his arm, but his hands merely slipped off the boy.

Howard shook his head again. "Come now, Mr. Hayden. This isn't about changing the past. It's about confronting it."

Conner ran to the house and pounded on the patio door. It made no sound. It felt as though he was pounding against a brick wall. He beat on the glass until his fists throbbed.

"Get out here!" he shouted. His throat was raw; his voice rasped impotently. He saw himself return to the kitchen and sit down at the table.

"Not even a glance outside," Howard said, peering through the window. "You weren't even thinking about him, were you?"

Conner ran to the breakfast nook window.

He glanced back at his son at the edge of the pool, reaching for the ball, floating just out of his grasp. He pounded again, screaming. "Look up! Look up! *Just look up!*"

After a moment his shoulders slumped. His voice was gone. "Please . . . ," he rasped, "just look up."

Splash!

Conner dashed back to the poolside. Matthew was floundering, beating the water with his hands, still trying to reach for the ball. Now out of desperation.

Howard's voice was cool and even. "If only he had been able to grab hold of the ball . . . But it was just a few inches out of his reach."

Conner tried to dive into the water but met with a force that knocked him backward, onto the ground. He tried again and again as Matthew struggled. He searched for something to throw to him, something he could reach. But every item, even the raft, was too heavy for him to move. As though everything in the yard was made of granite.

His eyes flooded with tears. "Matthew," he sobbed. "Oh, God, please . . . *Matthew!*" Conner looked back to the house and saw himself get up from the table again and return to his office. Unaware. Lost in his work.

He was supposed to watch Matthew. Marta had told him, "Play soccer with your son." She had told him before she left. But he had a brief to write. He had a case to research. He had . . .

Conner stared at the empty kitchen.

He had work to do.

He turned back to the pool, tears pouring down his cheeks, as Matthew's head sank beneath the surface. He watched his son try to call out, only to suck in a lungful of water. His arms flailed. His eyes were round with fear. His beautiful blue eyes. Filled with fear. He choked and coughed and gasped for air but only took in another mouthful of water.

Conner's mind clouded. The scene was too much. His legs buckled and he sank to his knees at the poolside. "Oh, Matthew . . . my beautiful little boy . . . my son . . . I'm so sorry. . . ."

Matthew was staring at him now. Right at him. Eyes round. Mouth open, drowning beneath the surface. Slowly, his legs stopped kicking and his arms grew still. His little body sank, legs together. Arms outstretched.

Conner could see his eyes grow calm.

Then glaze over.

55

"We're losing him." The voice was professional. Stable. But filled with urgency.

Rachel's eyes widened again.

No!

They had revived him. He had been conscious. Just a few seconds ago, he had looked at her. He was alive. . . .

Time seemed to slow down.

The ER staff bustled with activity. The EKG monitor blared a steady tone. Rachel watched them work. Their voices died away in an echoing canyon. She could feel herself growing faint. Her vision began to tunnel. She clutched her mother's arm, digging her fingers into her shirt.

"Mom?" Her voice sounded far away. Her mom's hand swept down across her shoulder and pulled her close.

God, please don't take him. . . .

The doctor charged the defibrillator again and checked the monitor.

"Clear!"

They backed away as he laid the paddles on her father's bare chest. Rachel could hear the thump and deep hum as the current coursed through his flesh. His chest lifted slightly, held for a moment, then sank back down. The monitor hummed a steady tone.

The doctor swore and shook his head.

Conner knelt at the poolside. His eyes stung as tears streamed down his cheeks. His body shuddered with sobs.

"Matthew . . ."

Howard stood over him, arms folded, shaking his head. "You didn't even come outside for another twenty-five minutes, Mr. Hayden."

Conner's eyes opened. He caught his breath.

Twenty-five minutes?

Had it been that long? He'd sworn he had just taken his eyes off the boy for a minute. He'd sworn he had been watching him the whole time.

"Tell me," Howard said evenly, "how did your wife react? It must have been difficult for her. To come home from the mall and find an ambulance in her driveway. To see that tiny bundle of linen on the stretcher.

And then to realize her worst nightmare had come true."

Conner nodded, his chest tight. Marta's reaction was violent, unabated sorrow. She had collapsed there on the driveway.

"I imagine it must have been difficult for her not to blame you."

Conner struggled for breath. His heart raced. They had stopped speaking altogether for the first several days. And she was cold for several weeks more. He knew she blamed him. She never said as much. But he could see it in her eyes. In the way she avoided his gaze.

Howard leaned over Conner's shoulder. His breath was cold on Conner's neck. "Yet somehow, I can't imagine you acknowledging your own culpability."

Conner stared at the pool. Sunlight glinted off the water. "I didn't. . . . I didn't. . . ."

"But you did find someone to blame, yes?" Howard straightened up. "Someone at whom you could direct your anger. Someone to be the target of your rage."

Conner shuddered. "Yes. . . ."

"Yes, the Almighty. It was *His* fault. He could have prevented it, after all. He could have intervened. . . ."

"Why didn't He? Why didn't He save my son?"

"Because He couldn't." Howard bent again to Conner's ear. His voice was low, barely above a whisper. "Or perhaps He didn't want to. Perhaps He wanted to teach you a lesson. He's nothing but a schoolyard bully after all, isn't He, Mr. Hayden."

Conner opened his mouth but could not speak. A chill crept over him, down his torso, up to his neck. His rash was spreading. They had given up on him. They weren't going to revive him. But he didn't care. He didn't care about fighting any longer. Numbness swept across his mind. A thick, black numbness.

"Or maybe . . . ," Howard whispered, "maybe He wanted *you* to know what it was like to have to stand by and watch your only son die."

Conner's eyes began to roll back. The sunlight faded away; the pool was changing color. Darkness crept across the water, swallowing everything in its path. The trees disappeared, the yard and the house. The entire scene melted away before him, and Conner found himself kneeling again on the edge of the precipice. Staring down into the vast chasm of darkness.

The multitude of voices rose up like a wave and washed over him. Endless rage and despair of embittered souls swirled around him now. He could feel their terror and sorrow and anger. The knowledge of separation. Lost in unending darkness. Multitudes of souls, yet each one completely and utterly alone.

Conner could feel the presence of more than just Howard behind him now. He could hear the whispers. The creatures had brought him back. Conner looked down at his hands. His flesh was now all but swallowed by the rash creeping across his body.

"You are going to have a long time to consider these things, Mr. Hayden." Howard's voice fell to a deep, guttural tone. "A very long time."

Conner turned around. Howard's gaunt, pale face gazed back at him. It was vacant and expressionless.

And the gray creatures emerged from behind him. More than two. Now more than a dozen. White, soulless eyes gazed at him. Burned through him. Mouths gaped open. Black tongues rolled forward. Thick saliva, like tar, dripped from their jaws. The stench of death and rot filled Conner's nostrils.

Howard's face was changing as well, melting into a hideous gray mask. His eyes faded to white. He straightened up and towered over Conner, looming up against the gray clouds. His clothing grew dark and enveloped his body with a black mist. It swirled around him, shrouded him, spreading outward like a great cloak.

Conner could feel the darkness bearing down on him, as if it were a physical thing. A weight crushing him. He struggled for words. "Who . . . who are you?"

Howard laughed. "I have many names." His deep voice rolled and growled. "I am the Hunger that cannot be filled. I am the Consuming Darkness that comes to all men. The Wasting that gnaws away at flesh and bone. I am the Devourer. I am Death."

The ground began to crumble. Conner felt himself slipping backward, off the cliff. He clawed at the rocks, digging his icy fingers into the ground.

Fear broke through the numbness and clutched him. He struggled to hold on. His hands flailed helplessly at the rocks. He tried to cry out, but his voice was dried up. He looked up and could see beyond the creatures, on the embankment behind them . . .

Something moved.

56

Rachel bit her lip and watched the frantic activity over her father. Tears streamed down her cheeks. What was the last thing she had even said to him? They had argued, and she had said something mean. Her mind spun back to their conversation.

"I don't even know who you are anymore."

The words echoed in her head, haunting her.

Her mother pulled her close.

"Sweetheart, we need to pray," she said, then whispered a prayer into Rachel's ear. Her warm tears dripped onto Rachel's neck, and her voice quivered.

Rachel squeezed her mother's hand and prayed along silently.

Oh please, Jesus . . . he's not ready. . . . Please . . . don't let him die.

In the ER, the doctor returned the defibrillator paddles to the station. One of the nurses turned away from the gurney and tugged off her mask.

Rachel gasped.

No!

She tore herself loose from her mother and ran down the hall. “Please don’t stop! Please don’t give up! He’s not ready to die!”

The nurse blocked her path. Someone shouted, “Close that door!”

The door swung shut in Rachel’s face and the nurse pulled her back. “Please, miss. I’m sorry. . . .”

“He’s not ready!” Rachel screamed through her sobs. She pounded on the door. “Don’t stop! Please don’t give up! He’s not ready to die!”

Rachel felt her mother’s arm around her again. The doctor stared at Rachel through the window. His eyes seemed filled with regret.

Rachel wept. *“Please!”*

Conner’s arms grew numb. He was losing his hold. The wind howled in his ears, pulling him backward. And Howard — Death himself — loomed over him.

But a small figure climbed up the slope behind the creatures. Conner struggled to keep his hold. More ground crumbled away beneath him, and his feet swung loose over the precipice. The wind howled louder now.

The voices hit a crescendo. Conner's eyes narrowed, then widened.

The boy!

The boy stood on the edge of the embankment. Conner blinked. He had lost him on the boat. He thought they had taken him.

The wind whipped around the child, tugging at his old flannel shirt. His hair blew back. His dark eyes were fixed onto Conner now.

Death seemed to sense this new presence. He spun around to face the boy, and the black mist swirled, trailing his movement. It shrouded his torso, coiling around his face and limbs. The other creatures turned as well and fanned out as if to flank their leader. Shoulders pulled back, heads stretched forward, gaping jaws opened in a chorus of guttural hisses.

The boy stood his ground, bracing his frail body against the wind.

Death bellowed a deep, thunderous roar. His voice sounded like a multitude of inhuman voices crying in unison.

"You will not interfere!"

The ground shook with his fury. Conner slipped again, kicking his feet to gain a foothold. The rocks beneath him were jarring loose.

The boy's eyes did not waver from Conner. He stood in the wind and the fury and shook his head.

Death stretched his hand forward. A tendril of black mist curled out like an enormous serpent and encircled the boy.

Conner cried out, "No!" But his voice was lost amid the howling wind.

Rachel pounded on the door. Another nurse removed her mask. They were giving up! They couldn't give up!

"Miss, I'm very sorry," the nurse beside her said. "There's nothing more we can do."

Rachel's mother was weeping. She tried to pull Rachel away from the door.

But Rachel's eyes were locked on the doctor. Her voice was hoarse, lost in her crying. "Please don't let him die. . . ."

The doctor drew in a deep breath and nodded. He reached for the defibrillator paddles again.

"Charging . . ." His voice sounded grim.

Black mist coiled around the boy, swirling up to his torso. Only then did his eyes move from Conner, up into the face of Death.

And he spoke.

His voice sounded like an explosion of thunder. It rocked the entire precipice. The ground shook. The trees snapped at their trunks as the shock wave spread outward, blasting the gray creatures off the ledge, like hapless flies blown by a tornado. The force of it stripped Death of his black shroud, leaving his pale, withered frame naked and exposed.

The sky erupted with light. It blazed down, flowing around Death's gnarled gray form, dissolving it like a twig dropped into acid.

The light pierced Conner as well, warm and clean, slicing through him, blinding him with its brilliance. He clung to the rocks as the ground shook. His raw hands began to slip as the ground dropped away beneath him.

Then the fury subsided.

Conner found himself in complete silence. He opened his eyes. Darkness yawned beneath him. He looked up. One hand clung to a rocky outcropping just below the top of the ledge. Dark clouds swirled overhead. His hand was slipping.

Slipping.

The boy's face appeared over the edge as the rock fell away. Conner felt himself drop. But he didn't fall. He looked up to see the boy's fingers wrapped around his wrist. His brown eyes narrowed. His teeth clenched. Conner reached up with his free hand and clutched the boy's arm.

Then Conner saw it. A gaping scar on the child's wrist. Conner clung to him as he swung over the abyss. The boy's arm stretched under Conner's weight, tearing the wound open again. Blood rolled down from his wrist onto Conner's hands.

The boy pulled. He reached down his other hand and pulled. Conner felt himself slowly moving upward. He kicked against the side of the cliff, searching for a foothold. There was no way this kid would be able to pull him up. Not alone.

He was just a boy. . . .

Conner's arms emerged over the edge. Still the boy pulled him. He pulled until Conner's upper torso was back on top of the ledge.

Conner swung his legs over and rolled onto his back. He gasped for breath, too weak to talk, still clinging to the boy's blood-soaked arm. The child swept his free hand softly across Conner's forehead, and Conner saw his other wrist. An identical wound marred the flesh. Deep, jagged, and thick.

Someone had done something terrible to this boy.

He looked down at Conner and smiled. Conner's eyes stung with tears as he gazed back into the wide brown eyes. Beautiful and deep, they seemed to hold some ancient secret. A vast knowledge of countless, indescribable worlds. Mysteries beyond imagining. As if the whole of the universe itself could be held in that one look.

It was a depth and wonder he could not fathom.

Conner wept. He wept with all that was in him. He reached his hand to touch the boy's cheek, but he felt so weak. Darkness was closing in on him. And the abyss still loomed.

Far off on the other side of the chasm, Conner could see sunlight. A lush green country. He turned back to the boy and tried to speak but could only manage a hoarse whisper. "Please . . . I'm not ready. . . . I just . . . I just want to see my family again."

The boy stared at him for a moment, then nodded.

Far away, Conner thought he heard a faint voice, as if lost in some deep canyon.

"Clear."

The boy touched his bloody hand to Conner's chest.

Conner's body seized uncontrollably as a jolt of pain surged through him. A searing . . . beautiful pain. It grew from the center of his chest and spread outward. It sucked the air from his lungs. His back arched. His eyes rolled.

White light pressed in from the corners of his vision. Conner could see the boy's face slowly melding with the light. Fading into it, becoming one with it.

He caught one final glimpse of that far, green country. It was fading as well, growing wide and deep in the brilliance. Surrounding it, enveloping it.

And for one brief moment, just before all was consumed in glorious light, Conner thought he saw the figure of a small boy running.

Blond hair, catching the sunlight . . .

57

Rachel pressed her face to the glass. The doctor pushed the defibrillator paddles onto her father's flesh.

His back arched upward, high off the table. His mouth opened with the sound of a long, slow inhale, sucking air deep into his lungs.

The doctor stepped back, his eyes wide. The nurses as well gasped and moved backward. The entire ER staff stood for a moment in stunned silence around the table.

Then Rachel's father blinked and exhaled. Long and slow. His body settled back onto the table. The monitor beeped; the line jumped. Once . . . Twice . . .

He breathed again.

"We . . . we have a sinus rhythm," someone said.

"Blood pressure is rising . . . stabilizing."

Everyone snapped back to work, and the

flurry of activity resumed.

The doctor glanced through the window at Rachel. She caught his expression for a moment before he looked away. It was a look of amazement.

"He's breathing!" Rachel said. "He's breathing again!"

Her mother was pale. She closed her eyes and whispered, "Thank God."

Rachel turned around and hugged her mother. They stood, holding each other tight, crying, laughing, and thanking God.

Six Days Later

Conner lay in the hospital bed, wide awake. His fingers pressed lightly against the dressing over his sternum. It was nearly four o'clock. Rachel would be here soon.

Friday night they had managed to stabilize him and kept him in critical care overnight. The next day his doctor ran a barrage of tests and scheduled open-heart surgery for Monday morning. But Marta and Rachel had been with him the entire time. They had practically camped out in the hospital.

Conner told them about his experiences. But he didn't tell them everything. He didn't mention Mitch or Helen or Devon or Ray . . . or even Howard. He wasn't sure he wanted to share those things with anyone. Besides, he had no idea whether or not they were even real. He had called the office on Saturday and left a message for Nancy, with a list of names and everything he knew about them. He asked her to compile whatever information she could find.

Meanwhile Rachel had bombarded him with Bible passages and books. She recounted every step of her own journey to faith. She shared everything she had found. Marta just sat there quietly and held his hand.

Conner had described being on the very brink of an abyss and told them about the boy who had saved him. Rachel, bless her heart, was convinced Conner had seen Jesus Christ Himself, or at least some image of Him. But Conner was still prickled by doubts. How much of this had been hallucination? He had lived his entire life as a skeptic. It was in his nature to question everything. To doubt everything. Whatever Nancy would come up with would go a long way in convincing him that his experience had been real. But Conner had difficulty sleeping. His dreams were filled with images he couldn't shake.

After the surgery, they had him up and about almost immediately. He had just finished a round of physical therapy on Thursday afternoon. It was shortly after four when Rachel poked her head inside his room.

"Hi, Dad!" She bounded over and kissed him on the forehead.

Conner grinned; he had been waiting for them all day. "Hi, sweetie." He kissed her back.

Marta entered a moment later. "Hi, Connie." She took his hand and squeezed it.

Conner pulled her to him and pressed his lips to hers. He could feel her neck tense slightly and then relax. He breathed in her scent. Her hand brushed up to his jaw.

After a moment, Rachel cleared her throat. "Umm . . . you just had, like, a quintuple bypass surgery. Don't you think you should, y'know . . . hold off on that a bit?"

Marta stood up, her cheeks flushed. "Yes, you should."

Conner laughed. "I've got a lot of lost time to make up for."

Marta smiled and touched his forehead. "They said you could probably come home tomorrow. I've got your room ready, like we discussed."

Conner smiled. Marta had set up a bed in his old office. The doctors wanted him to ease into stair climbing after a few days.

But his physical therapy was going well, and he hoped to be back up to full speed within a few weeks. Besides, they technically weren't even married. He guessed the people at Marta's church might frown upon them shacking up together.

He found himself staring at her again. The curve of her lips. The slope of her nose.

Marta glanced at him, then turned to Rachel. "Oh, sweetie, you know what I forgot? I left the card and the gift from the Brandts back in the car. Would you mind running down and getting that for me?"

Rachel sighed. "You know, if you want some time alone, just say, 'Hey, Rachel, we'd like a few minutes alone.' You don't need to come up with all these contrivances."

Conner chuckled. "Hey, Rachel, we'd like a few minutes —"

"Yeah, yeah." Rachel rolled her eyes. "I'll be back in ten minutes."

After she left, Marta curled an eyebrow. "Contrivances?"

Conner smiled and leaned his head back. "Are you okay with me moving back in like this?"

Marta shrugged. "Are you sure this is what you want to do? We have a lot of unresolved issues. I think we need to take our time and make sure we're not going to ignore the elephant in the room."

"I understand." Conner nodded. "And I know we have a long way to go yet. But I don't . . . I just don't want to put anything off anymore."

"Neither do I." Marta sat down on the bedside. "I want to work things out too. I always have. But there are a lot of things to consider."

"I've been thinking a lot over the last few days. And there's something I have to tell you. Something I *need* to tell you. . . ." Conner's eyes began to sting. He cleared his throat. He had practiced this. For five days, he had practiced this. "I know . . . When Matthew died, I know you had issues with me. I know you blamed me for what happened. . . ."

Marta shook her head. "Connie, I don't . . . I don't blame you. It was an accident."

"And I . . ." Conner swallowed. "And *I* tried to put the blame everywhere else. Everywhere but where it belonged."

Marta's eyes filled with tears. "Oh, sweetheart, don't. . . . You . . . don't have to do this."

"Yes, I do." Conner's jaw tightened as he fought his tears. "I *have* to do this." He tried to calm himself. He took a breath.

Marta bit her lip.

"You told me to watch him," Conner said. "You told me to keep an eye on him, and I made you think . . . I swore up and down that I had. I said I only turned away for a minute. But . . . but I wasn't even watching. . . . I was inside. I sent him out to the yard — I was irritated with him and I was . . . I was busy with work." Conner struggled to speak through his tears. He had dreamed of Matthew's face every night since the heart attack. It had haunted him. It haunted him still. The sight of Matthew struggling in the water. His eyes wide and fearful. Every night it replayed in his dreams. "I was supposed to be there to protect him. But I was too preoccupied. I sent him outside to play, and I didn't look out again for *half an hour.* He drowned because I . . . I wasn't where I should have been. I wasn't *what* I should have been."

Marta only stared at him. He couldn't tell what she was feeling at that moment. What she must think of him. She stood up and went to the window, wrapping her arms around herself. He could see her shoulders trembling.

Conner went on. "I won't blame you if you can't forgive me. I don't deserve it. I pushed you away. I tried to put the blame everywhere else — even on you and Rachel. I almost convinced myself that if you had just taken him with you that morning, he'd still be alive. But it was *my* fault. I might as well have held his face under the water myself."

Marta turned around. Her eyes were red.

Conner drew a deep breath and closed his eyes for a moment. "I need for you to decide if you can forgive me." His lips tightened. "Or if you never want to see me again."

Marta blinked her tears away, squeezing them down her cheeks. "It took me a long time to get over blaming you. When you denied it and when you tried to blame me . . . I hated you for that, Connie. For months I hated you." She sat down on the bed. "But when I put my faith in Christ . . . Connie, all that hate and pain began to leave. Slowly. I don't know how, because it wasn't my doing, but in time He replaced it with love again."

58

There was a knock at the door. Marta stood up.

Conner wiped his eyes and cleared his throat. "Come in."

Nancy peeked inside. "Hi, Connie." She cast a glance at Marta. "Is now a good time?"

Conner blinked. "Yes, come in. What do you have?"

Nancy came in with a legal pad and sat down next to the bed. "I've spent the last few days running down those names for you. Where do you want to start?"

"Whatever you have first," Conner said.

Nancy put her reading glasses on. "Well, there were the two boys from the South Side — Devon Marshall and Terrell Carter. Now —" she glanced over her glasses at Conner — "did you know these people personally?"

Conner shook his head. "Not exactly, no."

Nancy raised an eyebrow. "They were

involved in a gang-related incident. It seems they were the victims of a drive-by shooting last Friday night. Terrell was hit twice in the chest and died at the scene. And Devon was hit in the chest and shoulder. He was brought back to Cook County Memorial, where he is listed in stable condition."

Conner frowned. "Did you find out any details about Devon's injury? how serious it was at the time?"

"The police report indicated that neither boy was breathing when they arrived on the scene. The police attempted CPR on both but were unsuccessful at reviving either one. When the paramedics arrived, they . . . managed to get Devon's heart going again and stabilized for transport. But the other boy, Terrell, had already lost too much blood by the time they got there."

"So, what's going to happen to Devon?"

Nancy checked her notes. "Umm, he's going to be released into police custody. Apparently he was on probation, but he's only sixteen. He's waiting to find out what the state wants to do with him. He's spent some time at several juvenile detention centers."

Conner leaned back and nodded. They were real. He *had* met Devon. They had all experienced the same nightmare together. He felt dizzy but tried to shake it off. "I want to try to speak with him. I want to see if I can help him."

Nancy peered at Conner over her glasses. "I thought you said you didn't know any of these people?"

"Only as acquaintances, really. Just through professional contacts."

Nancy wrinkled her forehead. She glanced at Marta, who only shrugged.

Conner pointed to the legal pad. "Who's next?"

Nancy sighed and glanced at her notes. "Well, there's twenty-three-year-old Raymond Cahill Jr. of Thorton, Indiana. Deceased. He, uh . . . he overdosed on methamphetamines a week ago last Monday. His parents came home that night, found him unconscious in their living room, and rushed him to the hospital. He was placed on life-support." She flipped the page. "The doctors indicated he was brain-dead, and his parents had him disconnected four days later. He died late last Friday."

Conner frowned. "Are you sure about that timeline?"

"This was from the newspaper in Thorton."

Conner nodded to himself. He could still see Ray Cahill's body being dragged outside the house by those creatures. Dragged off into the darkness. He knew exactly where. He shuddered and stared out the window for a moment. Ray had been stuck in that place for what seemed to him like weeks but was in reality just a few days. His body was being kept alive while his brain was dead. Poor Ray was relegated to wandering through that wasteland until his parents disconnected the life-support and his body eventually died. He was one of those souls Howard had talked about, who clung to life for some time before death finally caught up with him.

Conner turned back to Nancy. "Who's next?"

Nancy peered at Conner a moment. "Well, this one's a little interesting. And a little creepy. Helen Krause, fifty, of Chicago. I, uh . . . I couldn't find anything on her from the police logs, and she wasn't in any of the local hospitals. I did manage to locate her apartment, though. . . ."

"And?"

"I contacted her building management and told them I was worried that something might have happened to her."

"Did they get into her apartment?"

Nancy nodded. "Yes, Monday afternoon, and . . . and they found her. Her body, that is. She had apparently died sometime over the weekend."

Conner took a breath. So she *was* dead. Howard hadn't lied about that. "What did they find out?"

Nancy cleared her throat. "Well — now I had to call in several favors with my contacts at the police, so you're going to owe me big-time for this."

"Fine. What did you find out?"

"Ms. Krause had apparently committed suicide."

Conner furrowed his brow. "Suicide? Helen?"

Nancy shrugged. "That's how they're classifying it."

"Why? What happened?"

"Apparently they found her on the balcony. She had several prescriptions she had been taking for depression and so on. They found an empty bottle on the dining room table."

Conner's frown deepened. "But . . . she didn't strike me as . . ."

"That's where it gets a little weird. She appeared to have had a guest over that night for dinner. Friday night. Which also happened to be her birthday. They found a 'Happy Birthday' sign taped on the wall, and she had stopped on the way home to pick up a cake and a couple Chinese dinners."

Conner nodded. "Her son. She said she had . . . that she was *going* to have dinner with her son, Kyle."

Nancy's lips tightened. "Yes, her son . . ."

"Yeah, I thought something may have happened to him as well." Conner leaned forward. "What's the matter? Did they find him?"

"Well . . ." Nancy bit her lip. "Not exactly."

"What is it?"

Nancy took a breath. "I managed to locate a business associate of hers. Her agent —" she glanced at her notes — "Rex VanKammen. I think I better let him tell you."

Conner raised his eyebrows. "He's here?"

"I asked him to wait outside for a minute. I didn't know if you felt like having company."

"Well, don't just sit there; bring him in."

Nancy sighed and went to the door. "Would you please come in?"

Rex was a thin man. Conner figured him to be in his early sixties. Thinning, gray hair was cut short and spiked. He wore jeans and a sports jacket over a black silk shirt. He shook hands and stood looking a little uncomfortable.

Marta moved her chair over for him.

Rex sat down and shifted in the seat. "Uh . . . Mr. Hayden, I was just wondering how it was that you came to know Helen? You see, I knew Helen her entire career. In fact, we had just got together last Friday and . . . well . . . no offense, but she never mentioned you."

"Ahh." Conner nodded. "Yes . . . well, I only met her recently. Umm, just last week, and it was regarding a case I was working on, so unfortunately, I'm not able to go into great detail."

"Oh." Rex nodded. "Oh, well, I see."

"Can you help me find Kyle? I was worried something may have happened to him."

Rex just gave Conner a strange look.

Conner frowned. "What's the matter?"

Rex cleared his throat. "I'm afraid there *is* no Kyle Krause."

Conner blinked. He tried to process what the guy was saying. "Excuse me?"

Rex drummed his fingers on the armrest. "How can I put this?" He scratched his head. "Kyle was . . . a figment of Helen's imagination."

Conner shook his head. "I don't understand."

Rex leaned forward. He seemed very uncomfortable. "Helen never had any children. And her closest relative is a sister somewhere out west. South Dakota or someplace."

Conner just stared at him. "Montana."

Rex nodded. "Well . . . I knew Helen when she first started in the modeling business. And she was tops. I mean she had a great look, y'know; she could really find the camera. So she was very successful in her day."

"Yes, she mentioned to me that she had done some modeling."

"Well," Rex went on, "a few years into her career, she met Nick Roselli. He was a photographer. And she fell for him pretty hard."

Conner recalled that Helen had mentioned Nick on the boat. "Yeah, she said Nick was Kyle's father."

"Yeah." Rex's lips tightened for a moment. "She got pregnant. And Nick asked her to marry him, but . . ."

Conner frowned. "Nick *wanted* to get married?"

"Yeah, he wanted to do right by her. He didn't want her to . . . y'know, have to raise the kid on her own."

"So what happened?"

Rex's gaze drifted down. "Helen wasn't ready for that. She wasn't ready to settle down. And she *sure* wasn't ready to have a kid."

Conner leaned back. "I think I understand."

Rex shook his head and sighed. "She had an abortion. And when Nick found out, he nearly hit the ceiling."

"He left her?"

"He left her." Rex nodded. "Poor Helen was never the same after that. I think Nick was the only man she had ever really loved."

"So what happened?"

"Well, Helen went through some major depression after that. A year later, she started talking about her baby."

"Her *baby?*"

Rex shrugged. "She went off the deep end a little. She went around talking about her and Nick's little boy, Kyle. The baby she had aborted."

Conner looked around the room. Marta and Nancy were sitting, speechless. He looked back at Rex. "So all this time, Kyle was just her own delusion?"

Rex nodded. "And she started going through men like they were candy. She dated rock stars and congressmen. The richer the better. But she never settled down. And as far as I know, she never fell in love again. I think, deep down, she was a very lonely woman."

Conner stared out the window. He had only known her a short time. But he hadn't really known her at all. "I think you're right."

"I tried to get her into therapy," Rex said. "And for a while she was doing pretty well. But then the modeling gigs started to dry up. You know, as she got older. Then about ten years ago, she started talking about Kyle again. Kyle was graduating high school. Kyle was going to college. She had every detail of this kid in her head."

Rex looked down. "She set up a lunch appointment with me once to discuss some business plans. So I showed up at the restaurant and found her sitting at a table for three, talking to an empty seat." He shook his head. "I was so embarrassed for her. She was talking and laughing and carrying on a conversation with 'Kyle.' The whole restaurant was staring at her. So I sit down and she asks me if I know anyone in the entertainment industry that could represent him. She said he wanted to be a comedian now." Rex rolled his eyes. "She even made me sit there and listen to part of his routine. I'm staring at an empty chair. She's listening to some joke of his and laughing her head off. I just made an excuse to leave. I couldn't take it anymore."

Rex sighed and rubbed his temples. "So I managed to get her back with a doctor again. And he had her on some medication. I thought these last few years she was doing better. Her consulting business was doing well. But if what you're telling me is correct, it sounds like she had another relapse. The police called me when they found her. And then I remembered last Friday was her birthday. I was probably the one person who knew her the best. The closest thing she had to a friend. And I didn't even remember her birthday. I was with her last Friday. We met for drinks that evening, and I had to give her some bad news. She was going for this ad gig and they . . . well, they wanted someone a little younger. I was probably the last person to see her alive."

They all fell silent. After a moment, Rex stood up to leave.

Conner felt numb inside. He shook Rex's hand. "Mr. VanKammen, thank you for sharing that with me. For what it's worth . . . for my part, Helen seemed like a . . . like a very nice person. She seemed to be caring and genuine. And I . . . I'm truly sad to hear she's gone."

"Yeah," Rex said. "Yeah, me too."

Once Rex had gone, Conner lay back and

breathed a deep sigh. For all her popularity in life, Helen Krause had died completely alone. He cringed inwardly at the memory of her cries, echoing through that dark forest. He would remember that sound as long as he lived.

After a moment, Nancy cleared her throat. "Well, there are a couple others you asked about. Like Mitch Kent, from North Chicago."

Conner sat up. "Is he still alive?"

Nancy raised her eyebrows. "It depends what you consider 'alive.' He's in a vegetative state, according to the doctors at Good Samaritan up in Winthrop Harbor."

Conner frowned. "What happened to him?"

Nancy glanced back at her notes. "He was . . . he was in an accident. A motorcycle accident, Friday night as well. He was riding north on Sheridan when a truck crossed the center lane and struck him. Umm, a passerby stopped and called 911. He suffered from massive head injuries."

Conner leaned forward. "Is he on life support?"

Nancy nodded. "Yes, for now. His next of kin is his father, who lives in Lake Bluff."

"He's not planning on disconnecting him, is he?"

"I haven't actually discussed that with him. Do you want me to set up an appointment?"

Conner stared at her. He recalled Mitch, sitting on the sofa in Howard's house. That was the last time he had seen him. Ray Cahill had been in a coma four days before he died and it had seemed to be weeks. What about Mitch? Was he still there? Alone in that . . . Interworld? It had been six days since their experience. It must feel like a couple of months had gone by for Mitch. He was there alone with Howard.

With Death himself.

Conner frowned. "What about the last one, Howard?"

Nancy nodded and flipped the page. "Right. Then there was Howard Bristol, sixty- to seventy-year-old white male, address unknown, somewhere in Indiana." She looked over her glasses again. "I found three that matched that description."

"Three?"

"Yep. One's a banker in Indianapolis. Another sells insurance in Gary. But one of them . . ."

"What?" Conner leaned forward. "What about him?"

"One of them — a sixty-seven-year-old farmer — has been comatose in the Merrillville Hospice Center for the last eight months. Stroke victim. Apparently his wife just can't bear to let him go."

Conner stared at her. "Comatose?"

Nancy shook her head. "I don't know what your fascination is with all this stuff, but to me, it's kind of morbid." She closed the legal pad and left it on the table next to the bed. She gathered her things and patted Conner on the head. "Now stop with all this work and relax. For goodness sake, you've just had surgery. Do you want to give yourself another heart attack?"

As she left, Conner leaned back and sighed.

Marta stared at him. "What was *that* all about?"

"Mmmm." Conner rubbed his eyes. "It's a long story." One he wasn't quite ready to share yet. But one thing he was sure of: his experience had been real. He could no longer ignore the God he had spent so much time hating. For God Himself had pulled him back from the brink of a terrible abyss.

Something Rachel had said earlier that week now echoed in his mind. *"He saved you for a reason, Dad."*

And though he knew it might be a while

before he ever found out what that reason was, something told him she was right.

59

Mitch opened his eyes. Gray light poured in through the living room window. He had spent another fitful night on the couch. He sat up and rubbed his eyes. His neck and back were stiff; his joints cracked and popped as he dragged himself off the sofa.

He stood up and stretched. Another night. He had made it through another night. He yawned and stumbled into the kitchen for some water. He poured himself a glass and downed it immediately. Then a second and third. He'd been so thirsty lately.

He leaned on the counter and hung his head for a moment. Every day it seemed harder to wake up.

There was a soft noise behind him. Mitch turned to see Howard at the table, shuffling a deck of cards. Howard glanced up and grinned. A wide, toothy grin.

"Mornin', Hoss," he said. "We need to make another gas run today."

"Mmph," Mitch grunted. "Great."

Howard chuckled. "Well, we need to keep the lights burnin', don't we?"

Mitch stretched again. He went to the cupboard for some breakfast and shook his head. Nothing but more stale granola. "Can we make another grocery stop on the way back?"

"Sure thing. How about we see if we can find us some beef jerky?"

"No." Mitch thought a moment, biting his cheek. "Slim Jims. I could go for some Slim Jims."

Howard snapped the cards. "Slim Jims it is!"

Mitch glanced down at the table and groaned.

Howard had the cribbage board set out. He looked up with a wry grin. "Up for a game?"

Mitch felt his jaw tighten. He had taught the old man how to play but had yet to lose a game to him. The guy just didn't seem to have any luck. Mitch glanced at the tally board on the kitchen wall. He had a streak going over the last ten weeks: 357 games to none.

"Aren't you tired of losing?"

Howard raised his eyebrows. "Me? Naw!" He snorted. "I'm bound to win sooner or later. Just a matter of time."

Mitch sighed and plopped down across from the old man.

Howard slid the deck to the middle of the table. "Low card deals first."

Mitch cut an ace. As he started to shuffle, he glimpsed a faceless, gray head peeking in through the window. Then it slipped away. Mitch stared at the window for a moment.

"Uhh . . ." Howard tapped the table. "You gonna deal, Hoss?"

Mitch fixed his gaze back on the old man. "Are you ever gonna tell me what happened to my friends?"

Howard's placid expression faded slightly. His eyes flitted down to the cards in Mitch's hand. "You let me win a game . . . maybe I'll tell you."

"Right." Mitch snorted and started dealing. "Like *that's* gonna happen."

Howard grinned. "Well, it was worth a shot."

Mitch wound up with three sixes and a nine. And Howard cut him another nine. Mitch laughed and shook his head. "Looks like you're gonna be keeping your secret a little longer, old man."

After a few hands, Howard sat up with an odd look on his face. He got up, stepped onto the back porch, and peered off into the gray horizon, tilting his head. Then he came back and snatched the keys to his truck from the counter.

Mitch scowled. "Hey, I'm about to skunk you. Where're you going?"

"Keep my seat warm, Hoss." Howard nodded out the door. "I think we got company. I hear a car out on the highway."

"Company? Again?" Mitch strained to listen for the sound. "I don't hear anything."

"You didn't hear anything the last three times, either," Howard retorted.

Mitch sank back in his seat. "It's probably just more old people."

They'd had a steady stream of visitors over the last several weeks. Mostly senior citizens and such. They'd show up for supper, all freaked out and disoriented, and by breakfast they'd be gone. Vanished. Just like Conner, Helen, and Devon. Mitch had gotten past being creeped out. It had become something of a regular business. But he was getting sick of it now. Everyone who ever came to this farm seemed to disappear mysteriously. Everyone but him. It was like he was living in his own personal . . .

Mitch looked up. His face was grim. "Hey, Howard?"

Howard paused in the doorway. "Yeah?"

"Seriously. Was Conner right about this

place? Am I dead? Is this hell?"

"Hell?" Howard chuckled and shook his head. "Naw, *this* ain't hell."

Then his smile faded slightly and he shrugged.

"It's Indiana."

ABOUT THE AUTHOR

Tom Pawlik has a BA in communication and works in the marketing field. He has also been active in Christian teaching, youth work, and music for over twenty years. His first novel, *The Way Back,* took second place in the 2004 Operation First Novel Contest run by the Jerry B. Jenkins Christian Writers Guild in association with Tyndale House Publishers. His second novel, *Vanish,* won first place in the 2006 contest. In addition to writing fiction, Tom is also an accomplished songwriter and musician who writes and records at his home studio. He and his wife, Colette, live in Ohio with their four children and one large dog. Visit Tom's Web site at www.tompawlik.com.

The employees of Thorndike Press hope you have enjoyed this Large Print book. All our Thorndike, Wheeler, and Kennebec Large Print titles are designed for easy reading, and all our books are made to last. Other Thorndike Press Large Print books are available at your library, through selected bookstores, or directly from us.

For information about titles, please call:

(800) 223-1244

or visit our Web site at:

http://gale.cengage.com/thorndike

To share your comments, please write:

Publisher
Thorndike Press
295 Kennedy Memorial Drive
Waterville, ME 04901